The Assassination Of Spiro Agnew

a novel

Steven Janiszewski

ISBN: 0615670253
ISBN-13: 978-0615670256

Published By

Los Mortales De Publicacion

Arvada, Colorado

Covers by Studio Sophia,
featuring old, public domain images
of the Mormon Temple and Temple Square
in Salt Lake City

For George Garrett and that punk on a motorcycle to whom he gave a chance.

The proper nouns in this book do not have referents.

"No assassin in his right mind would kill me, because they
would get Agnew as President"

Richard Nixon

CONTENTS

Chapter One

The Assassin and the Revolutionist

September 21, 1970, Salt Lake City, in a small 4-room adobe house up against the eastern slope of the roadbed for I-15, 1½ blocks south of the Sixth North Exit, Orrin stops singing at the sound of a knock on the front door and turns on an FM tuner to whelm whatever vestiges of his lyrics still float around the house. Humming, as The Hymn continues in his mind, he opens the door.

"My, ah, battery's dead. Can you jump it?"

It's the young Mexican, Tony Archuleta, who lives in the adobe house next door. Orrin doesn't know his name but has said hello to him on two occasions.

"Sure," Orrin says.

He steps off his front step into his topless CJ5, parked between his adobe house and Tony's. "You got cables?" he calls over his shoulder.

"Yeah," Tony answers, walking toward his Chevy in the unpaved and rutted private roadway between two rows of small 4-room adobe houses. Orrin backs his Jeep into the roadway, then pulls up slowly till the Jeep's winch gently kisses the Chevy's grille. No dent, not even a mark, a skillfully executed kiss. Tony had waved him on and had signaled him to stop before he stopped, had even yelled, but Orrin hadn't been watching him, or listening.

"Close enough?" he smiles, pulling the hand brake, easing the Jeep out of gear,

Tony nods. He's waiting with the cables as Orrin jumps out, unlatches and raises the Jeep's hood. "Comes in handy sometimes," Tony says, trying to make a little conversation, indicating with a tilt of his head that he is speaking of the winch.

"Sure does," Orrin manages to say congenially. But inwardly, he sighs: Oh, God. Who is this? What does he know? What part will he play? Is he just being friendly? Maybe. But why the winch? It's touching his car. My winch, his grille. First physical contact. Obvious, logical point to begin some friendly small talk. Too logical. Oh, God.

Almost but not quite brusquely, for he feels the brusqueness coming on and tries to suppress it, Orrin takes the cables from Tony and tells him: "Get in and start your car. I'll do this."

Tony does as he is told; he's used to doing as he's told, or acting as though he is. It doesn't matter to Tony who starts the car, and if Orrin wants to play authoritarian, why hassle him? Orrin connects the batteries, connects his powerful, expensive, and well-fed Diehard to Tony's pathetically dead, pathetically cheap, and sparklingly new Sun. Orrin's seen the Sun batteries in supermarkets. He knows they are worthless, and he knows this young Mexican (what's his name, Tony?) bought the Sun because he needed a battery, and he couldn't afford a good battery, but all things being as they are, he bought the Sun. He'll get by jumping it as long as he can, but that will become impractical soon. So, all things being a little worse than they were before, he'll buy another cheap Sun battery and another, spending more on batteries in a season that I ever have or will, using money that should buy food for his kids, listening to their cries of hunger as he adds another Sun to the stack of dead ones on his front step. (Orrin glances over his shoulder. Sure enough: a stack of three dead Suns on the front step of Tony's house.) Finally, Orrin thinks, it will get to be too much, and he will have to quit driving his car. Orrin shudders at that thought. The Chevy groans, then starts.

"Thanks," Tony says openly, as he gets out. He picks up a twig, breaks off a short piece and wedges it into the carburetor linkage to increase the idle. "Let 'er charge up a little," he says to Orrin's back as Orrin latches the CJ's hood. "Got time for a toke?"

"No, thanks." Orrin turns to face him. "I don't smoke dope."

"Oh, well, I, ah, kind of suspected you were a Mormon, but thought maybe, because of your, ah..."

"Because of my hair?" Orrin laughs. He touches the straight, black hair that hangs loose to the bottom of his shoulder blades, no ponytail or braids for him. "It's a long story, but I'm no hippie."

"Oh? Then you must be Orrin Porter Rockwell Christianson. I'm Tony Archuleta, pleased to meet you." He extends a hand. "Glad you're right next door."

"We pronounce it Christi-Anne-Son." Orrin takes his hand feebly, thinking: What?! My God, what does he know? How? He looked on my mail box. No, my name's not on it. He looked on my mail, the sneaky bastard. But I don't use my full name. It's too long.

"Is something wrong?"

"No, no, why?"

"You stopped humming. Your hand's cold. Your mouth's open. You're staring off at something. And your hair curled up a little at the ends."

"It did?" Orrin is concerned, touching it, bringing a handful around to check.

"It has straightened out again. Don't worry. Come on in and have a glass of water. I'm gonna tell you a story." Tony puts an arm around Orrin's shoulders, and they start in. "One that you don't wanna hear."

Orrin recognizes the floor plan of Tony's house as being the same as his, only the corresponding rooms are put to different uses. What in Orrin's is an uncluttered living room study (old, rugged couch, desk, bookshelves, tape deck, turntable, amplifier-tuner, speakers, 13-inch TV), is in Tony's a much cluttered living room nursery playroom broom closet hamper (old, sagging couch, two sagging chairs, ironing board, laundry, crib, two bawling babies, gigantic, console television, toys, books, scraps of paper, globs of lint, a leaf on the floor). A pregnant, squirrel-cheeked woman, brushing hair from her eyes, saying, "Hello."

"My wife, Rosita." Tony waves a hand her way.

4

"Hello," Orrin says, looking over her shoulder, through the archway, into what in his house is a simple bedroom, seeing a disheveled bed, a disassembled Honda Trail 50, two VW tires with rims, and cardboard boxes stacked along the far wall, with clothing hanging out of several of them. Above the boxes is a massive crucifix. There is something almost lifelike about the figure of Jesus. As Orrin looks closer, it blinks.

Tony clears off a chair. "Sit down. I'll get your water."

Orrin sits uneasily on the edge, not really fearing anything, but not wishing to make himself vulnerable by sinking in and leaning back. On the opposite wall: a picture of an eviscerated heart wearing a crown of thorns and dripping blood. The blood has trickled down the wall and there is a puddle of it on the floor, dried dark around the edges. Orrin has seen the Sacred Heart of Jesus before, on the bunkhouse wall. Mexicans work for his father. Alone, it is enough to sicken him. Blood on the wall and floor, he has not seen before. His stomach begins to turn, he pales, looks away.

"Don't worry," says Rosita, a baby on her hip, "Tony painted the blood. See." She touches the trickle on the wall, brings her finger away smeared red. "Oh, well, I guess it hasn't dried yet." She ponders. "Should have."

Orrin looks away again, but there is no relief in looking away. There is only Che Guevara, in poster form, on another wall, grinning and farting. The miasma of Che's flatulence envelopes Orrin and he gasps. Doesn't she notice? What is she saying? A glass of water enters his peripheral vision.

"Here, drink this. Get hold of yourself. You've got some close listening to do."

"Augh!"

"Rosita, change that kid and get him out of here!" Tony commands obvious authority, pointing to the baby on the floor, who has shit, like raw pumpkin pie filling, oozing out of his diaper around his legs. Rosita disappears with her babies. From the pocket of his fatigue shirt, Tony draws a Havana. He unwraps it saying, "I hope this doesn't bother you. It smells better than shit."

Orrin looks up to see what he's talking about, thankful, at least, that it's not incense.

"Don't ask me how I got it and I won't have to tell ya."

"The Corina cigar store?" Orrin ventures, seeing only a cigar.

"Good enough." Tony strikes a kitchen match with his thumbnail, and with exaggerated puffs, lights up. "Now," he says between puffs, "for your story."

Orrin sips from his glass, readying himself for he knows not what. How Tony knows about the winch, if he knows anything about it. When he sneaked a look at his mail and learned his name, if that's how he knows it, or how he knows it, if it isn't. These are possibilities, but he has no idea what is coming. The air is heavy with Cuban smoke, but of course he doesn't know that either. He knows only that it is cigar smoke and it offends his eyes and nose, but, as Tony says, it is better.

"My great-great-grandfather," Tony begins, and Orrin is immediately at ease, remembering that this is supposed to be a story that he doesn't want to hear.

"My great-great-grandfather was very poor. He lived, for a time, in a small village on the Rio Grande called Guadalupe-Bravos, not far from Colonia Juarez." Tony stops here to measure Orrin's response, to look and wait for a gleam of suspicion, to puff his cigar.

But Orrin says blankly, "Yeah, yeah, I'm with you so far. Go on."

"He was a sandal maker, sometimes. Sometimes, a farmer. When he was in Guadalupe-Bravos, he was a sandal maker and very poor, but handsome and virile. Ninos all over the place. On my great-grandmother. On women all up and down the Rio Grande. Something like twenty-four kids in all. He recorded the ones he knew about in his family Bible. I *know* that doesn't sound like many children to you, a Mormon, but it is fair, is it not?"

Orrin nods, "Fair."

"Well," Tony pauses to puff, "there are many stories about my great-great-grandfather. Many stories, and most of them true. We have the relatives for proof. But of the many stories, there is one I like best. It tells of the time he went to Colonia Juarez to sell sandals to the Norte Americanos there. There was a community of Norte Americanos springing up in Juarez. A new community. Not the regular outlaws. These were outlaws, okay. But they were more respectable. Families. They were Mormons, running from the Federales of the U.S.A., because they had too many wives."

Tony pauses. "You know about this group of fugitives?"

"Yes. My great-grandmother was born in Juarez." Orrin speaks somberly, vaguely, as though he never knew her, just knows of her, and what he knows is sorrowful.

Tony thinks his story caused the change in Orrin's mood and adds: "I wouldn't worry about it, Orrin. You know Romney of HUD? He was born in Chihuahua, and that's really Mexico. Hell, Juarez might just as well be El Paso," he says, knowing there is all the difference in the world.

"Yeah, I know. A lot of people were born in Mexico."

"It's a horror to determinists," Tony points out, "but there are more important things than where a person is born."

Orrin wonders where Tony got a word like "determinists" and what he knows about their theories, but not for long, because Tony doesn't let him.

"Well," he continues, "great-great-grandfather had heard of these Mormons living in and around Colonia Juarez with their many wives and offspring. He had children of his own and knew the need for sandals would be great among the Mormons. So he made sandals, sturdy and in all sizes, packed them on his burro, and headed for Juarez. The morning was not yet born when he started out. And as he trudged along he thought, truly, only of the Mormon pesos he would get for his sandals. You know how coyotes yap to each other just before dawn? I know you do, you lived on a ranch. Well, they did that. Two, three yaps from scattered coyotes, each in turn. He took them as a farewell, good wishes. And when the sun came up, it looked to him like one big, shiny peso.

"He went to Colonia Juarez to sell the Mormons sandals. That is all. He found the Mormons all right.

But to his surprise there were not so many men as he had thought there would be. There were a few. But the husbands of many had returned to Utah, where they kept one wife and a reasonable number of children. The Federales would suspect them if they produced one wife and claimed she had given birth to thirty-one children. Especially because it was said that the wife they kept in Utah was the youngest, prettiest one.

"Naturally, there was much loneliness and resentment among the Mormon wives left without a man in Colonia Juarez. Most of them spoke no Spanish and had little contact with the natives. They did not socialize with the other outlaws, and the letters from Utah came less often than the rain. But they were strong. They had seen many hardships and were bearing this one bravely. Though they felt abandoned, only few would let their feelings be known to others. But in their letters to their husbands they pleaded for rescue, for a visit, for a reply.

"My great-great-grandfather was a man with eyes to see and ears to hear, and he had a heart that throbbed with compassion, especially for women. He did not learn all this about these women by selling them sandals. No. They were not so open with a sandal vendor. But there was one among them, a Senora Snow, who had not the strength of her sisters. They called one another sister, did you know?"

"I know," Orrin says, having recognized the surname of his great-great-grandmother, preparing to reject out of hand anything Tony will say, "they still do."

Tony looks Orrin over, figures he has rigidified, puffs his cigar. "As the story goes, there were, in

Colonia Juarez, at that time, three Senoras Snow. The other two, their names are not remembered, knew of Gwendolyn's lack of strength."

That's her name. Gwendolyn Snow, Orrin's great-great-grandmother. He looks straight at Tony, saying with his dark brown eyes: "You lie."

"Oh, she was not weak by any standard. Just not so patient as the others. She said aloud and often that they had been deserted. Her letters were not pleas. They were demands. She did her work, all right. She gathered wood, prepared the meals, sewed, cared for the children. She did as much as any of her sisters. But she also learned the language of the natives and took a lover—my great-great-grandfather, and yours."

Orrin snaps to his feet, sloshing water all over and then flinging the glass, he screeches, "No!" in a voice uncommonly shrill for a twenty-year-old male. He whips his head from side to side and screeches, "No!" again and again. But his long black hair slaps him in the face. He stops, begins to shake, collapses in the chair. "So that's it," he manages to murmur in a moment.

"That's not all of it." Tony puffs again. "The best part, the funny part, is coming."

"Funny?"

"Si. You know the other two Senoras Snow, they watched her like a pair of hawks."

"Ah, for God's sake, Tony. Don't recreate a fabliau. I couldn1t take it."

"A what?"

"I don't know. Just spare me all the 'funny' details, will ya?"

"I knew I should've waited," Tony thinks aloud.

"Waited? For what?"

"Well, I didn't plan on telling you her name till the end, see. I wanted to go all the way through the story about how they fell in love at first sight; how my great-grandfather scratched the sole of her foot with his middle finger while fitting her with sandals, because the hawks wouldn't let him touch her hand; how he pretended to leave for Guadalupe-Bravos and snuck back and gathered firewood and stacked it in the gulley behind the Snow's, so when Gwendolyn came out to gather wood, they could make love and she wouldn't go back empty handed; how the hawks discovered him waiting for her one evening and almost blew his head off with a shotgun; how he escaped and tricked them into sending Gwendolyn to him with a forged letter ordering her to return to Salt Lake City; how their happiness was interrupted when Senor Snow arrived unexpectedly in Colonia Juarez and tracked them down and nearly blew his head off with a .45; how he escaped with his life and, knowing when his luck had run out, returned to Guadalupe-Bravos; how he later learned that Gwendolyn was whipped, reprimanded, and forgiven, and their child, a girl, raised with the others. I planned to tell you all this and then spring her name on you and tell you the child was your great-grandmother, and we are cousins."

"Well," Orrin sighs, "I'm glad you didn't."

"I think, Cousin, you would've laughed at their adventures, before you knew her name."

"I doubt it," Orrin says, thinking of something else. "One question, Tony. Could your great-great-grandfather read and write *English?*"

"Ah, the letter. No. He could speak a little, but read and write it, he could not. There was a Norte

11

Americano he knew, a professional counterfeiter and good at forgery. He was a fugitive in Colonia Juarez. He owed our great-great-grandfather a favor. And hated the Mormons. He welcomed the chance to pay his debt and fool the sisters. Had I told the story fully, the way I planned, you'd have learned that."

"Umm-hmm."

"You do not believe me?"

"I don't know. I'm tempted to. It explains a lot; brings things into focus. I'll have the Genealogy Society run a thorough check. I should've thought of it before."

"But that Senor Snow, he may have claimed the child. You never know. The records might have it wrong. Your hair and eyes, your skin, they do not lie."

****

Orrin sinks into contemplation. Tony puffs his cigar, watches him, and lets him go, undisturbed, waiting for him to speak. To pass the time, he picks from the floor and peruses a comic book, *Zap 4*.

"Do you know anybody else named Orrin Porter Rockwell, with a last name of his own tacked on?" He is asked some seven pages in.

"No. Not right off hand."

"No. I didn't think so. It's not exactly a popular name. Not like John or Mark or Matthew or Luke."

"Or Antonio," Tony adds with a grin, much like Che's.

"Have you ever heard of anybody named Orrin Porter Rockwell?"

Tony thinks. "Was there not, in the early days, a Mormon bandito by that name? Who preyed upon the wagon trains?"

"He wasn't a *bandit*," Orrin condescends, "and as far as anyone can *prove*, he is only responsible for the massacre of one small band of emigrants, and that he did not do single-handed, or without orders. He was, mainly, just a bodyguard for Joseph Smith, and then for Brigham Young. But he was also on call to right any serious injustices. He was a Mormon lawman not a bandit.

"He probably would've been forgotten completely right after his death if it weren't for his eccentricities."

"Oh, yeah?"

"Yeah. He had long hair, much longer than my own, which, by prophecy of Joseph Smith, protected him from bullets and any other bodily harm, as long as he didn't cut it."

"Kinda like Samson?" Tony observes.

"Yeah, and he wore a mustache and full beard. His wild, piercing eyes turned his enemies to jelly. His voice climbed to an ear-shattering shrill falsetto when he got angry or excited. He carried two sawed-off pistols in his coat pockets because he didn't like holsters. He was possessed by an angel, The Avenging Angel, and claimed that *he* never killed anybody. The *Angel* did it. When he was sent to get somebody, he was a maniac, persistent, and his tracking skills were common knowledge. Some outlaws, offenders of the Lord, turned themselves in to the nearest secular lawman for protection. One of 'em knew that he couldn't make it to a jail before Rockwell caught him and committed suicide in the desert rather than face the Avenging Angel.

"If it hadn't been for his eccentricities, he would've been just another Mormon lawman, just another member of the Sons of Dan, just another agent of the Lord, forgotten. But, he had 'em, and he was not forgotten. I *can't* forget him, 'cause he is my great-granduncle. And he's an angel himself now. "

"Jesus," Tony chews the cigar to the other side of his mouth, "what a lineage."

"He's really not *that* close a relative, Tony. Which makes me wonder. As far as I know, I'm the only person of our generation with his full name. None of his more direct descendants have it."

"There is a reason for this you think?"

"Yes. I'm beginning to. It's not entirely clear yet. But things are falling into place, and it's a little frightening."

"Frightening? To have the name of such a glorious man, why?"

Of course, Orrin can't tell him. No other mortal knows of Orrin's duty here on Earth, and no one will know, either, until it's done. But he must tell Tony something, to throw him off the track, if he is on it. So he tells him something true, because it comes to mind:

"Well, there's something just a little mysterious about the way my mother died. She was my father's second wife. He has another now. I was her only child. She died when I was born. Orrin Porter Rockwell is also the great-granduncle of all my brothers, but my father named me Orrin Porter Rockwell Christianson. It's just a little frightening was all I said. Just a little. I mean, I'm not scared stiff or anything."

"And your mother was the.... Let's see, she'd be the great-granddaughter of Senora Gwendolyn?"

"You've got it. And, if what you say is true, about her and that sandal maker, that just might be a clue."

Orrin pauses and then says as though confessing: "My father dislikes Mexicans. He pays his ranch hands pitifully, sometimes not at all. Says they waste their money anyway, have too many kids. Says they're lazy, no-account, low life. I think he hates them."

Slowly removing the Havana from his mouth, Tony corrects him: "Us, Cousin. He hates us."

Whatever kind of put-down or instant ethnic membership Tony meant to imply, it is lost on Orrin. He had noticed (it was impossible not to) that his father felt differently about him. Unlike his brothers, Orrin did not receive his father's Fatherly Love, which all good fathers give openly. But neither was he treated badly, as he would have been if his father hated him. No. Tony is wrong, Orrin thinks. My father doesn't love me, but he doesn't hate me the way he hates Mexicans. He... He *respects* me. That's it, respect. Even fearful respect. As Americans respect the Soviets. I guess there is a little hate in there. But he could have done me in. He had chances. If he hated me, he could have done lots of things. Given me away. Yeah, it's more mystical than our national feelings about the Soviet Union. It's closer to the way some people feel about God. But Orrin can remember nothing he had done to deserve such respect. He knows only that he got it and still would if he went home. Example: his father admired a good shot, a clean kill, and taught his sons, including Orrin, how to shoot. It was an important skill for them learn. But he never berated Orrin's poor marksmanship, never mentioned it. Orrin sees that Tony has again picked up the comic book and feels

15

he was rude to have withdrawn into his thoughts again so quickly.

"He never even joked about it," Orrin says.

"What?" Tony imagines Orrin's father not joking about his black hair, brown eyes, and skin just dark enough to look like he is suntanned, all over.

"When everybody else was riding me about being a rotten shot, he never even teased. He made them stop once. It embarrassed me, too, because he made it sound like they were being blasphemous or something, you know."

"Oh?"

"He didn't say anything to me, as usual. He just shouted, 'Shut up!' the way he had when they were making jokes about Joseph Smith and the Golden Plates. They shut up, all right, and never teased me again when he was around. But I don't think he did it out of love."

"I am disappointed," Tony says. "Your uncle, I like him better as a bandito, you know what I mean? I mean, back then I think I like the Mormons better, all around. They were oppressed, were they not? The underdogs, kicked around. I can see their need for a strong bandito. Their ruthlessness, then, was justified. But now they are in control, and their ruthlessness continues."

"Oh, come off it, Tony. Ruthlessness?"

"You have not been a Mexican for long, Cousin. Try it full-time. Join the Church. Try being a Roman Catholic Mexican in this Mormon State. The methods, they have changed. There is no long-haired Avenging Angel anymore. But the ruthlessness that possessed him remains."

"I'll be honest with you, Tony. I think you're indulging in self-pity."

Tony sucks his lips, bobs his head, acknowledging Orrin's honesty as the typical easy answer. "How long you plan to live here?" he asks.

"Next door you mean?" Orrin dodges, alertly sensing a trap.

"Yeah. Next door, or anywhere on the West side with the Mexicans and blacks and Japs and Chinks and Indians."

"Oh... I don't know. Till June at least. Maybe till I finish school." Orrin stops lying. "I don't even know why I'm here."

"What?" Tony says in mock disbelief, thinking he has slammed the trap shut. "You're not going to live your whole life out in that wonderful house?"

Orrin yields to the temptation to escape, and to obscurely talk about his mission. He knows it must remain a secret, but he cannot resist toying with it now and then, dropping hints (he fears he might, subconsciously, want to be discovered and stopped). "That just might *be* the rest of my life."

"Besides your lineage and your name, you've got a terminal disease?"

Orrin chuckles to himself. Some people might call it that. But he says, "No. But, you never know, tomorrow I might get hit by a garbage truck as I cross the road."

"Bullshit. You don't plan to stay here. You've got goals, hopes, just like everybody else, and for you they are possible. But some, some hope in vain."

"But they do hope." Orrin wants to keep him going in this direction, away from his careless clue.

17

"It is a curse. It is a blessing. Their hope is blind and senseless. But it will nurture revolution."

Orrin tells himself he should have known. But he is not completely sure. Maybe Tony is just talking. Nothing like a straightforward question to find out: "Are you a Communist?"

"Hell, no." Tony says with pride, thinking there is nothing like a straightforward answer to inform. "The Communists are fools. They don't know that God creates them constantly. They think that they have the power. The Mormons are more communist than I."

"What's with the poster, then?"

"Che is a selfless martyr who transcends Communism. I am not, nor ever will I be, as great as Che." He looks fondly at the poster. "But I am a revolutionist. And, now, Cousin, so are you."

Orrin is not so much different from anybody else that he likes or accepts appointments such as this. No one becomes a revolutionist by appointment, especially if they don't want to be a revolutionist and the person purportedly inducting them into the revolution has no power to induct. Orrin has more important things to do. He has no time for Tony's revolution. He laughs, begins to stand.

Tony stops him halfway up with a hand to his chest and gently pushes Orrin back into the chair.

"You will not have to shoot a gun or throw a bomb. There are plenty for those jobs. You will not even lead a march. There are Chicano liberals for that." There is disgust in Tony's voice. "I hate that word 'Chicano.' I do not use it for myself. My heritage," he taps his chest proudly with a thumb, "my heritage, my blood, is Mexican. Where does this word 'Chicano' come from?"

Orrin knows he's not supposed to answer.

"There is, in Mexico, a word like this 'Chicano'. It is 'Mestizo'. All are Mexicans. But some, they say, are still of *pure* Spanish blood—it is so nice—and some are still plain Indios, living in the mountains, primitive and uncounted, because the census takers won't go among them out of fear. They still have magic, they still have sorcerers, they are so primitive. The majority, though, are called Mestizo. They *feel* inferior to those few of Spanish blood, though most will not admit it. And the Mestizos feel and act superior to the Indios, though they fear the Indios' raw, primitive power." Tony rests now, collects himself. Then bursts:

"In Mexico, it is simpler. There are not so many races and just one nationality. Two races mixed and made a new one. So there are three. Here, we have hundreds. You know of them. All are supposed to be Americans. But some are more American than others, you understand?"

"I think so."

"You *don't!* I tell you where Chicano comes from and why it stinks of degradation. You say you understand. You don't understand. I'll draw a picture with a crayon. You hear of those Asian-Americans, those Afro-Americans, those Mexican-Americans. All modified Americans. Not True-Americans. Even Native-Americans are not the real Americans.

"I was born here, just like you. But I am Mexican-American. And you, though partly Mexican, are just American. Not Anglo-Mexican-American or even Anglo-American. Just American. Black hair and

19

all." Tony flips Orrin's hair. Orrin jerks his head away.

"I will not strike you, Cousin. You are not to blame. But you know how it is. Some people, white or light-skinned people, in their rush, leave off 'American.' They just say 'Mexican.' It's fine with me. As I have said, there are more important things than where a person's born. The 'Mexican' is deeper." Tony says, cupping his hands on his chest drawing in. "The 'American' is superficial, circumstantial. To me, Mexican is fine. But to some it is humiliating. They want to be Americans, or at least not be called Mexicans."

He stops abruptly, looks around, then whispers: "Some will even claim that *they* are not Mexican at all. They say *Spanish*. Again the pure, nice, European, *Spanish* blood. It is a tragic thing to hear from one with high cheek bones and dark brown skin. But they have learned that it is low to be a Mexican. They learned it here, of course. In Mexico, they'd be Mestizo, and that's not so low. The Indios are still beneath them, and, besides, they are the majority."

Tony resumes his normal voice. "So. We have the liberals. They think 'Mexican' is low. They do not like the word, and they know the foolishness of saying they are Spanish. So, they say they are 'Chicano.' They convince no one. If you ask another Mormon what 'Chicano' means, he will tell you it means Mexican. Ask one of your professors, he will tell you Mexican-American. No white man is fooled by a word. I say it is worse than Uncle Tom. It is *triquiñuela*. And they have done it to themselves.

"Anyway, they think they are progressive, and they will march. They want only minor changes. They are *afeminado*, but they pose as the Mexican threat to tranquility, and thus," Tony grins, "they are our shield. No, Cousin, you will not have to march or even show yourself in public. You have more important work to do. Work of consequence."

Orrin cringes. Tony couldn't know, but he talks as though he does.

"Do not cringe. It will not be difficult or dangerous. We are still preparing, and when it comes, we will not be alone, and it will not come only to Salt Lake or only through us Mexicans. You will be acknowledged by the Revolution. You will be allowed to survive, but your work will have been accomplished when the shooting starts."

To find out, and only to find out if Tony knows, Orrin asks, "What am I supposed to do?" He asks it doubtfully, implying that he is helpless and will be of little use. As though he had assumed that Orrin would come around, unsurprised, and without any congratulations or thanks, Tony gives him his assignment. "You will gather information on the secret mind control methods of the Mormon Church. We know that it has money, land, businesses, many financial investments. We know that it has its bureaucrats, its politicians, its mayors, governors, senators, congressmen, cabinet members. We know that it has its own welfare system. And we know about its militia. But we have only a vague idea how the Mormon Church controls the minds of its members so completely. I mean, how does it gets them to believe the *Book of Mormon*? In the face of reality, they believe that book. And do the head honchos of the Church believe it? We would like to know these secrets. You give me the information, and

I will decide what to do with it and give the orders. When the time comes. You need not be involved further, unless you want to be. In that case, we can train you."

Orrin is relieved and, at the same time, indignant. "And what makes you think I'd do a thing like that, even if I could? That story about the sandal maker?"

"No, Cousin. The story, it is true. You are part Mexican. But your loyalty, your devotion, they lie elsewhere. Not with us. I have certain information you might want—for reasons of your own. I have given it to the Chicanos already, and they have planned a demonstration. We have a fund-raising event scheduled. But, as I said, for reasons of your own, you might want to know when the Vice President of the United States of America will be in town." Tony pauses to observe Orrin's reaction, then adds: "It was a hunch. But I thought I might as well ask. I know the date, the hour, the agenda."

Orrin is slow to recover from the shock. When he does, he not quite convincingly asks: "Why should I want to know that? And, if I did—just assuming, *arguendo*, for the sake of argument, that I did want to know it—I could find out from the news. If I did...want to know...when Agnew...will be in town"

Tony is calm. "The reasons are your own. It is better that I do not know them. And, yes, you would see it in the papers and on TV. But you would not find out as much as I can tell you, or as soon as I could tell you. I could tell you now. If we come to an agreement. And, please, don't ask me how I know. That, I cannot tell you."

But Orrin thinks he is crafty. Tony's already told him all he needs to know. He can smooth out any one of several plans he's been developing, discover the essential details of Agnew's visit in the papers later, and pull it off without complicating his life by spying against the Church. If, somehow, Tony knows what he is going to do, and it looks to Orrin as though he might, Orrin feels certain he will not try to stop him. That is, if he is really a revolutionist, which Orrin thinks he is.

"Well, Tony, I'll have to think about it," he says, beginning to stand again. Tony pushes him back. He means it this time and sends Orrin into the deepest regions of the chair. "Think about it here, Cousin. Take your time. But tell me you agree."

Orrin's eyes flash wildly. He bolts to his feet yelling, brushes Tony to the floor as easily as he brushed aside blockers when he played linebacker in high school, and makes it out the door, almost flinging it off its hinges, before Tony can get up.

But if Orrin would look back, he would see that Tony isn't getting up. Tony has no intention of chasing after Orrin. Lying comfortably on his side, one hand propping up his head, he has returned to his comic book. But Orrin doesn't look back. He bounds into his Jeep, notices that the Chevy's stalled out, thinks it serves Tony right, and see if he jumps that Sun of his again. That serves him right, too. Orrin foresees Tony's children starving, while he keeps buying Suns. The stupid bastard. If he'll buy 'em, it serves him right. That scummy greaseball peppergut spic.

Orrin backs the Jeep into position between their houses, sprints into his house, locks the door behind him, and falls backwards onto the couch to think. The first thing he comes up with is that Tony is lying. That sandal-maker story is certainly a lie. And he's probably not a revolutionist, either. Just wishful thinking. Commander Archuleta, my ass. Agnew won't ever come to Salt Lake City. Tony's just trying, who knows why, to draw me out, to make me show my cards. After thinking of that metaphor, Orrin is sure that he is safe. He has no cards to show. He never touches them. Playing cards are for idle minds, and so is the Devil. And the Devil's Church. Tony belongs to the Devil's Church. He admitted it. All those idolatrous symbols on his walls, sickeningly evil. Gambling, idols, invocation of luck: all evil. Tony probably plays cards all the time. Just goes to show his value system. He stole that Honda and those tires, it's obvious. Runs a midnight auto parts. He'll probably steal my Diehard next. I'll epoxy razor blades to the hood. That'll fix his greasy fingers. Maybe not, though. He's so sneaky, might get it, anyway. I'll rig the Diehard with a bomb. It'll go off five minutes after the Diehard's disconnected. Blow him and his Chevy to Kingdom Come. That'll serve him right. Too bad I don't know how to rig a bomb.

Agnew's never coming here. I'll have to go someplace else. I've known that all along. It would be too easy here. He'll never come. Ho, ho, if he did though... I might even get away. Don't bank on it. It's possible but not important. If you can do it and get away, that's okay, but get it done. That's all that matters. You'll be taken care of, even if you're caught. Don't worry. Don't make any plans to get away. Don't complicate your mission. If, in the chaos, you see your chance, then go, but don't be disappointed if you're caught. I'll have to learn how to rig a bomb, Orrin is thinking as the telephone rings.

He picks up the receiver, "Hello."

"Hello, this is Commander Archuleta."

"Yeah, I know. What do you want? Make it fast. I'm busy. I'll hang up soon."

"Do you know Dan Watersman?"

"No."

"I do. Very well. He is the top narcotics detective in Salt Lake City. He's in charge of the Greater Salt Lake Drug Task Force, works directly with the DEA. I'm on his payroll, one of his Mexican informants."

Orrin doesn't believe him but says, "So?"

"I have never given him bad information. If I tell him there's a long-haired pot dealer living next door to me, one who peddles to elementary school kids— he hates them worst of all—if I tell him that..."

Orrin hangs up. He has nothing to fear from the narcotics squad. Tony's lying, anyway. Who'd trust that spic? Surely, not a policeman. The phone rings again. Orrin lets it ring, but Tony, lying on the floor in comfort, can and does wait him out. Orrin decides to tell him off, picks up the receiver and starts to say, "Listen."

But Tony is already talking. "He won't bust you right away. He'll compile a dossier. He'll have you watched. He'll corroborate my tip. He'll search your house while you're at school."

"He won't find anything." Orrin squeezes it in, visualizing the poisons, the commando knives, the daggers, straight razors, hatchets, hammers, the garrotes, stashed around his house.

"He'll think you're smart, that's all. He'll have a narc approach you, try to score. He'll have another one try to sell you a *large* quantity of weed. Cheap. I can get you ten kilos of Panama Red for five grand,

Cousin. He'll still be watching you when Agnew comes to town."

This time Tony hangs up. Orrin lunges for the phone book, finds the Archuletas, no Tony, dials information, dials it wrong, dials again: sorry, unlisted number. He runs outside, tripping on the doorsill, landing face first in the private roadway, planting seven pebbles in his cheek. From his vantage point, though his view is marred by ruts and rocks and notices of fantastic sales at Sears, Orrin can observe one important fact: the Chevy's gone. And so, he assumes correctly, are Tony and his wife and kids.

"Raspberries!" Orrin squeaks as he picks himself up, choosing not to interject a fricative plosive "Fuck!" because of his observance of the Mormon doctrine of salvation by works.

****

Orrin sulks the evening away, knowing he is trapped and finding no solace in listening to his Mormon Tabernacle Choir tapes, watching out the window for a light in Tony's house, thinking of turning Tony in as a Commander in the Revolution, or as a dope-smoking, petty thief. But, of course, there is no justice. The charges wouldn't stick. Tony'd slither out of them and tell Dan Watersman his vicious lie."

"My anonymity'd be gone!" Orrin laments, before retiring at nine. He has always retired early, risen early, learned it on the ranch, likes his life that way. But he is confident that, when necessary, he can endure long periods of sleeplessness, just because he is so rested. He *knows* he can, he's done it, but the memory is unpleasant, so he forces it from his mind and goes to sleep.

As always, The Hymn is with him. It is planted so far down in his soul that it knows no hours, no states of mind. It is always there, continuous, reeling off the stanzas, creating new ones. It is his lullaby, the sound track of his dreams, his morning song. There are times, of course, he doesn't hear it, when he is concentrating on something else for instance, as his studies at the University, but it is there, as background music, hardly noticed till there's a lull in concentration, hardly noticed but controlling his behavior, or at least his attitude—his own Muzak. But more than that, it's his attitudinal gyroscope, or gyrostabilizer, his automatic pilot. He never strays for long from thought about his mission, and even when he does, he really doesn't. Everything he reads, or sees, or hears, everything he senses, everything he thinks is related to his purpose. Either it is useful or it isn't. It sheds new light or doesn't. It is interesting or dull depending on its applicability to killing Agnew. If Orrin is obsessed, it is The Hymn that keeps him. Without it, he would be free, and common decency would repel him from indulging murderous thoughts. But The Hymn is there, autonomic, more so than his heart. Through the influence of a lullaby stanza

Put your weary head to rest
Drift away.
You will need your sleep for strength.
Don't delay.
I have my work;
I will not shirk.
Put your weary head to rest.

Orrin arrives at pure and instant sleep. But, as sleep-time measures things, this lasts only an instant. Then, there's Agnew and a crowd of people on Temple Square. (Dream scenes are shot MOS; The Hymn and an occasional wild line, usually from Orrin, are the only sound.)

Now's your chance, while Agnew's here,
Get him now.
Do your duty like a bull
Not a cow.
I have my work;
I will not shirk.
Now's your chance, while Agnew's here.

Orrin's in the crowd, now, hatchet under his coat, a framing hammer on his right hip, a commando knife on his left, a dagger in his cowboy boot, a garrote around his neck, a spring-loaded, poisoned needle in each finger of the glove on his left hand.

Just one prick and Agnew's dead,
Merely touch him.
Do your duty with a heart full
Of your Hymn.
I have my work;
I will not shirk.
Just one prick and Agnew's dead.

The poison needles are something Orrin hasn't thought of yet. He'll "think of it" tomorrow, in a flash. The Hymn will let him take credit for the thought. Agnew's headed for Temple Square. Whenever any dignitary visits Salt Lake City, he gets a tour of Temple Square. If he is well-favored, he gets to make a speech in the Mormon Tabernacle. The Tabernacle lends prestige, the Church's blessing, and a peculiar, mystical, acoustical quality that enhances anything said by anyone, exalts it to divine, melodious wisdom. There's no telling in this dream if Agnew's just touring or is going to make a speech. The police are clearing a corridor through the cheering crowd. The Vice President has many fans in Salt Lake City.

Agnew thinks that he is safe,
Among friends.
But your duty says that here
His life ends.
I have my work;
I will not shirk.
Agnew thinks that he is safe.

His bodyguards are close, but Agnew's ranging from one side of the corridor to the other, shaking hands and waving, making leisurely progress. The Chicanos and the hippies are demonstrating peacefully outside the walls of Temple Square, but the police think that they are threatening to erupt at any moment, like a Molotov piñata.

There're more cops outside than in,
And that's good.
They are looking the wrong way,
As they should.
I have my work;
I will not shirk.
There're more cops outside than in.

Orrin's at the front of the crowd, on the edge of the corridor, watching Agnew approach. Because of the ultimate identification Orrin the dreamer has with Orrin the dreamed, there is no need for any verbal communication of what Orrin the dreamed is thinking, feeling. Orrin the dreamer knows that the dreamed is hoping Agnew will reach out for his hand and, ZAP, the needles will be buried in his wrist. If

Agnew doesn't reach out to him, Orrin's prepared to blitz. His heart thinks that his body is running wind sprints; his lungs agree; his legs are having fits. That cop, there, he's in the way. Put the hammer in his face. The guard'll try to take me out, but he'll go for the hammer. Just slide off and let him have that arm if he wants it, but get to Agnew with your left hand. If you can't get any closer, pull out the hatchet and throw it at his head. While Orrin's getting this information from himself, The Hymn continues (the theme is omnipresent; stanzas are inserted by The Hymn at appropriate moments).

Agnew's coming over here,
Cheer him, Yea!
Make him want to take your hand,
Give him Yea!
I have my work;
I will not shirk.
Agnew's coming over here.

And he is, too. Agnew's headed straight for Orrin. All things indicate that he will take Orrin's hand. Ah, God. Orrin readies for the clasp. So easy. Agnew reaches out. Orrin raises a steady, deadly hand. His heart has stopped. He's really going to do it! The Hymn assures him it is true. Then, a gigantic water balloon with arms, legs, and head, envelopes Orrin from he knows not where. Through the heavy water man, Orrin sees Agnew hustled safely passed. He also sees the letters D A N, fluorescent red, Microgramma Bold. He is smothering and cannot move. The needles in his glove, though triggered, have no effect. They do not penetrate or even scratch the thick water balloon.

Orrin the dreamer is smothering, too. Attempts to move are stifled. He's on the verge of waking up. But The Hymn doesn't want Orrin to wake up gasping and remembering, maybe taking it from here and thinking for himself. It wants to make sure Orrin gets the right idea.

Cut to Orrin in a labyrinth of bookshelves, working in a lonely carrel, filling yellow pads with notes. Dimly lighted, musty peace, tranquility. Easier than he thought.

Yes, agree to Tony's deal,
Give him secrets.
They are open, anyway,
Give him secrets.
I have my work;
I will not shirk.
Yes, agree to Tony's deal

Chapter Two

Secrets of Mormon Mind Control

In the morning, Orrin has a lot to think about. He has an eight o'clock class that starts at seven forty-five, so he's up at six, fixing breakfast, humming The Hymn. Clean-living, hard-working, early-to-bed and early rising Mormons, like Orrin, make up for smoking, drinking, carousing, and fornicating with food. Quality does not concern him that much. It is quantity he's after. Take for example Orrin's standard breakfast: hot oatmeal with sliced banana and raisins; a quarter-pound of bacon; hash browns; three scrambled eggs; four slices of buttered toast; orange juice, and milk. He prides himself in preparing the various elements of his breakfast all at once, at measured intervals, so that they are all ready to eat at exactly the same moment. In the beginning, it required intense concentration. When to start the oats, the bacon, when to toast the toast. He ran around the kitchen in a frenzy, scorching potatoes, burning bacon, buttering cold toast, or if he put it down again to warm, burning it, too. But now, he moves with the grace of a dancer, the speed and assurance of a veteran short order cook. Now, he thinks, he can think of other things (hum The Hymn) and cook his breakfast easily.

He thinks about his father, Clifford Milton Christianson. The Hymn doesn't care. It has planted its seeds, and no doubt they will grow. Is the tune not on his lips at this very moment? Are the words not ever present in the deepest regions of his mind?

Clifford Milton Christianson: the youngest of four sons. While he was still in his mother's womb, his father's horse stepped in a prairie dog hole and broke its leg. But that was not the worst of it. The horse broke its leg, and Clifford's father, thrown, tucked and rolled, perfectly. The fall didn't hurt him a bit, but as he completed his move, as he rolled spread-eagled onto his butt, he landed in a cactus patch—big, healthy prickly pear cactus. In the movies, in cartoons, someone's landing on a cactus always gets a laugh. He grimaces and grabs his ass; his life is not endangered, nor greatly changed. Clifford's father came to rest in a cactus patch with his legs spread open, and his Levis, old, worn thin, were no great hindrance to the needles of the prickly pear. Though he jumped right out of there as soon as he could, he had needles in his legs from the tops of his boots to his spine, a needle in his rectum, two in his right gonad and one in his left, more needles lacerated the epididymis and vas deferens, and one stuck painfully in the tip of his penis.

The high desert canyon country around Moab is hot and dry. Sweat evaporates immediately from most parts of your body, but your crotch, sealed in underwear and Levis, resting protected from the wind against warm saddle leather, retains its salty perspiration, as do the insides of your legs. Orrin knows all this. He knows his grandfather was in the hospital at Grand Junction, Colorado, for a week as surgeons removed the needles and treated the infection as best they could. Maybe, Orrin speculates, if they had had penicillin back then, things would have been different. But he must stick to what has happened, stay away from what might have happened "if this or if that," if he is to get anywhere. They *didn't* have penicillin, and his grandfather fathered no more children. Four. Only four. It is pathetic even now. Back then, with a ranch to run and leave to offspring, it was tragic. At least they were four sons. That was something for the old man to be thankful for.

Clifford Milton Christianson: the youngest of those four sons, after the World Wars, the only son. Orrin knows his father's brothers all joined up to save the world and got themselves killed. This information and many tall tales and bits of family history including the story about the cactus, Orrin got directly from his grandfather, a rugged, weathered old man he dearly loved. He died one spring of a stroke and didn't even fall off his horse. Eighty-six and pushing cattle out of canyons with the kids. Oh, he hired Mexicans to do most of the work, but he insisted on participating in the roundup, the branding, and trucking up to the mountains every spring, and he was the Boss.

His grandfather would sit in his big leather chair with Orrin in his lap or, when Orrin was too big for that, at his feet, and tell him about the nature of things. Turning the bacon, buttering the toast, Orrin remembers how much it meant to him—listening to that old man. Asking questions, getting long, exciting answers. Orrin and his father rarely exchanged even perfunctory greetings. If, for instance, Clifford wanted Orrin to do something, he'd route the order through one of his other sons. "Joseph, you and Orrin put that new universal joint in the Jimmy and then go pick up the strays they drove out of Salt Creek." That's if they were all together. When they were scattered around the ranch and Cliff wanted Orrin to do something, he would find another of his sons and have him relay the message.

Orrin has been no more than twenty-five feet from his father, seen him walk at least a hundred and fifty yards to Mark or Hyrum, Tim or Joe; seen him talk and maybe point, then had his brother walk up to him and say: "Dad wants you to. . . ." Orrin often felt the word to follow should be "die." He reminds himself, now, not to dwell on the way his father treated him, not to dredge particular incidents from his memory, instead, to search his memory for the reasons. He regrets not having asked point blank one evening, "Grandpa, why does Dad fear and respect me so much that there can be no true father-son relationship between us? Why?"

His grandfather died well before he was able to articulate a question like that. But he could have asked why his father didn't like him, which is what he had thought most of his life. It was not until recently that he had become aware of the true state of affairs, realizing that "like" and "dislike" were secondary considerations not gotten to because of the overwhelming fear, which spawned, for some unknown reason, respect rather than maliciousness. If he'd had the courage to ask his grandfather why his father didn't like him, Orrin is certain he would have gotten the answer. "There I go 'ifing' again," he says out loud as he scrambles his eggs.

****

Clifford Milton Christianson married his virgin high school sweetheart two months after returning from his mission to South Africa. Everyone knew that they would wed as soon as he came back, knew they'd have been married sooner; and, that Cliff would have skipped the mission, if his father had not insisted that he serve, for his brothers' sakes. Only the waiting list for Temple Marriages could have forced them to wait two months, and it did. Even then they had to settle for the St. George Temple. It was not the Salt Lake Temple, which was hopelessly booked solid till November, and they simply couldn't wait that long. But still it was a Temple Marriage, and it sealed them to each other forever. Their marriage was as beautiful, as fulfilling, as fruitful as they had dreamed it would be. Before she died five years later of Rocky Mountain spotted fever, Elizabeth bore four healthy, clean-cut sons.

At the time, Cliff was studying Animal Husbandry at Utah State and may have brought the tick home with him from a field trip. He's always thought that he had done so. He was quick to accept the responsibility for his wife's death and almost as quick to shift most of it to his father. He had been around cattle and sheep all his life. He'd burned ticks out of his legs, even out of his groin, but he had never seen a case of Rocky Mountain spotted fever, until his father sent him away to university, and he had to go on field trips to unhealthy herds. When Cliff got right down to it, his father had caused her death—his father and Utah State.

Cliff's father had a healthy respect for any education that did not attempt to discredit the Church or demoralize the children, especially if it might help him turn a profit, and though it had not originally been Cliff's responsibility to learn the new fangled ways, he was determined that one of his sons do it, so it had to be Cliff. He was not a good student—better than he would have been at Philosophy or Mathematics, but still not good. He became even worse during his wife's illness, and after her death he flunked out and came home to face the quiet rage and restrained disgust of his father, who held back only because of his son's grief.

He allowed Cliff to sulk around the ranch for a couple of months, dabbling at this and that, playing with his sons, and, occasionally, with a glance or a sudden phrase, implying that his father was morally culpable for his wife's death. His father was not stupid; he read the looks, the implications, but he made no reply, knowing it would be better for Cliff to learn on his own that he was wrong. Besides, he was truly sympathetic. Unfortunately, the only way he could show it was by leaving Cliff alone, keeping quiet on the subject. Under the circumstances, to say that it had been God's Will, which he believed, would have sounded like passing the buck. So, rather than start a religious argument, he remained silent and let Cliff's grief take its course. Then, he climbed on Clifford's back, coaxed him, spurred him, rode him out and sent him back to school. He was not the first, nor would he be the last man to lose a wife. With grief, as with everything else, enough is enough; and too much, unhealthy.

This second time around Cliff attacked his studies with apathy and determination. He was still not a good student and didn't care much to have an education, but he had to finish in order to get back to his sons, and he knew his father would let him have no peace until he graduated. He returned to university with, say, enough determination to overcome his apathy for one semester; for he thought he had only one semester to go. But after enduring the readmissions procedures he found that he had two, "a whole darned academic year" he wrote his father. His hopes to get it over and be home for good by Christmas and maybe start looking for a new mother for his sons were blasted. He knew appeals to either the school or his father would be futile, so he didn't even rough them out in his mind. He accepted his bitter fate and decided to make the best of it.

What he did: he studied during the day, except on Sundays, every free moment he could force himself and at night and on weekends went looking for the next mother of his children. For he had realized one day, while unconsciously ogling a group of coeds, that the Utah State University campus was a much more promising place to look for a woman than Moab. Also, he remembered with a tear and a twinge of pain that he had already married the best woman Moab had to offer. Which made him wonder if maybe his father wasn't wiser and more benign than he had thought: tough on the outside but with a heart as warm and rich as homemade pudding. "Maybe he knew it'd work out this way all along." This proposition fit the Father Myth perfectly, so he believed it, always willing to give his dad the benefit of any doubt. He even found himself thinking that his father, who acted in strange ways, would make an excellent god.

Cliff had converted and baptized two hundred and fifty-three souls (no blacks) during his two years in South Africa, which is neither an outstanding nor a poor performance, but none of them had asked about the possibility of becoming god of his own private universe when he left this world. Cliff had been instructed not to inform potential converts of the possibility, because the concept might be too complex for the essentially monotheistic Gentile to grasp right away. Let them learn about it when they have become more immersed in Mormon thought. Chances of a convert earning a universe of his own aren't too good, anyway, so why mention it and maybe lose a soul that could otherwise be saved? Chances of Cliff's father becoming god somewhere weren't too good, either. He swore too much, drank coffee everyday, and drank whisky, sometimes. Worse than that, though, he wasn't married in a Temple and never had his marriage solemnized. But Clifford liked to think that if the whole thing weren't so involved with petty rules and ceremonies, his father would be a shoe-in and make a darn good god.

Presuming his father's blessings, he began his wife-hunt in earnest, feeling the excitement that goes with any hunt and cautioning himself against "buck" or in this case "doe fever". He silently laughed when he thought of that one. And Cliff was a good hunter, anyone could tell you that. He knew what he was after and where to find it. He frequented church socials, singles groups, evening religion classes, and fireside discussion groups, the Sunday meetings at University Wards 1,2, and 3. He joined the LDSSA. The girl would have to be a special, hearty, breed to take on a man with four sons and be prepared to give him more, many more, but if she were to be found, Cliff knew he'd find her in those places.

The second Sunday in November, during Sacrament Meeting at University Ward No.3, Clifford scanned the congregation. He had never scanned a ridge or canyon, sagebrush flat, or cedar grove more carefully than he scanned that group—and never spotted a finer prize. She was beautiful, big-boned, not fat though, and not an Amazon. But she looked strong. The subtle darkness of her skin was so integral to her beauty as to go unnoticed. Perhaps Clifford placed too much trust in his concept of natural habitats. Finding a woman of Mexican blood in that congregation, or in any of his carefully chosen haunts, would be to him like finding an alligator on the slick rock. But just as there are lizards on the slick rock, so are dark-haired women in the congregation—an innocent Mediterranean influence. Not that the Church actively dissuades Mexicans from joining—that is not its policy. It actively converts Mexicans. But most Mormon Mexicans are in Mexico, where Mormonism is the second largest Church. There are few in Utah, and they are usually unseen. But she was visible, pristine. She didn't know that a Mexican sandal maker was her grandfather, so she had no secrets to keep or to betray.

Clifford spotted her that Sunday in November, introduced himself the next week, had her sealed to him forever in the Logan Temple on the twenty-first of May. Her name was Linda Johnson, too common for her he thought. He liked Mrs. Clifford Christianson better, and he called her Lin. She gave him strength to carry on, more time to cram for finals, and a fertile field to plow. He barely graduated in June and returned to the ranch with a healthy, pregnant mother for is sons. All was going well.

****

Orrin knows that a lot of white people in the West think Mexicans are scum. Orrin's father is not unique in his hatred, more demonstrative and intense, perhaps, but not unique. Taking his father's hatred as a given, a constant, assuming that Tony's story is true, and that his mother was indeed of Mexican blood, assuming also that his father discovered this, Orrin can come up with a thousand scenarios of confrontation, railing, even violence, but none that justifies his father's fear/respect for him. His father is too arrogant to fear a greasy little Mexican, even if he is his son.

Nostalgia, a need to know, a yearning for his grandfather, an innate trust, a faith that tells him his grandpa still lives and can be contacted, all this and a specific, spiritual gift enable Orrin to have an audience with his grandpa, while he cooks his breakfast. The scene—he and Grandpa in a cloud bank—flashes on his mind's eye like a movie on a screen, and he asks the question he should have asked before his Grandpa died. "Grandpa, why doesn't Dad like me?"

If you were there, within ear-shot, you'd hear him ask that question, but you wouldn't hear the answer. Grandpa is seated and settles back into the cloud, betraying his anticipation, preparing his reply—then moves forward, leaning with his forearms on his legs. His face is about a foot from Orrin's, and he looks straight into Orrin's eyes. "Dag nabbit, Or, your father's scared to death of you, and dang well should be, too. He had no business shooting down your mother like he did. I'll tell you now; I had no part in it. I knew right off, soon as he brought her in the house, she had some Mexican in her. I guess old age has mellowed me a tad, 'cause when I saw her belly bulging with a grandson and the way she loved that no-good Cliff, I fooled myself into thinking there wasn't really none in her at all. Cliff had seen her genealogy, 'course, and she'd seen his, before they married. That was standard, well and good. You know it well as I do. Snows and Johnsons, Hatchers, Fletchers, Williamsons, Smiths, far back as you want to go, nothing to suggest a trace of Mexican. Well, I knew, deep down, somethin' wasn't on the up and up. Then one day, when your mother was nigh on nine months on with you, your father got this typed-up letter from the Snow Family Organization. It said in backwards, upside down, left-handed ways that there had been some sort of mix-up down in Mexico, and Linda Johnson's grandfather might not have been Erastus Snow, though he *was married* to her grandmother and fidelity was assumed. The secretary who typed it up and sent it out said she was getting on in years and was a little absent-minded and apologized for the delay. It didn't help your father much, knowing she was sorry. He cursed her old age up and down, then threw up on the letter.

"He looked at me and said, 'Do you know what this means?' I thought I did, knew it all along. Figured it was something he'd have to live with. I gotta tell ya, Or, I didn't give your dad his due. He hates Mexicans more than almost any man I knew in all my days on Earth. He didn't get that much hate for them from me. I've never in my life just shot one down. But your father, now, he went crazy—the cold, calm-eyed kind of crazy when he was through with his cursin' and throwin' up. I thought maybe he had purged himself, but I shoulda known better. Let me tell ya, Orrin, he walked away from me cool and calm-eyed as could be, and when I saw him next, he was a blabbering, jellyfish fool, scared shitless. I could smell his shit above the guts and gun smoke. Your mom, she was in the kitchen when it happened, slicing homemade bread for sandwiches. Cliff snuck in quiet like and just stood there with that single-action .45 pointed at her back. She was singing "Put Your Shoulder to the Wheel":

Put your shoulder to the wheel,
Push a-long.
Do your duty with a heart
Full of s-ong.
We all have work;
Let no one shirk.
Put your shoulder to the wheel.

Can you believe it, Or? She was standing there working her fanny off, making sandwiches for Cliff and his kids, singing that beautiful hymn, and when she turned around, Cliff shot her. Right in the belly. Now, you know dang well what kind of damage a .45 can do at close range."

Orrin nods, "Yeah."

Orrin remembers his dad's single-action Colt .45. He saw him shoot a trapped coyote with it once. Blew it right in half.

"Well, let me tell, you, now," his grandpa is saying. "Cliff thought that he would just wipe you both out with one shot, and he should've, too. But when I got there, like I said, Cliff was wallowing on the floor in his own shit, speaking in tongues. Your mom was splattered on the wall and cabinets, in the sink, all over. And I looked down at her body on the floor, and I saw this little fist poking out the hole in her belly, and this little wrist and forearm, and they were coming further out. I swear I almost fell down on the floor with your dad. It was a miracle, Orrin. You, yourself, a living miracle.

"By the Grace of God, I kept my wits about me and helped you out of there. 'Course I didn't bring you out the normal way. I helped you out the way you'd started out yourself. Sure as I'm sittin' here, Orrin, I swear you woulda made it without my help. I swear you woulda wriggled outta there and lived. The umbilical cord was gone. I didn't do hardly nothin'. I washed you off, wrapped you up, and called the doctor and the Sheriff. You were not as premature as I had expected. You were healthy, crying, strong. You had a head of hair like no kid I ever saw before, and I thought of Orrin Porter Rockwell, right away. You didn't have a scratch on you! The impact of that hollow point should have popped you like a bubble, but it didn't. The doctor checked you out, no internal damage, no concussion, nothin'. You scored a perfect 10 on the APGAR scale.

"Your dad was hauled away and charged with murder. I got him the best lawyer in Utah. The judge, the prosecutor, everybody knew us. He was acquitted. The jury said it was self-defense. She came at him with the bread knife."

"What about my brothers?"

"They were outside, playing. 'Course they heard the shot and came running in. I shooed them back out again as soon as I could. Joseph, who was about six and a half, would have the clearest memory of it, but he don't remember much, 'cause he didn't get to see too much. We never mentioned it, and he never brought it up himself, but I'm sure he must have images, emotions still hanging around, working themselves into his dreams. He has a lot of bad dreams. But don't worry about your brothers. They're all right. This whole thing is between you and Cliff.

"He's sure you're gonna kill him someday, but he's too dang scared to lay a hand on you. He won't even look at you for long. He knows he missed the best chance he had to do you in, and knows it was a miracle against him that you lived. He's positive you're an agent of the Lord, sent to destroy him. And you're doing it just by living. He thinks that you can shoot straighter than anybody ever, straighter than O.P.R., himself. He thinks you miss on purpose, so's everybody'll think that you can't shoot. Then, when you shoot him, nobody will suspect you done it. He thinks you got the same Avenging Angel in you Orrin Porter Rockwell had, and that's what scares him most. 'Cause if you do, ain't nothin' on this Earth can stop that Angel from killin' what it's supposed to kill. Nothin'. Not even you. As Joe Smith once said, 'The Angel has done the work, as I predicted, but Rockwell was not the man who shot; the Angel did it.' You take care o' yourself, Orrin. Don't let your breakfast burn."

The smell of burning oats, potatoes, bacon, burning bacon grease... The frying pan's in flames! Orrin snuffs out the blaze with Arm & Hammer Soda, cleans up the mess, drinks orange juice and milk for breakfast. His stomach will begin to growl about half-way through his first class.

Chapter 3

Into The Maze

Driving in his open Jeep to school, Orrin stops for a freight train. It's stopped, too, and he's in for a wait. Every other morning he's crossed the 28 tracks before the morning freight pulls in, but he's running a little behind schedule this morning. He's about to back up, turn around, and drive the extra blocks to the overpass when he sees what looks like two duffle bags roll out of a box car, flop on the cinders to the right of the road. Neither moves. Then the one with dirty, frazzled, holey, once high-topped but now low-cut, jungle boots sticking out, that one stands, drags the other over to the Jeep. "What town is this?" His mail of corroded medals jangles as he swirls his free hand at the city. Railroad dirt is thick on him, but the eyes are there, blue beneath the bill of his fatigue cap. Grimy teeth between soot-black lips.

"This is Salt Lake City, Utah, Sir."

"Ah-ha, and Hooah!" He exclaims. He tosses the duffle in back and jumps into the Jeep, "Take me to the fort."

"Fort Douglas?"

He slaps Orrin on the knee. "Ah, you spics are all alike. Of course, Fort Douglas. How many forts are there in this two-bit town? Let's roll, boy. Any gooks in the area? You know they're all together, don't you? You should know that. It should be known, generally and privately, too. Corporally, even. It should be spread around. You got to watch out for them gooks. All of 'em. We ain't got no friends over there. Back here in the world, you don't know that. You think everybody is Jesus Christ Himself. But gooks ain't Jesus Christ. Gooks is gooks. Got any salt water taffy on ya, Gomez? Might as well get used to it, with the lake. Hey, where are all the sprinklers? I could use a shower."

Orrin's headed for the overpass by now. He's sure this guy's a nut, and he's going to take him to the V.A. Hospital, not the fort. Both are on the perimeter of the University, not far from his first class. Angry at first, he was ready to beat the raspberries out of this dirty bum and throw him out. Now that he knows he's got a freaked-out Vietnam vet in his Jeep, he's just ignoring him. McKinstry is used to it, though. He keeps talking. If talking to someone who isn't there is the same as talking to somebody who isn't listening is the same as talking to yourself, which McKinstry feels is true, then everyone who prays is as mad as he. He presented that to the Chaplin one day, hoping for rebuttal. But the Chaplin wasn't listening. He couldn't even shock attention out of him, not with words.

Half the time he doesn't listen to himself. He withdraws into an emptiness as vast as death. He's sure that he is a non-entity. Now and then he'll surprise a stranger, as he did Orrin, and be briefly recognized as a living human being. Without exception it is a transient recognition, moving on to more important life, a hummingbird, a bee; or, to a train of thought. Bishop Berkeley was partly right: perception and existence are indeed related, in subtle, psychological senses. A person, object, place, event, exists (in those subtle senses) in unfair proportion to the extent that it is perceived. The good bishop's escape hatch, though, has slammed shut on McKinstry. He doesn't know that God is there, perceiving everything, and he never heard of Berkeley.

Winner of every medal, ribbon, certificate of valor, and debt of thanks from all the allied nations in Indochina, Stephen B. McKinstry is not a person. Regular Army life robs a person of his individuality and some say of his humanity, but it is a human individual's paradise compared to what McKinstry moves through. He doesn't live it, he would tell you, he just moves through. He is rarely told to do anything, and it's never anything of consequence. He has no duty anymore. He is an officer in charge of nothing and does his job. A year ago he was court marshaled, because he asserted his existence at Fort Bliss. He burst out of a doorway, tackled a captain, held him down, touched noses, and screamed: "I'm here, Mother Fucker! See me! I'm fucking here! Admit it!" They admitted it, with a court marshal. McKinstry's silver-tongued lawyers pleaded post-traumatic stress syndrome and argued McKinstry's five voluntary tours of duty in Vietnam, his charismatic leadership abilities, his fearlessness, his rise from draftee to field commissioned second lieutenant, and won McKinstry an acquittal. He was transferred to Fort Douglas (which is being phased out), the better to perform. That was a year ago.

Field commissioned draftee Stephen B. McKinstry, hero of an unromantic war—no whistle-stop appearances, no speeches, no selling bonds for him. The one big call, he found, for veterans of his war is to denounce it at anti-Vietnam War protest rallies. And he will not do that, even if they ask him, but they don't. There is an overabundance of long-haired winners of the Silver Star stepping forward, ready to sell their souls for a little recognition here at home. So, for a year, in box cars, flat cars, cattle cars and hobo camps, McKinstry spread C-rations and the word. "You got to watch them gooks. They're all together." While they ate, his companions pretended to be listening. When they were through, they went to sleep. Through no fault of his own, through random traveling, he ended up in Salt Lake City, the Chicago of the Rocky Mountains, as far as railroads are concerned.

****

Over the tracks, Orrin falls into his habitual route. The Jeep seems to drive itself, seems to need no driver. Once, when he was headed for the grocery store, Orrin became distracted by a thought and ended up at the University—seven miles in the opposite direction. He has to pay attention to get the Jeep to go anyplace else if it so much as crosses his route to school. But, he thinks, this habit does more good than harm. Today, he pays little attention to the driving and has this time to think.

Unlike most of us, Orrin questions not the validity of information obtained through conversation with the dead. His mind is at ease concerning his father now. He isn't going to kill him, and neither is the angel. The angel's after Agnew, and Orrin has to go along. There's nothing he can do about it. He isn't conscious of the angel, if it's there at all. That doesn't matter much. Orrin himself is obliged and ordered.

To hoist responsibility onto an angel is not his way. He will make no reference to it when he is arrested. If the legend that is sure to grow around him wants to add an angel, well, he wouldn't want to dictate to a legend what it can and cannot have.

In a sentimental, reminiscent mood, Orrin willingly subjects himself to painful memories. Memories he refused to indulge the night before, memories called up by all this angel information from his grandpa. Before that weekend (or was it longer) in The Maze, he had never thought of killing anything, let alone a person. It was just not in him. Now it is. Maybe it is an angel, an avenging angel, infused in Orrin. But if so, it is camouflaged in the triune nature of his being—in his soul, his spirit, and even in his flesh, to the point where he cannot distinguish it from himself, as the first O.P.R. apparently could. It has integrated with him completely and has made him something else, something that is indistinguishable from the angel or from what he was before. There is no telling what it is. Maybe it was part of him all along. His grandpa and his father think so. Maybe it was there all the time, awaiting orders. Why else is he alive? The laws of nature and ballistics say he should never have seen the light, never breathed a breath of air. Orrin doesn't know the answers. His understanding of the world has changed upon learning the circumstances of his birth.

When memories of The Maze rush him in the Jeep, he does not resist. It was this Jeep, this Jeep he's had since he was sixteen, this faithful, sturdy first set of wheels he saved for, cared for, trusted. This Jeep took him and his beloved Laura to the edge of The Maze.

Laura, Laura, Laura

What more is there to say?

Orrin's first and last attempt at poetry, inspired by Laura, the only person, place, thing, or experience that could have inspired him to try it even once.

Love: pure and simple love, as only the young can have it; as only those young not caught up in peer group security demands can love; love without the slightest unconscious consideration for social, economic or personal need; not to need at all but only love; not having grown accustomed to, dependent on, proud of, or sexually proficient with but loving in the purest, simplest sense; love that is not built on time together, obligations met, worldly accomplishments, or sexual virtuosity; love of two young people for each other; a love by no means courtly or platonic, by no means vulgar or self-serving; love as natural and innocent, as joyous, as emotional and purely spiritual as love can be; love so overwhelming, guilt cannot accompany or follow any of its expressions; love warm enough to melt feelings of insecurity before they form; love that frees rather than enslaving; Orrin's love for Laura; Laura' s love for him.

The Maze is an abyss, a big hole in the Colorado Plateau, cut off from the east by the meandering gorges of the Green and Colorado Rivers—you can see portions of it from Dead Horse Point, but only portions. The San Rafael Swell and Henry Mountains, behind The Maze, are more visible from Dead Horse Point. It's as if there's nothing between you and them but a hole. The Maze is a labyrinth of canyons crowned with pinnacles and natural bridges, monoliths—solid rock washed clean and cut and broken up for centuries, entire geologic periods, by rain, frozen seepage, and tributaries of the Green and Colorado. The Maze—an abyss cut off from the west by desolation, high slick rock desert, sand, and a fault line so dramatic the only way in is on foot with ropes (or you could parachute). No ATV would make it, no mule. There's no place for a helicopter to land, except maybe on a monolith, but then you'd still be high above The Maze.

One night when Orrin was over at Laura's house and they were sitting on the couch holding hands, her father came in and asked him: "How would you like to have a good look at The Maze, Orrin?" Laura's father, a local Jeep dealer, continued, "I sold a Wagoneer to a lion hunter out of Hanksville the other day, and we got to jawin' about some of the trails round here, and he asked me had I ever drove right up to The Maze before. Well, I told him I sure hadn't. And he said it was a true test of a man and his machine to get there, and once you got there it was worth it. Said there's a way down into it marked off by-two explorers—the Abbey-Waterman trail it's called. Said he didn't go down into it, though. We could go this weekend. Think of it. The Maze!"

Laura's was a Gentile family; her mother, alcoholic; she, the only child. Orrin didn't care. Her father liked Orrin, seeing in him a son, someone with whom to do things—like visiting The Maze. The three of them had been on other four-wheeling trips before—Orrin and Laura in his Jeep and her father alone in his, usually behind them. They had been to The Land Behind the Rocks, Elephant Hill, the Needles District of Canyonlands National Park, all rough four-wheeling, and they thought themselves equal to any challenge others had already met.

Orrin didn't bother to ask his father's permission or even tell him that he was going. He knew there was nothing at the ranch that his brothers or the hands couldn't handle, and his father didn't much care where he went, as long as it was away from him. His grandfather was long dead or he would have told him where he was going and talked to him about The Maze. As, things were, though, he didn't tell anybody. He just met Laura and her father at their house Friday afternoon and they took off.

Laura's father had to close down the dealership for the weekend, because his salesman had quit and driven to Salt Lake City, on Thursday. He'd said Moab was dead, and he couldn't stand to look at another Jeep. A note on the dealship door, reading," Gone To The Maze, " was the only notice the world had of where they had gone.

They gassed up at Green River, filled the main and reserve tanks of both Jeeps and eight five-gallon gas cans. The extra gas was in and strapped on Orrin's CJ5. The food, the water, gear, everything else was stowed in Laura's father's Jeepster. Green River is the last place to get gas for thirty different back country Jeep trips. The attendant had gassed up so many four-wheelers that he was tired of hearing about where they planned to go, what they planned to see, how they planned to get there. Most of them go into some section or another of the Book Cliffs, and he assumed that was this group's destination. Laura went to the Ladies' Room. Orrin talked things over with her father. The attendant went about his work, then told them how much they owed, wished them luck, and offered S&H green stamps. He didn't ask them where they were headed nor notice that they did not head for the Book Cliffs when they left. His new eight track stereo and his sidekicks in the station beckoned him, commanded his attention. Johnny Cash at San Quentin or The Best of Merle Haggard. Which one, he must decide, is he going to purchase next?

They found the dirt road mentioned by the lion hunter and were bouncing east across the Green River Desert toward The Maze before they had to use their headlights. While it was still light enough to see, Orrin had to stop so Laura could pick some sunflowers—the only growing thing, besides the prickly pear and the red sand dunes. But, God, those golden flowers, and the way she fixed them in her hair.

There was no moon whatsoever, wouldn't be a sliver of moon for two more nights, and it was dark, dark as night can only be in the wilderness, far away from any city lights. The lights of Salt Lake City make it possible to climb partway up the nearby mountains on a moonless night, their soft glow floating up the slopes like lazy dawn. But they were far from any city lights, far from any busy highway with its passing rays of hope. They stopped at a fork in the dim Jeep tracks, postponing the decision till morning, ate canned beef stew, crawled into their separate sleeping bags by the light of a Coleman lantern. Orrin and Laura respected her father's presence. And when the lantern was turned out, stars were the only things they could see.

Orrin thought maybe he must let his eyes adjust, then he'd be able to make out Laura's form, not a foot from where he lay. They talked as if to disembodied souls, through a solid wall of darkness. When his eyes adjusted, he still couldn't see her. He tested the cliché; couldn't see his hand. Human communication, to be fulfilling, requires two senses be in contact. This is the motivation behind the video phone. People like to see who they're talking to. But being denied the sight of her, Orrin removed his hand from his nose, positive now he couldn't see it, and reached out for Laura.

"What's that?" Out of the void.

"My hand."

A grunt, a stir from Laura's dad.

"Take it."

"Where is it?"

"Here."

Some time later, after they had found their hands and gone to sleep, Orrin woke up when Laura slipped hers free. He listened. She crawled out of her bag, walked off.

"Laura!"

She didn't answer his stage whisper. Toward the Jeeps she sleep-walked in the sand, toward the bathroom at home, in her mind. In that absolute desert stillness Orrin could hear her breathe. She was not far off. He heard her whisk her panties down, heard the pssssssssssssst. Oh, Lord, he loved that girl. She whisked her panties up, returned, crawled into her bag. She didn't take his hand again. Orrin didn't mind. A sudden wave of tenderness for her lulled him back to sleep.

In the morning Laura combed and brushed out her hair, decorated it with fresh sunflowers. Looking over the alternatives, Orrin and her father decided on the less-used, northeasterly towaring trail. Already it was hot out there, ninety-three, and the morning was just born. All evidence of Laura's nocturnal pee was gone; Orrin didn't mention it, nor did she.

Thirty miles or so toward The Maze through the desert, they started climbing. The vegetation thickened—a lone juniper, then a stand, pinon pine, more sunflowers. Canyons grew, orange, red, narrow, deep on each side of the trail. Up, up, grinding up into the rising sun in low range second gear, the little V6 sucked gas like a big V8, sputtered, backfired. He switched to the reserve tank and they kept climbing. The pinon pine and juniper were thicker now. Monoliths, spires, buttes, painted canyon walls appeared between the trees. Nothing unusual yet. They lived among the things. Up, up, the trail to an inexperienced driver wouldn't be there. Largely improvisational, never straight, with occasionally a vague old rut to guide the way, the trail became rocky, rougher, steeper. The soil and sand were blown and washed away. The hearty trees clung to slick rock. Defied the burning sun with green.

Suddenly they came to the end. The big jump-off. Land's end. The Maze below. It was spectacular enough but no more maze-like than a hundred other places. Orrin stopped, waited for Laura's father to walk up to his Jeep. "This must be the head of the Flint Trail," her father said, "the roughest part."

"You mean that isn't The Maze down there?"

"Hell, no. Does that look like a maze to you?"

"Kinda, yeah."

"Ah, come on, Orrin. That's no more a maze than a hundred other places and you know it."

"That's what I thought. Just what I thought."

"Well, that ain't The Maze. It's further on, and when we see it, there'll be no mistaking it for something else. You think it's called The Maze to fool tourists?"

"Okay, okay, calm down. It's not The Maze. How do you expect to get down this cliff? You gonna winch us both down off of here?" He pointed to the winch on Laura's father's Jeepster. "Your cable isn't long enough."

"Let's look around for the trail then," her father suggested.

They didn't look long. The trail, blasted in the cliff by uranium prospectors years ago, started at the only break in the sheer wall of the plateau. "I don't know," Orrin said, looking it over, and Orrin was no sissy. "How long ago was that lion hunter out here?"

"Couple years ago he said, maybe three. He said it was rough."

"Yeah. Let's walk down a ways." Orrin held on to Laura, helped her over rocks. The trail was intricately eroded, crowded with boulders, divided by crags. Narrow, steep, and tilted out toward the edge, it traversed and switchback-ed down the cliff. "If we do get down, how are we gonna get back up?" Orrin asked after he'd had his look.

And Laura's father told him: "We'll figure that out a whole lot better when we're down there tryin'." Adding casually, "Might even get to use that winch."

Back on top they sat beneath a juniper, drank heartily, ate a snack. They refilled their tanks from the cans in Orrin's Jeep, then started down the cliff in first gear, low range. If Orrin's speedometer were all you had to judge by, you'd have to swear he went down the cliff zero miles per hour. Rocks he would have bounced over on another trail had to be crawled over or the bounce and the outward tilt of the trail would combine to send the Jeep sideways off the cliff. Orrin expected to go over any minute, anyway, bounce or no. His seat belt alone kept him in the Jeep, in a suitable position to do the fancy pedal work, the strenuous steering demanded by the Flint Trail. He scraped the wall, and even with the CJ's short wheel base had to back up to negotiate the switchbacks. He wore new blisters on his calloused hands fighting crags for the right to steer. When he finally made it down, he felt he had accomplished something, though he couldn't open his hands completely till Laura rubbed the tightness from his forearms.

"Those uranium prospectors must have been crazy," Orrin said, looking up at what he had just driven down."

"Oh, I don't know," his lover's father argued, "they stayed out of The Maze."

After resting, drinking, agreeing on the difficulty of the trail, and deciding they were a couple of thousand feet lower and a mile or so further south from where they were on top, they took off in a northeasterly direction, following a trail that existed more in their minds than on the rock and sand.

Laura wasn't so much an outdoorsy girl as she was in love with Orrin. She was, however, not a frail, city girl. Living in Moab all her life she'd been conditioned by the sun and wind, the slickrock, the desolation of the desert. Baking out there, in the middle of nowhere, with Orrin and her father the only other people within a hundred miles didn't bother her. Perhaps she did not experience the same feeling of communication with the rock, the wilderness, the stillness; perhaps she did not appreciate the power of the land or value aloneness in the same way or to the same extent that Orrin did. But she liked the scenery. Especially the monoliths, the knobby pinnacles, the spindly spires. She liked the massive canyons and the arches, too, but not as much. Most of all she liked being with Orrin. If he just sat in a cold small cave forever, she'd stay there with him. She wouldn't even think about it. She'd just stay. It wasn't what he did, outside of love her, or who he was, or where. She loved him. She'd just sit there in the cave the way she sat there in the Jeep— with him. But she did not ponder life with Orrin in a cave, nor did she follow him around like a puppy, nor feel cheated if he wished to be alone. She didn't worship Orrin. She didn't even think they were "meant for each other" in the predestinarian sense of the phrase that gives meaning to the circumstances and coincidences of their pasts, of their parents' love lust. At that time, Orrin was the only long-haired male in Moab. Laura liked his hair long, just as she would have liked it short. She attached no value, no stigma to his hair. She would have loved him bald or with hair down to his knees.

She was neither the prettiest nor the most popular girl at school, not a cheerleader, not a member of the pep club, but Orrin thought she was beautiful, thought she looked like Julie Christie. She watched Orrin play football from the stands but wasn't thrilled. She wasn't disappointed, either, when he missed a tackle or was blocked out of a play. She didn't care about football, didn't know that Orrin was a mediocre talent who made the team because their school was small, and because, as coach said, "he gave 110% all the time." Coach did not even think about asking Orrin to cut his hair. The only people who gave him any shit about his hair were outsiders, who shut up fast as soon as Orrin looked them in the eye.

She was young, with all the energy of youth, but not a giggly girl. Mature you might say, but she was not mature to the point of practicality. Innocent, though she gave herself to Orrin. Pure, because she did. Honest with herself and others, she naturally had few friends but knew beyond the doubts most girls have that what she shared with Orrin was pure and simple love. She wasn't worried about its lasting or what would become of her when she was old. She didn't want to run off and get married. She didn't want an engagement ring to dangle like a trophy for the other girls to see. She didn't talk about her boyfriend. Bouncing, jolting, crashing around the crumbling base of a butte, her mouth clamped shut so she wouldn't bite her tongue off, Laura loved Orrin as much as she would've loved him in a feather bed, or on the Sealy in her father's trailer.

So around the butte they bounced and crashed and jolted, and Orrin was glad his wide, high, off-road tires had six full plys of steel. Fifteen, twenty miles further on, crawling like tractors up and down hills, in and out of washes, along a ridge, they come upon the brink abruptly. Nothing out in front of them but sky—a vast blue veil. As if the earth just fell away, which it did. Below them, far below them—the northwest quadrant of The Maze. They both had seen a good deal of nature's barren sandstone wonders, a good deal of remoteness, hazy depths. Traveled widely in that useless, threatening, inhospitable wasteland around the oasis they called home. The trip to where they were standing would leave a city slicker pop-eyed and out of film, dehydrated, weak, sun struck, and sore. But Orrin was used to the massive beauty and the colors; he appreciated them more than a tourist could, but they didn't take him by surprise and awe him senseless; he was used to the sun, the danger, accepted them as contingencies of off-road travel; and his ass was tough from many stiff-suspensioned bounces. Still, after taking his first look out, then down in to The Maze, Orrin stepped back carefully from the edge.

Laura's father pulled his Jeepster up alongside Orrin's CJ5, stopped, got out, walked over to them. "Yup," he said and kicked a spray of sand and rock into The Maze. "If I was an Indian, I'd say that down there was holy. Either holy or pure evil. Evil spirits live down there. Evil spirits or the god of rock or something. Anyway it ain't meant for humans." Laura's father was a Gentile, so he could indulge in such speculation. Orrin knew that the Devil maintains his headquarters in the sea; and, that his agents, formless demons, are all over, not just in desolate hell holes like The Maze. He did agree, though, that The Maze did not appear to be a place for humans. It was a long way down there. He couldn't see the bottom, just the tops, the sides of standing rock.

They stood quietly scanning what they could see of The Maze, each spellbound by the sheer magnitude, disorder, the beauty of that great hole. Borges, say, or a conniving B.F. Skinner-type behavioral psychologist could not design a labyrinth to match The Maze. It's obvious they could not construct one on the same scale that other people could visit, as you can visit The Maze. They have not the power, material, or time. That's not the point.

They couldn't dream up such a mess—vast and, yes, beautiful, deep, and awe inspiring, but a mess nonetheless. For even in their dreams men are confined to their minds, minds that to work at all must impose a system, strange and private as it may be, must try to make some kind of sense, if only to themselves. One can see a pattern, reason, design in anything the human mind creates. Borges has a reason or two for his labyrinths—they, themselves are full of reason—so does Skinner. Borges tells a story. Skinner fools a rat, then teaches it. The Maze, however, is the effect of many causes, but it has no reason.

"They marked their trail with pointer stones," Laura's father said, tearing his eyes away from The Maze long enough to glance at Orrin, gauge his response.

"Who did?" Orrin asked, skeptical but excited, staring off at a sculptured sandstone woman far out in The Maze, cloaked it seemed in blue. A thin blue wisp through which her red flesh throbbed.

"Explorers. Abbey, Waterman. Wanted to see the bottom of The Maze."

"Before that lion hunter?"

"Oh yeah. Long time ago."

Laura, for the first time in her life obsessed with depth, stood closer to the edge than the men, looking down. "I bet we could find it anyway," she said. "I bet we could find it and follow it all the way down in there," her voice sounding like it had already gone, "all the way down in there to the bottom."

There was never any doubt, even before they saw it, that they would climb down into The Maze and have a look around. They found the pile of rocks marking the beginning of the trail—a notch in the white rimrock. Orrin looked it over, decided there were enough hand and foot holds to make it down without the rope to the sloping bench about two hundred feet below. He went down first, helped Laura and her father with their descents. They traversed the bench for a mile and a half, as walking down a steep red ramp, following the pointer stones all the way, though they could have walked just as easily and in the same general direction—down— anywhere on the bench. But they told themselves a trail isn't marked for nothing, and when they had finally crossed that burning expanse of stone, they were affirmed. They found themselves atop foreboding yellow-orange bluffs, the trail continuing along down at the only possible point of descent.

The Maze was taking on a new look already and they were not yet half-way down. Now they saw the sides, the curves, the angles, crevices, and the bulk of multi-colored rock. And though they could not see so much of The Maze, they saw more detail, and it was vast and massive and they could not see the bottom. They stopped to rest and to drink. Orrin turned, looked up at the rimrock, far away now, and high up there (the bench sloped more than he had figured), the white rim looked flawless. The notch they had climbed down was not apparent.

The trail down the bluffs was just a series of toe and finger holds, ledges and other protuberances they could move on. Then, they found a thoughtful piton, planted just where it was needed, where they had to use their ropes. Laura would do or try to do anything to be with Orrin. If he rappelled a hundred feet down a sandstone wall, then she'd be right behind him. She had been a tomboy once and was still strong but feminine—a tigress, Orrin often thought. She rappelled better than her father did, if not as well as Orrin. She wasn't scared, but she was nervous. A moment's hesitation. She closed her eyes, pushed off. Orrin was waiting for her at the bottom and she hugged him around the neck and kissed him with her sun-dried lips and thirsty tongue till he had to protest. For another mile the trail balanced down a narrow, steep, broken ridge. They followed it as it angled down then dropped off sharply and ended on the floor of a skinny canyon. They were at the bottom of The Maze.

Just as they had not seen the bottom from the rim, now, when looking up, they could not see the rim. That last ridge and sheer sandstone walls rising six or seven hundred feet above them were what they saw. And there were no more pointer stones. Either those explorers made it down then went back up again, or they figured you were on your own once they'd led you into The Maze. Which Orrin saw as fair. He'd not have made it this far without their help, and it was not an easy chore marking a trail over solid rock. They'd have little time to see The Maze themselves if they spent all of it piling stones. Besides, it didn't look too complicated. You could go up the canyon, which probably boxed soon because the fault line was still close, or you could go down the canyon. He'd been in narrow, steep, high-walled canyons before and didn't feel threatened. Neither did Laura.

Her father had voiced no complaints during the entire three and a half hour descent, which was longer than he'd expected, and he was bushed. It was cooler in the bottom of that canyon than on the slopes, just over 101, and shady. He sat down, uncorked his canteen, said he'd wait right there while the kids took a look around, if they still wanted to. Warned them not to linger or get lost as it was getting late and they still had to climb back out. "And don't be too damned sure of yourself, either, Orrin," he said as they walked away, down the canyon. "Remember what this place looked like from up there."

"Yeah, but we couldn't see this part," Orrin answered, thinking he had discovered the truth behind The Maze: a complicated exterior façade, but when you get right down to the bottom of it, a simple canyon. "We'll just turn around and follow our tracks right back here." He looked down where they had walked: no tracks. He ground his heel into the hard sand, but even that made only a shallow half-moon indentation. "Well, we won't go far. We'll stay in this canyon then follow it back up." Simple enough.

"Okay," her father said, "see you in about an hour."

"About an hour."

They had continued walking slowly while talking and when Orrin agreed about an hour, he had to shout and it echoed off the walls, as if The Maze could talk. But, of course, it cannot talk, nor can it care, nor does it know of time.

Chapter 4

The Natural Bridge

"You think it's called The Maze to fool tourists?" Laura's father had asked him up on top.

That question did not occur to Orrin as he and Laura strolled down the canyon, but it does now, as he remembers. Before they'd gone thirty yards, the canyon had curved so they couldn't see Laura's father anymore, branched left and right and been joined by two other canyons; but they weren't worried. They could keep track of this. Bear right going down, left coming back. They weren't going far, just strolling along, holding hands, looking around. Mark a trail? What for? They weren't going far. They'd just turn around and head back up the canyon.

Orrin had never been lost in his life. Liked to think he had a natural sense of direction. The canyon meandered now, and more empty canyons emptied into it. It forked madly. When they looked up one of its dry tributaries, they saw the largest, highest, widest, most dramatic natural bridge they'd ever seen. And they'd seen all the famous ones. Perfect, yet asymmetrical, orange-red in this light, among the sameness of those canyons, this finally was a landmark. They would look for it again.

Orrin remembers The Maze more treacherous than he thought it then, as they casually walked through it, as if it were a park. The floors of the canyons were not steep. There is not much of a drop between the bottom of The Maze and the rivers (Green and Colorado) and The Maze is broad. Of course, there was no water in the canyons, and, if Orrin had not known the fault line was behind him, he'd have had difficulty telling if they were going up or downstream. He has cursed his foolishness many times since then, but he cannot recall exactly how he felt. He did not feel like a fool. He felt at ease, happy, comfortable, relaxed. They had not been walking fifteen minutes. At their leisurely pace, could not have gone more than three-quarters of a mile, probably less. The canyon had just forked again. Laura stopped.

"What's wrong?" he asked.

"Let's go back now, okay. This all looks the same. Let's go have a closer look at that natural bridge, then get back to Dad and head on out." The sunflowers had become loosened through the day and wilted but were fine and lovely dangling from her hair.

"Ok, sure." Orrin had a hunch she was worried, maybe even scared. But (though she did feel lost) she wasn't worried. She trusted Orrin. They drank some water, turned around and headed up, bearing left. Some fifteen minutes later they had not come across the natural bridge. Orrin stopped this time, looked around. High, red, pink, orange, smooth sandstone walls. "This isn't the same canyon we came down."

"How can you tell?" Laura was not being sarcastic.

"It's not as wide. This one must have snuck in on us from the right as we went down, and we just turned up it. Come on." He turned her around and they went back down till they came to the original canyon, then they turned left. They walked about a hundred yards, around a bend, and the canyon boxed.

"Rassssberries!"

"Orrin. Are we lost?"

"Momentarily. Just let me get my bearings."

"Do you have your compass?"

Orrin looked at her briefly with disgust; for it was not the right direction they needed, but the proper canyon. It would do them no good to be roughly parallel, going the right way, with an insurmountable wall of stone between them and Laura's father, between them and the trail out. Besides, he didn't have his compass.

Everybody thinks that if they were lost somewhere, they'd be logical and cool. They'd sit down as soon as they realized their situation, build a smoky fire and wait for rescue. Orrin would've been happy to do that, to be someplace where it was possible. Oh, they could survive without a fire. They'd have to, no wood around. And if they just sat there in that box canyon, the water left in their canteens would get them through the remainder of the day and maybe through tomorrow, if they found shade and didn't move. But after that they'd dry up, fast, and die.

"Orrin!" He'd been standing quietly, thinking.

"Okay, Laura. I've got it now. We can't stay here. I know where we went wrong. But first let's try something. Let's see how close we are to your father. I don't think we're far away. You see that wall?"

69

pointing to the right, "the canyon on the other side's the one we want, I think. Call your dad."

"DAAAADEEEE!!!" Laura bellowed, surprising Orrin with her volume. Her summons echoed off the three walls of the canyon, back and forth and up, off higher walls, and down the canyon, booming, fading: daaaadeeee!!! daaaadeeee!!! daaaadeeee!!!

A long half-minute after all the echoing had stopped and stillness had engulfed them, Laura set herself to yell again. Orrin squeezed her hand, signaled with a raised forefinger to wait and listen. They waited. Listened. They could hear the heat waves rising. They could hear their lungs, their hearts. Besides that they heard nothing. Stillness. Stark, vast, desert canyon stillness, the catalyst of meditation or madness depending on one's mind. If you wonder why old prospectors talked to their burros, this is why. That stillness makes one long for sound. If you don't supply it, your ears will do it for you, cacophonous, ringing, buzzing, tinkling sound, voices.

"Try again."

She bellows louder than the first time, and the echo has more resonance but the same result.

"You still think he's on the other side of that wall?"

"I don't know. I don't even know if this thing," pointing to the boxed end of the canyon, "is the fault line. It doesn't have to be, you know."

"Well, what are we going to do?" The shadows were longer now; all they could see of this canyon was in shade. But the sky above The Maze was clear blue. It was not yet sunset.

"Your dad's a heavy sleeper, right."

She nods. Other times they've been glad he was.

"Well, maybe he's asleep. I still think I'm right about that canyon."

"Okay. Let's go then. I don't like just standing here. This place is... I don't know. It makes me feel small."

They walk back down the box canyon, stop at the first canyon that breaks through the solid, high, right wall, look up it. Ordinary canyon, for The Maze. They can't see far without committing themselves to it because it bends.

"This is it. I'm sure," Orrin says, and they commit themselves. It's easy walking and just like all the canyons they have walked today, just like the canyon they came down at first. It forks and bends, has tributaries. Then they come across a huge, lone, sandstone boulder in the middle of the canyon. It doesn't block their progress or their sight. They can walk and see around it. Up ahead: more boulders littering the canyon; then a pile of them atop and strewn down the sides of a pile of fine red sand that rises a hundred feet and covers the entire floor. And they can see high above that pile, angularly spanning the canyon, almost as high as the canyon's highest walls—a tremendous, lovely natural bridge.

They look at each other simultaneously. "It's gotta be." Orrin says it first.

"I know! I know!" Laura screams gleefully, accenting her words with nymphetish jumps. "It's gotta be that same old bridge we saw when we were going down. Come on!"

Vermillion now, but the light has changed, the face of it is different, but they'd seen it from the other side. The general sweep, the arc and size of it assure them that it has to be the same natural bridge they

71

had seen earlier. There could be no other natural bridge of that magnitude and cut within so small an area as they'd covered. No. There could be no other natural bridge exactly like it in the world. Laura is ecstatic, squealing, dragging Orrin by the hand. Orrin thinks for a moment it might be wise to rein her in, but her excitement is contagious. Soon they are running broken-field through the boulders, up the pile of sand, slipping, huffing, laughing. Precious body fluids gushing from their pores and gone forever in an instant, gone to quench the dry air's thirst. Half-way up, the pile of sand is completely covered with boulders. From here on it's hopping, jumping, and following along one boulder till it ends then jumping to the next. Harder work. More sweat. They slow from delighted scramble to trudging climb, stop laughing, breathe with difficulty. The dry, hot air burns their lungs, rasps their throats, dries them from within. When they reach the top they're winded, thirsty, weak. The wrong technique. A strip of shade cast by the bridge is a place for them to rest and drink some water, for they must drink now, deeply. They must rest, relax, recover, let the water permeate their bodies. The water's warm, almost hot. They caress it with their mouths and swallow slowly. Down the other side of the pile, down the canyon that way, they can see where it empties into another canyon, just as they could see the bridge when they were in that other canyon. "There it is, Laura," Orrin indicates with his canteen, "we just turn left, up that canyon, and we'll be back to your dad in no time."

"Orrin, don't you think it's weird how we got turned around so fast? I mean, I know this has got to be the same bridge and that's got to be the canyon, but we sure got turned around."

"Yeah, well, it's a maze all right," Orrin says, meaning: The Maze tricked me briefly, but I found the way. I can take care of myself and my woman, too. I was never really lost. I know my way around. Orrin knows that is what he meant, knows now that he was an arrogant fool. He knows it driving to school, remembering, but he doesn't know it sitting in the shade cast by the natural bridge.

"How much time till Dad expects us?"

"None. We shoulda been back by now. I hope he waits. At least till we get to that canyon. Then we'll bump into him if he comes looking for us."

They leave the shade refreshed, start down the pile of sand and boulders. It is a shorter, steeper slope, and when they're off of it, the canyon is congested with more boulders and is steeper than any they've been in today. It is not a canyon running down the gentle incline to the mighty rivers but a cross canyon, joining two that do. The natural bridge is at the summit of the canyon and because the length they're walking now is shorter than the length they walked before, it is steeper. Orrin figures this out as they walk single file between the dwarfing chunks of sandstone. Walking steadily, unhurriedly, they make it to the mouth and find a fifty-foot drop-off, a waterfall at one time, where it joins the canyon they want.

Neither says a word. The drop-off is not that difficult to descend. Looks fairly easy. But there was no drop-off at the tributary with the first natural bridge. Turning, looking up toward the bridge, they are too near a massive rock to see anything but it. Laura begins to sob. Orrin cuddles her.

"Oh, Laura, don't. It's gonna be all right. Come on." He cuddles her and talks to her and in a while she stops.

"What are we gonna do?" She wants to know.

"You okay now? Sure?"

"Yeah. What are we gonna do?"

"Well, we're late. So your dad is either still waiting for us, looking for us, or gone for help. Either way, we'd be better off if we got back there, or at least closer. I don't think he'd find us here." He doesn't mean to say that. He means to be diplomatic, but his relationship with Laura is not based upon diplomacy.

Laura's through sobbing now. She can take the truth. "You're right," she says, "we have strayed pretty far. Think we ought to backtrack?"

He smiles. She knew what he was going to suggest all along. She probably didn't know the other alternatives he had weighed—following the canyon down below back up to the fault line and looking for another way out—following it thirty-some miles down to the Green River, if they could, and waiting there for rescue or floating down the river on a raft of driftwood to civilization—just sitting down right here. But that doesn't matter.

Half an hour later (the going's steep and they don't want to wear themselves out) they top the pile of sand and boulders beneath the natural bridge. The entire canyon is shaded now, even the bridge itself, so they sit down right where they top the pile, rest and drink. Laura studies the canyon wall supporting the natural bridge. Though the sky above The Maze is cloudless, it is streaked with purple, turning deeper blue.

"What would you do, if you were Daddy?" Laura's still studying the wall, up and down, carefully.

"I'd look for us. I'd be sure to mark a trail, and I'd come looking."

"Nope," she says dogmatically. "Daddy knows' he'd never find us; He's no romantic. He'll wait. He'll give us another hour or so. He would yell. Notice we haven't heard anybody yelling for us. I'm sure he's yelled by now. Then he'll get back up that trail and drive fast as he can right back to Green River. He'll call the Jeep Posse, the Helicopter Rescue Crew, the Light Aircraft Pilot's Association, the Civil air Patrol, Park Service, Sheriff's Office, everybody, then he'll get back down here with bullhorns, water, food, medicine, and as many people as he can drag along. That's what my Daddy will do. I know him."

"Well, I hope he doesn't."

"Why? That's the only logical thing to do. It's the only thing he could do, Orrin. Don't you see?"

"I see that if he left right now it'd be late dusk when he made the rim, if he could make it by himself."

"He could make it."

"Okay, he could. But by the time he got to the bottom of the Flint Trail—you remember that?—it'd be black. The way that trail twists and winds, he'd have to use a spotlight to see it 'cause his headlights'd be shining off into space. It'd be slow, if possible at all. Laura, driving up that thing would be rough as hell in the daytime. I know. Driving down it was the dumbest thing I ever did. It ain't meant for Jeeps. It's for mules or those little ATVs. There's no way he could make it. Not at night. He'd kill himself. Tomorrow, with luck and his winch, he might get up it, but it'd be a long hard grind, and he'd have to let his Jeep cool off before taking on the desert."

"I Think you underestimate my father, Orrin."

"No, I don't. Nobody could make that trail at night."

"Well then, we might as well just wrap our arms around each other and wait to die." She looks right at him, pauses, but he doesn't say anything. "That, or we can climb that wall to the bridge, where a helicopter could see us and drop a line. Might even make it to the top of the wall and follow that right back to those bluffs, then hook up with the trail out of here."

Orrin looks closely at the wall. There is a crack in it, angling down from the bridge to the pile of sand and boulders upon which they sit. The ridge of that crack and the crack itself, if not a chasm, could possibly be climbed.

"It's shady now," Laura continues, "and we could take it easy, save our water. The helicopters'll be the first things here, no matter when Daddy gets through, and if we're down here they'll never see us. Even if they did, they couldn't get us out."

"Look, Laura, if we go up there, we'll cook tomorrow. Starting right at sunrise. We'd need these canteens, full of water, to make it through a day on that bridge. But, if we stay down here, we can find some shade. If the choppers come, we can signal them. They'll drop us water and guide the men on foot to us. We'll be better off down here, believe me."

She thinks about it. Looks straight up at the narrow ribbon of sky; all the sky the canyon lets her see. "Do you know what the chances are of some guy in a helicopter seeing your canteen flash? They'll zip over this skinny canyon in half a second, Orrin. And they ain't gonna see it unless they're in that little strip of sky."

Orrin knows that's not entirely true. Though the chopper could not see him in the bottom of the canyon unless they were directly overhead, he can play the reflection off the canyon walls, and that would be more widely seen.

"Another thing, Orrin," Laura's going strong, "it gets just as hot down here but there's only a little while that the sun shines right down to the bottom. And that's the only time you'd able to signal. They ain't gonna spend all day' hovering over us, waiting for the sun to be just right.

"Orrin, if we stay down here, we're just hiding from them."

She ends with that, waits for him to speak. Let's the idea grow on him. Allows him to convince himself. Even now her argument is somewhat valid. They *would* have been difficult to spot down there. So what if the shade of canyon walls enables them to live a little longer? Will it be long enough for rescuers to find them still alive in that deep, narrow place? There are higher walls, above the walls that they can see, higher sculptured walls with steeples, pinnacles, arches—women cloaked in haze. The showplace of The Maze is high above these narrow canyons. They are so far down their ears popped twice while descending from the rim. What are the chances of someone in a helicopter peering through the layers of The Maze, as it were down through geologic time, piercing that, all that, and spotting them in the shade millions of years behind, three thousand feet below?

What are the chances of a helicopter's flying over this particular canyon, only one of thousands in The Maze? Pregnant probabilities. Pessimism, the only child they carry, will kill them as it's born.

So why worry about those things? The helicopters might not come at all. Laura's father might try the Flint Trail tonight and kill all three of them. Why climb up on that bridge and broil in the sun till you're too weak to get down, then broil till you're dead, when nobody will even know you're out here? But, on the other hand, what if her Dad waits and makes the trail tomorrow. And you stay down in the canyon, drying up more slowly, but drying just the same, and the helicopter flies past, so close that you can hear it, circles back across the canyon, then continues. Looking for you, but the sun is wrong so you can't signal, and you're too weak to climb the wall up to the bridge and too late anyway, because they probably won't be back. The Maze is too immense.

What if this and what if that. He could "what if" them right out of their chances for survival. He must act. Assume one set of circumstances as the real ones and act accordingly. Assume, for instance, as Laura does, that her father will make it to Green River sometime tonight—though that's absurd—and early tomorrow, before they're cooked, a helicopter will pass over and spot them, if they're on the bridge.

No. He cannot make that assumption. If he assumes anything, he must assume Laura's father has a little common sense. He will wait till morning to assault the Flint Trail, roll into Green River sometime tomorrow afternoon. At least two privately owned helicopters out of Moab will make a quick pass over

The Maze before tomorrow night. The main search will not begin until the next morning.

"Okay," Orrin finally says, "we'll go up to the bridge. But not now. Not until four o'clock tomorrow afternoon. That's the earliest anybody's gonna be here."

Laura doesn't like that idea. She stands up, boiling, her eyes spewing hatred. Once lovely sunflowers hang like shrunken heads—trophies of the warrior she's become. "You stupid Mormon! How do you know that?! You don't. They could come this evening before it's dark. They'll be out in force at first light tomorrow morning. And we'll be down here in the shade, hiding from them. Besides, your hair's too long. It's sapped all the moisture from your goddamn Mormon brain and you can't think. Can't see, either. Can't even walk back up a canyon... God damn it, Orrin, you got us lost! Ain't that enough?

"No. Not for you. You got to cast aspersions.... You got to put my father in a category with an idiot like yourself. Just 'cause you can't drive worth shit doesn't mean he can't make it up that trail. He *realizes* what kind of situation we're in down here, even if you don't. He'll get through tonight. By hook or crook. He'll get through because he knows our lives depend on it.

"Where'd you get that black hair, anyway? You're the only goddamn Christianson I've ever seen with straight black hair. Oh, I'm sure you think it's cool to have long hair like that murderer you're named after. But I'll tell you something. There's a lot of people think its strange. Think you're strange. They don't know you're just plain stupid."

She turns away. Hops to another boulder. Walks to the end of it. Broods. She has said enough for now. Perhaps—if Orrin were not Orrin and didn't love her as she is, blow ups included—perhaps she's said too much. You may think so, but she doesn't. A love that frees rather than enslaving, that's what they have. Laura is free to say anything she feels; Orrin's free to take it. He is not obligated (by anything) to slap her down, cower to her barrage, return a barrage of his own, or break up with her in retaliation. He understands the complex motivating factors, and since there is no one else around, she must vent her fear on him. Blame him, yes. But he will not deny that he is mostly responsible for their situation. Insult his intelligence, yes. But he is confident of his mental acuity and does not take her insults to heart. As for the questions about his hair and Orrin Porter Rockwell, he's asked them himself, so why can't she?

He lets her brood. She'll come back, and she'll do what he says. No matter what she calls him or says about him, she trusts his judgment. No matter how much she wants to think her dad's a superman or god or something, she knows Orrin is right about the Flint Trail. That's one reason for her blow up: she knows Orrin's right but doesn't want things to be that way. At least that's how Orrin sees it.

She turns to face him and says louder than necessary, though they are a considerable distance apart, "I don't care what you do, Orrin. I'm climbing up there right now, while I still can. Tomorrow afternoon we'll be stiff and thirsty and hungry and I won't feel like climbing that wall." She waits.

"Well?"

He says carelessly: "Go ahead."

It's not the easiest climb in the world—seven hundred feet straight up and she doesn't know what that crack's like. She won't try it alone.

"You're a real bastard, aren't you? You know I'm out of water. You know I'm scared and dirty. You know my skin's all cracked and my lotion's in the Jeep. You know all that and you'd let me go up there alone."

"You won't go."

"Don't be so damned sure!"

"Come here."

She hesitates but comes. He puts an arm around her shoulder, draws her close. She wraps her arms around his ribs, hides her face in his chest. "Please, Orrin. I really don't think I could make it tomorrow afternoon. Besides, there might be one of those Air-Tours planes coming over. You can never tell. They like to fly over this place at dusk. The tourists really dig it 'cause the colors are so weird. And they'd pay extra to see a couple of lost teenagers on a natural bridge.," she gently grabs a handful of his hair, "especially if one of them looks like a wild man. So it would be worth the Air-Tour's while to help us. They could radio a helicopter. Give them the exact bearings of the bridge, and we could get out of here tonight."

Driving to school, Orrin can't decide just what it was. Her pleas or her suggestion that the Air-Tours might be out. Or her blatant optimism. Something broke him down enough to say: "Well, let's go have a look at that crack."

****

The crack in the wall was not inviting. Narrow, deep, a whole slice of the wall was peeling away and

81

would eventually crash down, adding more boulders to the pile, widening the canyon and the bridge, if it doesn't come down, too. They'd have only the thin sharp edge of it to climb. Either cling precariously to that edge or wedge themselves in the crack and laboriously inch their way up seven hundred feet, with only the pressure they exert against the wall and the slab to keep them from falling. Either way would be difficult and dangerous.

"Oh, Jesus," Laura says. "I was hoping it would be shallow, filled in or new or something so we could walk in it like a stairway."

"Yeah, that would've been nice. Then we could wait till tomorrow afternoon, like we should. But you've got a point about what kind of shape we'll be in tomorrow afternoon. We couldn't climb this thing tomorrow. It'll be a miracle, almost, if we're able to climb it now."

"It's not that bad" Orrin."

"Almost. If not a miracle, we'll need a lot of luck. And it won't be easy, even if we have the luck."

"Well, I think we should at least give it a try. See how hard it really is before we convince ourselves that it's impossible. If we get up there a ways, and it looks like it's going to be too much, or we're too tired, we can come back down. At least we'll know we tried. That should give us some kind of peace as we lay dying."

That's the second time she's mentioned it, Orrin thinks. I wonder if she really sees it as a possibility. Probably not. If she does, she probably thinks that talking big about it will make it go away. But she's not facing up to it at all. He says: "If you think it'll put your mind at ease, if you think it'll let you die in peace, we'll try it. But don't be disappointed if it doesn't work out that way, okay."

"I think we'll make it to the bridge. That's what I really think."

They are on a boulder roughly perpendicular with the crack. Orrin reaches up, grabs the edge of the slab that's separating from the wall with both hands, pulls and jumps. His feet come down on the thin, steep edge, but he looses his balance. Thrusts a hand out against the wall. And there he is: two feet and one hand on the edge of the crack, one hand bracing against the wall, leaning over the narrow crack itself. He looks down at Laura. "It's not going to be easy."

"I know, I know. Just get me up there with you and let's give it a try."

Orrin's position is good for neither climbing nor helping Laura up. He squats, moves his other hand to the wall, wiggles his feet till his heels hook the edge. Then, testing, he slowly removes one hand from the wall. He is stable. Twisting around as much as he can, he reaches the free hand down toward Laura. "Here, grab hold with both hands, and, when I say jump, you pull on my arm and jump up here. Don't worry about pulling me off. I've got all my weight leaning into the wall. I'll help pull you up."

"Okay," she says, believingly, and takes his hand.

"Are you really out of water?"

"Yes."

"Well, then, shuck your canteen."

She does, then takes his hand again. Readies herself. "You ready?" he asks. She nods.

"Okay, Jump." He grunts "jump" more than he says it and he pulls mightily. Laura does her best but doesn't make the edge. Still holding on, she scrambles frantically. Orrin pulls. His propping arm collapses, and now it is his forearm and head against the wall that hold him up, above the chasm. He pulls and Laura scrambles, and she finally gets one knee up on the edge of the slab that is peeling away from the wall of a narrow sandstone canyon somewhere in the northern portion of The Maze.

With her knee as a fulcrum, Orrin's constant pulling easily levers her up, almost over the edge. "Ohahohssstugh!" she complains as she whips one hand out to brace herself against the wall. Bringing her other foot up to the edge, letting go of Orrin completely, throwing that hand, too, against the wall but higher, she stands with apparent lack of fear, moving her hands swiftly upward along the wall, then recklessly removes one to rub her knee. "What'd you do that for?" she asks, as though he tried to hurt her. "Cripple me for life."

Uncomfortable as he is, and seeing the ease and safety with which Laura stood, Orrin stands also, flexes his cramped muscles. "You think you can make it now, with that knee?"

"I'm all right."

"As soon as you're ready, then."

"I'm ready."

Standing on the thin edge, leaning over the crack, bracing themselves with their hands against the wall, they sidle slowly, carefully, obliquely up, toward the bridge. The edge is steep. Their downward legs and arms strain to stop a sideways fall and also push them upward. The wall is warm, though it's been in shade for hours. Their palms leave momentary sweat prints. It may be easier to picture it like this: the bridge is about as high as a seventy-story building. If you've ever walked up that many stairs, you've got some idea of the length and strain of the climb. But, remember, they don't have the stairs. Imagine a narrow street somewhere lined with say ninety-story buildings, windowless and red. Look up. Spanning the street, about seventy stories up, is a bridge. You can't get in these buildings, of course, and there are no elevators on the outside. But the facade of one building is peeling away where it was cracked by an earthquake. You get on that and climb sideways up to the bridge. Their legs begin to tremble from the strain before they are one seventh of the way. To rest is work; for they must still hold themselves up with pressure against the wall. They are not one seventh of the way and already it's a long way down. In their positions they cannot help noticing, cannot help looking down the crack they're leaning over.

Neither says a word. They have no strength to waste on words. They sidle up the thin, sharp edge of the slab that is peeling away. Up, toward the bridge, their muscles squeezing precious liquid from their bodies. A hymn that gave the early Mormons strength, begins in Orrin's mind:

Put your shoulder to the wheel,
Push alo-ong.
Do your duty with a heart
Full of so-ong.
We all have work;
Let no one shirk.
Put your shoulder to the wheel.

It comes unbeckoned, and it remains. It gives him strength. Keeps him going. And he keeps Laura going by example. Then—it is not a miracle, nor is it luck, except perhaps that they made it that far—the edge of the slab begins to widen. Gradually. From a thin, sharp edge, it changes to a blunt quarter of an inch in thickness. Even that makes it easier to stand on; Orrin feels the difference through the lug soles of his climbing boots. He turns his head, looks over his extended arm and up, seeing that the edge continues widening. He must tell Laura. She ought to know. She's below him, standing yet on thinness. His voice quavers, high and thin: "It gets wider up here. Don't give up. Keep coming." It echoes in the chasm, small and tremulous, but dissipates before it can echo in The Maze.

She hears him, but she doesn't answer. It will be enough for her to move. And she does, slowly, shakily. She moves slowly up the edge, shaking with exhaustion, fear. And it widens, further up, to six, then, in a little while, to eight broad inches. Hesitantly and carefully, the equivalent of fifteen stories up, Orrin turns his high foot, points it up the edge. Leans on it. Removes his high hand from the wall experimentally, then in one quick, gentle movement shifts his weight, turns his body, brings both hands over to the edge, up and in front of him. Safe and in a better position for climbing, he scampers up the edge to where it's fourteen inches wide. He rests and waits for Laura, who is still sidling up the edge, leaning over the crack, too scared to change her position. When she reaches him, he wordlessly helps her move completely onto the ridge.

She clings to him. Breathes convulsively. Quivers as she stares half-way across the canyon. "We've got a ways to go yet, Laura. It gets easier, but it's still a long way up there. If you'd rather go back down."

"No," she almost says. It rides out on a short, convulsive exhalation. Orrin pats her back and comforts her. Five long minutes later, Laura's breathing normally. She asks for water. They drink from his canteen.

"Orrin, do you think we can make it to the bridge before dark?"

"If we hurry, maybe. If this ridge stays wide enough to walk on."

"Well, then," she says bravely, as if Orrin's caused the delay, "we'd better get going."

The ridge stays just about as wide, wide enough to walk on, and steep enough to require hands. It is easier than before, but still not easy, not as easy as climbing stairs, for instance. And there is still the drop, growing on both sides of them, to nurture fear. Still short-lived sweat, still fatigue. And fourteen inches isn't much to walk on, hold to, or trust when you're that high up and going higher. The height has them wired. Useful, nervous energy. Though it's possible to not look down so much now, they can't help glancing. And even when they're staring up the ridge; up toward the bridge, the depth sneaks in peripherally. There's no ignoring it, no denying its existence. It's all around them. Even if they shut their eyes, they see its afterimage, feel it, narrow on one side of them, narrow, black and seeming deeper because it is so narrow. Wider, lighter on the other side, but just as deep. This, on either side of them, is no imaginary abyss into which one falls and fails forever. If they fell (and they are hyper-conscious of the possibility) they'd fall a good long time, but not forever. The boulders down below will put a sudden, violent stop to whatever ecstasy the fall might bring. They know how big the boulders are, and now they look like gravel. The summer before this time, one of the boys at their school, a big, sturdy boy named Michael, fell ninety feet off a cliff near Moab onto a pile of boulders. A better climber than Orrin, Michael turned as he fell and landed on his feet. He lived, but he broke both legs, both arms, his shoulders, collar bones (all compound fractures) fractured his Skull, his ribs, ruptured his spleen, broke his hips, and he was not yet back in school.

Among the thoughts of falling, remembering what had happened to Michael when he fell ninety feet, and calculating how much higher they are right now, accompanying these thoughts, the inspiring, steady Hymn rolls on, continuous, reeling off the that single stanza. "Put Your Shoulder to the Wheel," a standard Mormon hymn with a strong, simple, lasting tune. A white religious work song. It is the first song he remembers hearing, the first song he sang. And when he heard it for the first time it was familiar. He'd known it before his ears touched air. And the tune was there and understood, an integral rhythm of his life, before he learned the words. And it is with him now, enabling him to use his nervous energy to climb, enabling him to overcome his fear.

Half-way up, Orrin hears tiny noises coming from behind him. Laura's saying something. He backs down to where she's stopped. Lying on the ridge panting, she says nothing. "You all right?" Orrin asks.

She doesn't answer. Then, in little while, she pants: "You..." pant, "In a..." pant "race..." pant, pant, "or something?"

"Yeah. I don't want to be on this ridge when it gets dark."

But he lets her rest, anyway. And while she rests, he rigs his belt and the web strap of his canteen into a safety device. Not as good as the rope—which they left in the piton on the yellow, orange bluffs so they could climb back up it—his improvisation still serves its purpose. It connects Laura to Orrin, not far behind him, either. From here on, Laura clings to the strap with one hand, touches sandstone with the other, and Orrin pulls her up the ridge. All she has to do is keep her balance and move her feet fast enough to keep up—not easy chores.

The Hymn now booms in Orrin's mind, drowning out all other thoughts, threatening to burst a capillary, but not. The Hymn controls his heart beat, coordinates his muscles, rations out adrenaline. Moves Orrin in a slow, monomaniacal, quadrupedal dance up the ridge. Though she cannot hear the music, though she does not have The Hymn, Laura falls into step behind him and makes the work much easier. And The Hymn, on its own, creates another stanza, appropriate to the task:

Get your young love to the bridge,
Keep a-moving.
It's not far; you've got the strength,
Keep a-moving.
I have my work; I will not shirk.
Get your young love to the bridge.

Of course, Orrin would not be able to do it, hymn or no hymn, if he weren't in excellent physical condition. If he'd poisoned his body with one cigarette or cup of coffee, one glass of beer or Coca Cola, if he'd spent his days sitting around on his spine listening to records or the radio, slouching against the drugstore front, or driving a car with power steering, if he'd spent his nights carousing and fornicating, or just carousing and returning home late and beating off five, six times until the wee hours of the morning, if he'd been high or low on any drug at all, ever, if he'd turned his back on work and chosen the easy life, if he'd turned down the wholesome food at the family table for a hamburger and fries, if he'd preferred the artificial coolness of the indoors to God's hot, dry, healthy desert air, if he'd done the things that many young people do (young Mormons are included), chances are he wouldn't make it to the bridge. But he hasn't done them, and he has The Hymn to help him utilize the power of his healthy body, a body that has more power lurking unused in it than he ever thought it could have.

But he doesn't think about it. He doesn't marvel at his new-found strength; for The Hymn still booms. And Orrin climbs, stronger than he's ever been before, but not with superhuman strength. It is evident when they finally reach the bridge, just as the last blue-dark of dusk is fading into total darkness, that every calorie of energy, every foot-pound of work, every ounce of strength came from and was done by his human body—nothing supernatural about it. He is totally, blissfully exhausted. No football game or workout has left him so completely drained. No wind sprints' have explored this unknown volume of his lungs. But, then, he's never taken on such a task with such single-minded, hymn-controlled determination. And The Hymn is his. It's in his mind; though independent, it does not come from outside of him. It did not pull him up that ridge.

It didn't give him strength he does not have. It just found his strength for him and concentrated it, all of it—psychic, physical, emotional, on the work he chose to do. And now The Hymn subsides, slows his body down to rest. Leaves room in Orrin's mind to think of words to say to Laura. But remains. They've been standing on the bridge, now, two or three seconds when Orrin gets around to saying: "We made it, Laura! We made it!"

Laura's limp, sagging in his arms. He cannot see her. It's dark out there, up there, and, again, there is no moon.

****

Orrin lays Laura on the bridge, which is flat enough on top, twenty-some feet wide and seven hundred feet above the pile of boulders. Spanning the canyon angularly, its length is greater than the canyon's width. He fumbles in the dark at his improvised safety device and has to undo it entirely to free the canteen. Propping her head up with his knee, he moves the spout, by touch, to Laura's parched and open mouth. She is breathing; he feels it, on the back of his hand. "Take some water, Laura."

"Please rest, Orrin. Please. I can't keep up. Let's rest."

"Okay, we're here now. We'll rest. Just take a little water, and we'll go to sleep."

"We can sleep right here. The bridge'll be there in the morning. Please rest, Orrin."

Orrin pours a little water into her mouth, measuring the amount by the shifting weight of it in the canteen. She chokes momentarily but swallows, losing none. He gives her more: a healthy swig that takes half of what is left, which isn't much. Then he drinks, careful to leave some for the next time Laura's thirsty, screws the cap on tight and lies down close to Laura, with his arm beneath her neck, around her shoulders, his hand lightly on her breast, her head resting on his shoulder. He still breathes deep but slower than before. The air is cooling rapidly, but the sandstone is still warm. Orrin stares into the stars, relaxes with the metabolic knowledge of his strength. "You crazy Mormon," Laura sighs weakly, snuggling up.

"It's been a long day, Laura, but it's over now."

In a minute, maybe two, Orrin hears the breath of Laura's sleep beside him. But he cannot drop off so quickly. His body is still winding down. Turning from the stars to kiss her, a sunflower blossom gently rasps his nose. Still there.

Oh, God, he prays, let this innocent be saved. Let her vision of helicopters coming with the sun come true. Let them swarm, like bees around a sunflower, above this bridge, this wonder you created for only few to see. Let them pluck this blossom from the stone before she's dried and wilted. He turns his bloodshot, sun tortured, wind-burnt eyes up to the stars again. Oh, Lord, let her live to know The Truth, to be my wife on Earth and in Your Kingdom. Let her live to ask forgiveness, as I do now, for our sins together. Lord, it was not lust. I love this girl, this woman. And she loves me. And she will know The Truth, Lord. She will seal herself to me in Your Temple. She will provide wholesome earthly homes for worthy souls. She will raise them with The Gospel and prepare them for Your Kingdom. We will, both of us, together. Please. Let this innocent be saved. I ask these blessings humbly in the name of Jesus Christ, Amen.

It is a kalpa, an aeon, it seems—a wind rises up and dies; a satellite, traveling slowly across the sky, comes into then passes out of view—before he finally slips into unconsciousness. It seems he's just arrived at sleep, but who can tell? He is so tired. But it seems he's just arrived at sleep when he awakes. There is no sweet weight upon his shoulder, no breast beneath his hand. He is suddenly, uncompromisingly awake. And he screams, high and loud, with every cubic centimeter of his lungs, for there is no need to stage whisper tonight: "LAURA!!"

It echoes off sandstone walls impregnated with tormentors shrieking back at him from all sides, from the safety of thick darkness. Distorting it to intimate satanic laughter. Orrin clasps his hands over his ears, falls to his knees, and whimpers: "Laura, Laura, Laura," softly to himself so the echo cannot have it. "Laura."

He waits, rocking back on curled toes, then forward, till he's sure the rock is silent. Then he crawls on hands and knees, blind as any man has been, searching the entire length and breadth of the bridge methodically and without hope. He hears no sound other than his own. His breathing, whimpers, movement, nothing else. If she were on the bridge still, anywhere on the bridge, he could surely hear her in this stillness.

He thinks, maybe I am over concentrating. Maybe she's asleep and breathing softly over there somewhere, but I can't hear her 'cause I'm concentrating too hard on myself. Like on the ridge. She's got to be here somewhere. She's got to be. She couldn't... He tries to remember in which direction from their sleeping bags she walked last night. Toward the Jeeps. And not far, either. She could very well be on the bridge. At home a bath adjoins her bedroom. She probably knows, asleep or not, exactly how many steps to take, and when to turn and sit. Just like her, the little cutie. "Laura," he says aloud but softly, "where are you, Laura? Comeback to bed now." But he remembers that she cannot hear him, either. Not last night, so why now? But last night she came back. So, if she came back last night but couldn't hear me, and she hasn't come back yet tonight, then she can hear me. "Laura," he says. But maybe she's on her way back now, so like last night, she cannot hear. Maybe there's a shallow pocket in the bridge, or in the walls, and she got into it to take a bath. She was dirty, itchy, probably wants a bath. That's it. I'll have to feel around until I find her. She's got to be here. Somewhere. "Laura."

All through the night he crawls, sure that he has missed a spot, the spot where Laura's waiting, asleep and innocent. The Hymn, allied with his weary body, tries various techniques, spins new stanzas, lullabies, rationalizations, common sense (one such stanza goes something like this:

Go to sleep now, get some rest,
Wait till morning.
You will need your rest to search
In the morning.
I have my work;
I will not shirk.
Go to sleep now, get some rest.),

but Orrin does not stop. He can't ignore The Hymn. It is persistent and in his mind. He can't block its entry with his hands over his ears (he tries); it's already in. But it doesn't stop him. Nor does his body, which leaves negotiation and persuasion to The Hymn and simply refuses to work, collapses repeatedly. But every time it does, Orrin forces it to continue. As the night grows old, Orrin's hope, which is based on nothing but subjective necessity, grows as weary as his flesh. Carelessly, he crawls along the edges of the bridge, feeling in the cold night air as well as on the sandstone. He might just let his body collapse right now, in this position. Let it refuse to work, let it fail him now. He wants it to but can't allow it. Laura might still be, must be, on the bridge, and she will need him.

It gets colder, and Orrin knows first light will be there soon, before the sun burns up into the sky, and it will be light enough to see. There is an alienating, isolating, crippling quality to darkness, true, but in the darkness lies a reason for hope. She's got to be here somewhere; I'm just passing by her in the dark. How do I know how much of the bridge I've not felt? She could be in any of those spots I've missed. But first light, dim before the sun, will settle everything, one way or another. Anticipation. Dread. If the light will promise to reveal Laura, safe and sleeping in an untouched corner, let it come. God speed it on. But if it must reveal barren stone, then let the light stay where it is. No promises can be made, of course, and the light will come. Revealing whatever's there. Orrin makes a last ditch attempt to find Laura with his hands, and when he comes up against a wall, he knows not which, he sits against it, waiting with his eyes closed.

His body is relaxed immediately. The Hymn tries a lullaby stanza on him, now that he is still. But Orrin is busy. Eyes shut, head hung to his chest, curtained by his hair, Orrin's deciding what to do. He is, has been all night, resigning himself to what the light will show him: naked stone, devoid of Laura, soil, water, life. Underneath it all, Orrin is hard-nosed; he knows the probabilities. He will be ecstatic, overwhelmingly relieved and happy if the light reveals Laura somewhere on the bridge, but he does not expect that. So. What to do? (The answer's obvious when he reaches it.) The sun will be up soon and begin to objectively, non-maliciously, but effectively burn life out of him till he is as lifeless as everything else in The Maze. He knows the probabilities, and he will probably die out here. He is sitting there, despair, unlike the night, growing stronger as the day approaches, thinking of how best to die—just sit here and wait it out? Walk off the bridge? Try to stretch my time by finding shade?—when it comes to him in an existential flash. He must live!

Probabilities to the Devil. He must live for Laura's sake. It is childish to think of walking off the bridge to join her. (As tired as he is, exorbitant energy comes with the existential flash, as though he just shot up some speed. He bursts to his feet, tosses back his hair, and meets the rising sun with a flexing stretch.) He must live, get out of here, get back to Moab, see his bishop, get the procedural wheels in motion, have Laura baptized after death. He looks around. She isn't there. He peers down, toward the bottom. Everything down there is so small, he'd-need binoculars to pick her out. But her body, sweet as it has been, does not concern him now. They'll have to check her genealogy out up in Salt Lake and there'll be all kinds of paperwork, but it can and will be done. He's sure she'd want it done. He can even, with more paperwork and ceremony, have her sealed to him, so that in God's Kingdom they'll be man and wife.

He finds he has been sitting against the wall with the crack, his canteen not three feet from him. Near it, dry and dead, a lonely sunflower blossom. He had touched neither in his blind and futile search. And just as well. If he'd come across that flower in the dark, no telling what he would've done. Even now it wrenches sentimental tears and forces him to stoop and pick it up.

Chapter Five

Angelic Transport

It is one thing, an important thing, to decide to live. But it is quite another, especially in Orrin's situation, to figure how. He can say well enough, "probabilities to the Devil," but they probably won't listen or obey. His mind is (seemingly) clear and working fast. He arrives at his decision quickly. Scans the remaining canyon walls above him to see if it is possible. There is only one direction he is sure he must take to get back to his Jeep: Up. He must go toward the fault line, too, and he has a vague idea from the sunrise which way that is, but the canyons are a mess. He will go up. If a helicopter ever comes, he'll be easier to spot the higher up he is. And maybe, just maybe, when he gets up wherever he can climb to, there will be a ridge, a fin, or something, leading right back to the bluffs. At least, if he gets up higher, he might be able to see the Big Drop-off, and head for it. He doesn't think he's far from it; if he only knew where it was and how to get there from where he is, then he could make it. "The only way to find out is to climb up out entirely of this canyon." His mind is working fast but only seeming to be clear.

And lo, it came to pass that in an un-named canyon in the northern portion of The Maze, Orrin of Moab found another crack. Not at all like the first crack, this one is perpendicular, across the bridge in the opposite wall, extending like an poorly built chimney to the lip of the canyon, some one hundred and fifty feet above. Compared to the first crack, this one's easier to climb, and compared to climbing to the bridge, this climb's short. But Orrin is exhausted, so it takes him hours to climb the chimney. Compared to Laura's death, what he finds up there is not depressing, frightening, or confusing, but compared to anything else, it is the most confusing, frightening, and depressing scene in which one could find himself. Immediately in front of him as he stands up after topping the lip of the canyon, is a monolith; huge, it soars a... He's tired of estimating heights. He knows though that the famed monoliths of Monument Valley are just about this size.

What hope is there of finding his way back to the Jeep when everywhere he turns, if not a monolith like this one, then a fin—high and subtly curved with now and then an arch like a window showing nothing but a vast and empty space soon filled with another shape of stone, a row of goblins, pinnacles—or a butte, or mesa, or a towering set of spires, a maze itself within The Maze, is there to block his vision?

With all that depth below him, it seems impossible that there could be this much height above. But he remembers there is more above these buttes and monoliths and fins. He remembers looking down on them from the rim, seeing only tops and sides, looking far out in The Maze at a throbbing sandstone woman clothed in haze. From another angle she would be a spire. But now he's here, between the layers of The Maze. His lips are dry. He licks them with a dry tongue. The canyons will still impede his progress, even more now than before; now he cannot cross them with impunity. He is bound to this side of the canyon he climbed out of, unless he decides to go back down. But you know all the arguments against doing that. And there'd be no sense climbing this monolith, even if he could. It goes nowhere. He is confined to this narrow shelf, this slanted pause between deep canyons and soaring heights of stone, stone that vibrates with the heat, its edges loosing definition.

Predominantly red, the stone might just as well be heat itself. Flames. Fire. Their edges, all their surfaces, fluctuate; the air is mobile with the discharge of their heat. Yes, flames. He will not broil, Orrin thinks with a twinge of desperate humor. He will speed broil. No need for turning. Sun will broil him from above, sandstone flames will broil him from the below, from all sides. His juices consumed immediately by the dry, hot, thirsty air. Which way to go? A simple, ludicrous decision to be made with no criteria at all upon which he can base it. And probably both are wrong. He probably should be on the other side of this canyon. If flames could cast a spot of shade, and he could find it, he'd lie down and sleep. He is exhausted. If there were to be a moon tonight, he'd travel tonight. There *is* shade, somewhere. Sun cannot shine down on things this large without a little shade resulting, even at high noon. But there's none around. The sun's behind him, the shade, on the other side of everything.

The steady, strong, inspiring hymn is with him, reminding Orrin of the stupid girls in stupid plaid short skirts urging the high school football team to victory when they're behind forty-six to nothing. But he cannot shut it up, and he finds it offers a solution to his problem of the moment. It suggests that he get going, and so he does, following the narrow, slanted shelf to his right for no particular reason, maybe because he's right handed.

The water in his canteen sloshes small and pitifully, begging him to drink it now and end its misery. He should've already drunk four times that much today. The white foam's growing in his mouth, and when that's gone, and soon it will be, his tongue will swell and fill his mouth. Walking makes it worse, of course, but even sitting in the sun on the sandstone flames would dry him rapidly. And he must get out. He's sure now no one is coming. Waiting for them would be insane. Attempting to feel his way out of here at night when it is cool and absolutely black would be insane. Walking in the blazing sun, walking on, through fire is insane. But what's a guy to do? The Hymn concurs and fills his mind with inspiration, drawing on what's left of Orrin's energy to keep him on his feet and keep them moving. If he makes it through the day, till the sun goes down, till the air and sandstone cool, then he will drink, and it will stay in him long enough to do some good.

He will not die of dehydration, *per se*, in a single day. But there are symptoms that accompany dehydration—vertigo, weakness, a tendency to pass out—that may, in these surroundings, be enough to do him in. The fire gyrates. The shelf he walks on is narrow, and The Maze is swirling, but he manages, God knows how, to walk on it. And while he does, while monolithic flames and skinny towering flames, and flames with holes, and flames he touches with his hands and body so he can stand on flames that move beneath his feet, while flames and sun and pale blue sky whirl, The Hymn spins this stanza through his discursive thoughts:

Go ahead, now, drink your pee,
It will save you,
Fill your canteen up with pee,
It will save you,
I have my work,
I will not shirk,
Go ahead, now, drink your pee.

What? Even in his condition, Orrin is repulsed by the suggestion. He would have never thought of it himself. The Hymn repeats the stanza, over and over. But The Taboo is strong, and Orrin staggers on, refusing to consider the disgusting possibility of drinking his pee and thinking, for himself, that he will drink the water in his canteen right now. He stops and sways on the shelf like a drunk stopping suddenly on a sidewalk. He almost falls. He unscrews the canteen lid and lets it hang by its chain as he carefully sips his last, hot four ounces of water. Hot but wet. And standing there, open canteen in hand, he feels the urge to pee. The Hymn turns up the volume and sings this to him:

Fill your canteen up with pee.

It's for Laura.

You have got to drink your pee.

It's for Laura.

You will get out.

There is no doubt.

Fill your canteen up with pee.

Augh! God. Disgusting. But what the hell? What's it going to do? Poison me? He laughs weakly. Yeah, I might die, if I drink my pee. That's what's gonna kill me. He moves the canteen back to his mouth and bites hold of its spout with his teeth. The expanded buttonholes in the fly of his worn and faded Levis release the copper buttons willingly at one downward, sideways pull. He fishes in his shorts. Not even his genitals are damp, and they should be, protected as they are. But they are dry. He pulls out his skillfully circumcised penis and holds it in his left hand. Takes the canteen from his mouth and holds it down in front of his dick, so that he can—he can't believe this—pee into it. And it goes right in, even as he sways, unsteady on his feet, as if it is directed by some higher power, but not as much as he expects. It does not fill his canteen half way.

Go ahead, now, drink your pee.

You can't save it.

You must drink your pee right now.

You can't save it.

I have my work.

I will not shirk.

Go ahead, now, drink your pee.

Orrin shudders, shakes, but raises the canteen to his lips and drinks. The taste is horrid, salty, uric-acidity, and bitter, too, but he drinks it as The Hymn repeats its encouraging, pee-drinking stanza, and it gives him a tingle of energy, and it is wet. He screws the cap back onto the empty canteen, stuffs his organ back into his shorts, buttons up his fly. He wishes he had a mint right now, because the aftertaste is strong and bad. He feels in his shirt pocket and, praise God, finds a round cellophane-wrapped mint he picked up at the last café. White with red swirls. Habitually, environmentally conscientious, Orrin puts the wrapper back in his pocket after he pops the mint into his mouth. He must get out of here.

The Hymn strikes up the standard, put your shoulder to the wheel stanza, and Orrin starts walking again. He has some energy from his breakfast of pee and candy, and The Hymn helps more than he could know. It helps him move, and it helps him stay on the narrow shelf that whirls with the rest of his surroundings around him like the bedroom of a drunk with the bed spins. And The Hymn helps him stay awake. Helps him fight the fatigue from his Herculean efforts of yesterday and from his sleepless, anxious night. It will let him, help him sleep when shade is found, if found, but not until—as long as it can keep him from it. Besides all that, The Hymn, by filling Orrin's mind, protects it, helps block out the buzzing, tinkling, ringing sound, audio hallucinations that will come to anybody in that desert stillness and are attracted strongly now to Orrin because of his condition.

He moves and keeps moving, it's true, for motion's sake, knows not where he's going, following the shelf like a rail. Where else but where it leads? Through the sky, across the Sun. The shelf cannot cross canyons. It turns with tributaries, following their lips. His lips are blackened, curled back and bleeding. Dry blood. He is thirsty, but he doesn't have to pee again. He'd drink it gladly. He's gagging on his tongue and regurgitated bile. How long has he been walking? Since he was eight months old. All morning, half the afternoon. It makes no difference; he must get out. No one else will think to baptize Laura. And even if they did, they wouldn't seal her to him, so they could be together for eternity.

A high pitched, constant bell, electric, far away, accompanies The Hymn, the swirling universe. Around and round, like walking through the rotating tubes in the fun house, lost and sick. Flames lick his clothes, his hair, His once lovely, oily hair has dried: black straw. The ringing grows intense. It's coming from the sun. And the sun is fast approaching. Higher, louder, the ringing will shatter Orrin's mind. And POOF, his hair bursts into flames. He screeches, but he cannot hear his voice above the bell. When he awakes he finds that nothing's changed. He feels his hair. It's still there, burning but not consumed. His eyes are gritty, burning, dry. But, more, they've filmed over. How long has he been out? He wonders. The world still spins. It's still bright and hot. He feels uninjured—didn't fall, or if he did, not far. Maybe he wasn't out at all, completely. Maybe it's another day. The bell's still ringing. Far away some class keeps ending or beginning so the bell just never stops. The Hymn's there, too—weak, but there and reassuring. It doesn't urge him to continue, and he wouldn't if it did. He lies on sandstone flames, right arm, right leg dangling, his head turned to that side, eyes fixed, watching through the veil that has grown across his vision, watching sun and pale blue sky and flames pass by. Poor Laura. He'd cry if he could. But there's no moisture left for tears, no energy for sobs and sighs.

He has no strength for anything. He doesn't hold his eyes open. They stay open, as if he were already dead. And as he lies there dying it seems his eyes change focus. Remembering it, that's the closest he can come to a physical description of what happens. His eyes change focus. Instead of focusing as best they can on the whirling universe, they are now, with no help from him, focused on the veil that covers them. At least that's how it seems. And he doesn't like it. The heat, the vertigo, exhaustion, swollen tongue, and even the burning hair he can take. But this, this so unnatural, different kind of sight shivers him. He cannot squint, cannot even blink to change it. His eyelids are shriveled back, like strips of bacon overcooked, and will not respond to him. He's burning up, but the marrow of his bones is cold. He aches. He thinks that it is death beginning, but it's not death. It's fear.

He sees something that puts The Fear in him. It first appears as a small, white, nebular light. And Orrin's certain death is near; he hopes so. But The Hymn calms him with its gentle music, no lyrics. It seems to understand, to be in contact with the light. Orrin feels it. He can't explain—not even to himself, remembering. But he feels it. Feels that the light's reached out and made contact with him, with The Hymn, which is of, by, in, and for Orrin Porter Rockwell Christianson, but also independent. Moving across a great expanse and not rushing any, either, the light grows nearer, larger, throbbing softly into shape. The human shape. Long, long hair. Is it a woman? No, a man. It is Orrin Porter Rockwell. There's no mistaking him. Those piercing eyes belong to no one else. Those piercing, deep set, shadowed eyes—the look of a madman or an agent of the Lord? Even Rockwell's enemies agreed that he had something frightful in his eyes. The Gentiles said that it was madness but respected it as something else, because it is. Receded hairline. He is almost bald on top, with long, white, rumpled hair flaring out across his shoulders. Wiry white moustache and beard. The deep canyons angling down from above his nostrils into his beard, the hair, the wild eyes, present a paralyzing countenance. Orrin can see how they *could* anyway, but they don't to him.

They beckon. No words are spoken, no gestures made, but Orrin gets the idea. This spooky old man, this angel, or hallucination, whatever he is, is supposed to inspire or frighten his namesake into getting up and traveling on, putting his shoulder to the wheel, and God knows what else. Nice try. He's tired. Burned and sick beyond inspiration. Preparation for this vision went too far. He had to be prepared, of course, and he can see this whole chapter of his life falling into place as preparation for this moment. Ha. It isn't gonna work. What he needs is some real help. A helicopter would do. If this crazy, mute old ghost can show up, why can't a helicopter come? There are reasons, probably. But he doesn't care. No. He is not going to get up. He can't. Orrin Porter Rockwell can stand there and beckon till The Maze turns into a tropical rain forest, if he wants. Orrin Porter Rockwell

Christianson isn't gonna move. The Hymn...oh, of course, The Hymn will try to get him up. It's in cahoots with this old codger. Let it sing and scrape his soul for energy. It will find none. It has scraped it all and licked the scraper. The Hymn won't budge him, true. But Orrin underestimates his predecessor, among other things.

Porter Rockwell says to Orrin, "Wheat!" which in his own slang lingo means "All right, if that's the way you want it." He usually said it, screeched, it before he slugged or plugged somebody. It served the same purpose, more or less, as karate shouts, or war cries—though he would sometimes use the term in normal conversation as an affirmative or a threat.

If there was ever anybody who hated a part of his body, that would be Orrin Porter Rockwell. A good-sized man for his day, muscular, thick-necked; impressive, he was cursed with tiny hands. Hands that looked as though they stopped growing when he was five. He hated them. Forced them to do more work than hands four times their size, made them hard as rock and tough as leather, fast. His tiny hands could crack a man's jaw or draw a sawed-off pistol from his coat pocket and avenge the Lord with lead before his victim finished listening to "Wheat!"

And so it is with Orrin. He's lying there hearing "Wheat!" thinking, what can that word mean? Is that really what I'm hearing? Is the old man saying it? When he feels and sees the old, tiny hands vise-grip his arm pits. He feels himself, his dead weight, lifted, and, then, he feels that he is moving through the air, above The Maze. Just as Habakkuk was carried by an angel from Judea to the lion-pit in Babylon, with some stew for Daniel, and then back to his own place again, through the air. Only this is slower, Orrin thinks. And that quicker angel picked Habakkuk up by his hair.

Porter Rockwell stinks of horses. He has a way with horses. Stole horses from the Gentiles in Missouri, stole horses from the U.S. Army, from the Indians, from the hapless emigrants. He's really into horses. Raised horses on his horse ranch in Skull Valley. Go there now, you're in the middle of Dugway Proving Grounds. Dodge the bombs, protect yourself from nerve gas and whatever else they're proving. Look around, you'll find his house, what's left of it, a target now. 'Course it always had been, one way or another. Everything the Mormons had was in the crosshairs of the U.S. government. They figured Brother Brigham had an Empire out here and they didn't like it. So they commenced to harass and trouble us, shoot Zion full of holes. First thing, they bring us into range with the possibility of statehood. Then, with propaganda of their own and the wild-eyed, Gentile, Eastern papers, get the entire population of the other states against us for polygamy. Run good folks like Great-Great-Grandpa into Mexico, put others, just I as good, in Federal Pens. For what? For loving. For having the capacity to love, to care for, to provide for, fulfill the lives of more than one woman at a time. For bringing God's Kingdom down to Earth. For loving. They pour everything they've got into that campaign, and all the while there's a U.S. Army Fort sitting right up on the bench above Salt Lake City, its cannons pointed down our throats. They take that bench, the mountains, canyons up behind it; all of it was ours, all part of Zion; they say it's theirs now. U.S. property.

Military Reservation. They like that kind of thing. Take away our land and sap our strength. Indian reservations. No one will contest their right to give some of Zion to the Indians. So they give them huge chunks, as big as Massachusetts. National Security. The U.S. Government needs Tooele Ordinance Depot, Hill Air Force Base, Dugway Proving Grounds, the gigantic Wendover Bombing and Gunnery Range, Camp Williams, Fort Douglas, and, absurdity supreme, a Naval Supply Depot on the shores of The Great Salt Lake. Conservation, Reclamation. Other good excuses, as if we weren't doing it ourselves. No. The U.S. government's got to take it from us. Make more National Parks, National Monuments, National Recreation Areas in Utah than in any other state. They called one Zion, Zion National Park. Add insult to thievery. It's theirs now, they said so. But it's not enough for them. They make every stand of juniper that isn't part of a National Park or National something else into a National Forest. And the Bureau of Land Management confiscates our range. We need permits to run our cattle on *our* land. When they get through, they've got eighty-five percent of Utah. Eighty-five percent of Zion belongs to the United States. The Government. The rest is still ours but they've put a damper on The Saints, they think. They treated us the same way China treats Tibet. They thought we would suffocate and die. But instead, we grew. Not as we would've, grown if they'd left us alone, but we've grown. And they're running scared. They can't nationalize Salt Lake City, Temple Square, and all our Wards and Stakes. Temple Square National Monument? Not today, not tomorrow, never. So they offer Sperry,

Litton, Hercules, and Thiokol, to name a few, huge contracts, if they'll locate in the Salt Lake Valley, hire mobs of Gentile workers, and complain about the Mormons, demoralize the Mormon children, try to wrest control of local politics. Buy up Mormon land and smear it with developments. They've poured so much Gentile blood and money into the Salt Lake Valley, that now only half the people there are L.D.S. It's so bad, now, if you don't know a man, you've got to ask him his religion! It's war. It always has been. From the beginning it was war. It's war right now. But they've convinced most Mormons that it's not, that the U.S. government is great. It's almost blasphemous the way our brothers and our sisters see the U.S. government. They don't know it's out to obliterate us. Make us as weak as all the other churches. They don't know that all that "economic development" is war. They don't know the FBI and DEA subsidize drug traffic into Utah, support the dealers, thwart the efforts of the local, Mormon police. But that's okay. That's a tactical mistake. The Gentile kids and Jack Mormons buy most of the drugs, anyway. But some drugs get into the weaker Mormons, and that's chemical warfare. Deadly. As deadly as the nerve-gas that "escapes" from Dugway Proving Grounds now and then to kill us and our sheep. As deadly as the fallout that blows over us and falls on us. The government knows the prevailing wind currents, the weather patterns. It knows the fallout won't make it up to Canada and break a treaty. The government is sure of that. It will all fall on the Mormons. Porter Rockwell stinks of horses, and the stench of horses, catalytic, starts Orrin's mind, and maybe keeps it on the track. But Porter Rockwell has said nothing that comes through Orrin's ears. Nothing except that first word: "Wheat!" Remembering it now Orrin isn't positive his mind followed that progression, named those names, cited those events, threw that brief history together. He creates it now, as he rides to school in his open Jeep, as his own objective correlative. Because he knows he experienced an anointing, an initiation into a temperament he didn't have before The Maze. And now, recalling that, those things just come into his mind, just as the stench of horses comes again into his nose. Thought-induced perception.

Focused on the film that covers them, his eyes perceive the world as a fuzzy blur. The colors he knows are bright, come through to him washed out, filtered. Strands, great clumps of old white hair impair his vision further. But he's too weak to care. He's moving. He knows that. He's going through extensive changes, a spiritual metamorphosis. He feels that. An instrumental version of The Hymn, featuring the organ and the harp, plays in the background, while its lyrics are being updated.

****

When he comes down like a piece of ripened fruit on the sand and rock beside his CJ5, the music stops. When he awakes, awakened by a thunderstorm that causes flash floods throughout The Maze and slams its giant drops like flat-nosed bullets into his open eyes, The Hymn is going strong. And it has words again, new words to make new verses for a new and different Orrin Porter Rockwell Christianson. Still weak, he barely manages to slide a hand across his eyes. They sting and burn. They ache;

they feel bruised, but the forceful drops have started anyway to disintegrate the film. The thunder, somehow, sounds like large-bore, sawed-off, celestial pistols being fired in celebration of his life. That's egocentric, but he can't help it. That's what it sounds like to him. Does he remember seeing two pistol butts protruding from coat pockets? He thinks so, yes! He remembers them and more. His great-granduncle in angelic form? It must've been! His religion says that it can and does happen, and he has more or less accepted that, without really expecting see one of them. In short, he finds it difficult to believe. His parched, black lips, his swollen tongue, his entire shriveled body take in water like a sponge.

It's difficult to believe, but he has no choice. How can he, who was somewhere down there in The Maze near death, and is now beside his Jeep being refreshed by a God-sent thunder storm, how can Orrin not believe? He can't not believe. He does believe. A drop or two of water trickles down his slowly shrinking tongue; he swallows it gratefully and painfully; for his throat is dry and doesn't wish to work. The water has no chance at all of reaching his stomach. He takes more, a very little at a time. His throat, now primed, is more cooperative. The storm, violent and short, ends just as suddenly as it began, and inspiring shafts of sunlight break through the dissipating clouds. What water didn't crash down the canyons as muddy walls will be gone, into he thirsty earth or back into the air, in half an hour. It will be hotter than before. It always is.

Orrin crawls under his Jeep, rolls onto his back—shade there this time of day. He shuts his eyes with his hand, massages them. They pop open again, as soon as he moves his hand away. His vision is even more blurred now, and his eyes more bruised. It was stupid to rub them. He rests, looking up toward the Jeep's drive train. It is possible for him to do all this under there (for those of you who don't know) because Jeeps of necessity have more clearance than passenger cars, and Orrin's, with its 3-inch lift kit, 17-inch wheels, and 31-inch tires, has more clearance than a showroom Jeep. He has been thankful for the extra space before, when it has kept him from high-centering, but never as thankful as he is now. He rests, and in a while his eyes finally blink, without a conscious effort. Good sign. Directly above him, the front drive shaft comes into focus. Beautiful. That little baby makes all the difference. He turns his eyes away from it and scans the sand around his Jeep. No other wheels. Laura's father made it this far, anyway, and left. Help might just be on the way, but Orrin's not counting on it.

Far away, a monolith basks obscenely in the sun, water vapor rising from it. If Orrin tries, as he does, he can imagine that it looks like a man's head, or at least a caricature of a man's head. A huge, oversized, stupid-looking (how can sandstone look intelligent?) head. Sandstone—he thinks, still looking at the monolithic head, or head-like monolith—can look passionate, blazingly passionate, but not intelligent. Intelligent as sandstone. It doesn't work. It *looks* solid, strong, impressive, but in truth it's full of holes, extremely mutable. That monolith, for instance, wasn't always what it is. It was just plain sand once, got pressed into stone, shoved up in the air, washed, and it won't be a monolith for long, in rock time. Sandstone is a pretense: sand pretending to be stone.

That head *looks* solid, strong, impressive, but it, too, is full of holes, extremely mutable, and worse than pretense, it is illusion. Enough of that, he thinks, no one's head is that shape, anyway. Something must be wrong, to see it as a head. The Hymn spurts out its first new stanza at this moment, fast and not loud, mumbling, as though it's not quite sure of itself.

Kill An ag no stop ou los,
That's your job.
Do you duty with a shout,
Not a sob.
I have my work;
I will not shirk.
Kill Ana gnos to poulos.

Then goes back to its instrumental version, strings this time. Orrin is puzzled. "Kill?" He wonders. In the first and last lines, "kill" is the only word he's sure of. Does it mean me? I'm to kill something? Naw. I've never killed anything in my life, he thinks, waiting for that benevolent surge, that tidal wave of love, kindness, compassion, that has always filled him when he's taken dead aim at a deer or something, squeezed the trigger and missed. Truly, he has never *wanted* to kill anything in his life, and he hasn't killed anything, either, as far as he knows. Not even a wasp or cockroach, a rattlesnake or coyote. He swerves dangerously off the road to avoid jackrabbits. He is not a killer. He waits there in the shade beneath his Jeep, but the surge, the tidal wave does not come. Instead, he finds himself coldly trying to decipher what it is he's supposed to kill. "I'm not well!" he tells himself. An ag. What the heck's an ag. No, stop, ou los. It is confusing, baffling. Is The Hymn speaking tongues? But that is not what bothers him most. He wants—against what he's known all his life as his will—to figure out what it is so he can kill it. He knows he'll kill it. That's what gets him. He doesn't even know what in God's Creation it is yet, but he feels an ontological imperative at work on him. And he has no love, no pity, no compassion whatsoever for whatever it is, and he will kill it. As soon as he finds out what it is and gets the chance. "No. I'm not well at all. That's it," Orrin tells himself and rolls' out from under his Jeep into the sun, figuring that if he busies himself, he won't think about it.

He is right on one point: he is not well. He cannot stand on his own power. He must use the Jeep to pull himself up, and he must lean on it. In the passenger's seat he finds a plastic gallon jug of water holding down a note. GONE FOR HELP Cryptic, lucid, boldly laid down across an old, void automobile contract with a black marker. One gallon of water and a Jeep full of gasoline. He could drive longer than he could live. In the last line it has it: Ana gnos to poul os" Something like that. It must be tongues. He curses Laura's father for not leaving at least one of the five-gallon water cans and some food.

Ah, God, his capacity for sympathy is shot. The man must've been frantic, worried sick, weary from climbing out of that hole. He hopes the poor guy took time to transfer a few cans of gas to his Jeepster before taking off. What a horrible sense of impotence to run out of gas somewhere in the middle of the Green River Desert with your daughter lost and dying somewhere in The Maze. He jerks physically at the thought of Laura, not dying, dead, down there. Surely, dead. He is not without feelings for Laura. He must get out! Get back to Moab.

He hauls his body into the driver's seat. Fishes in his pockets for his keys, starts his Jeep. Reserve tank: full. Main tank: half. Enough for now. Kill an ag no stop ou los. Kill ana gnos to poulos. The Hymn does not repeat the lyrics. It just plays music, which brings them back to Orrin. But the words make no sense. None of them. Least of all "kill."

Ah, ah, ah, he wails, pushing it into first, did I kill Laura? Didn't I kill Laura? God knows it wasn't what you'd call premeditated murder. But, just the same, am I not responsible? I could've fastened her to me again, before we went to sleep. Why didn't I? I knew about her going to the bathroom in her sleep. Just the night before, I'd listened to her. A vile mixture of bile and water spews forth from his mouth, splatters on the steering wheel, the windshield, drips down on his legs. Kill? The vomitus evaporates almost immediately, leaving only stains and a pungent taste in Orrin's mouth: the taste of "kill." He must wash it from his mouth. Wash it from his mind, if impossible. Out damned taste.

He is not well. The sun has baked his brain. He drinks carelessly from the gallon jug. The taste remains. From the glove compartment he takes a cellophane bag of assorted dried fruit, stowed there for emergencies. Flings it on to the seat beside him, busts it violently with a karate chop, and pops a slice of dehydrated apple into his mouth. It sits there like an old, dried turd on his still somewhat swollen tongue. More water from the jug, held in his mouth and swished around with the apple as he chews it. Faint glimmer of long forgotten fruity taste. He swallows it and pops the clutch, turning the wheel viciously to miss The Maze. But the Jeep's still in low range and, though he popped the clutch, acceleration is not great; it is slow, ponderous and powerful. He misses The Maze easily but is forced to look at it briefly as the Jeep swings away. If he didn't know what's down there, what it's really like, the thing would lure him in again. It is so beautiful, so unlike man. It kills, but it is not a killer. No. It doesn't kill, just makes it easier for you to kill yourself, by accident or plan. He leaves it in low range but moves up through the gears, maintaining revs, and soon he's roaring along like a madman: fourth gear, low range, about twenty miles per hour.

Kill? He didn't fasten his seatbelt—something he always does when he's off road—and he's bouncing like a puppet in the seat, holding himself in with his grip on the steering wheel, which doesn't help his steering any. Bouncing from one side of the ridge to the other, hitting rocks he shouldn't hit, missing all the nearly open spots, he arrives at the point to turn off it down one steep bank of a gully and up the other. Has time to shift down only into third. Kill! Can't stop to put it into first, as he should. He barrels down off the ridge too fast, almost flies over the windshield. The gully's narrow at the bottom. He crashes into the other bank before he's off the first. Starts up. But the steep bank saps the speed immediately. Torque, that's what gets you up a slope like this. Torque and traction, not speed. You grind up these things. His foot's, as they say, in the carburetor, but the Jeep's lugging out in third. He's almost stopped, then he'll have to brake, or roll down backwards, slide backwards even if he brakes, rollover maybe, kill the engine, surely. Kill? He double clutches fast, with the pedal on the floor, grinds it into second, pops the clutch. No good. Might've made it if he started up in second, but partway up, almost started down, no. Again, still slightly moving, forward progress almost stopped, again he double clutches, starts down backwards, slams it with an ugly crunch into first. Synchromesh my eye. Floors it, pops the clutch. It doesn't want to, almost dies, but the omnipotent low-range first gear has its way. Up he starts. Grinding slowly, properly up the bank. Go baby. I'll be good to you. He stops it when he tops the bank, pulls the handbrake, shifts into neutral. He heaves a sigh, apologizes to his vehicle, drinks carefully, takes more fruit: an apricot, prune, apple, he doesn't notice. Drinks some more. Fastens his seatbelt and proceeds sanely, though he is still troubled by The Hymn. Troubled by The Hymn's new lines and his attitude toward them, an attitude he doesn't like.

Entering the campus, thinking back, Orrin realizes he was troubled by his "self" those first few hours after The Maze. Driving through the barren wilderness, his "self" is a stranger to him. It is eager to solve the riddle of The Hymn. Eager to kiil the answer. Well, if not eager, something too much like eager for Orrin's taste. Orrin is not a killer, at least he didn't think he was, didn't feel like a killer. He tries to divert his attention from those things by driving skillfully around the crumbling base of a butte. Not just carefully, but that too; for skill is care. Care with something more—a dash of virtuosity. More concentration is needed, and Orrin gives it gladly, becoming one with his machine, or more precisely, making his machine a part of him, an extension. So, Orrin and his four-wheel drive extension crash and bounce and jolt skillfully as one. But Orrin has another extension that is one with him and more independent than the Jeep.

The Hymn continues, driving Orrin more skillfully than he could ever hope to drive his Jeep. Orrin must get out of the desert wilderness alive, in order to obey the ontological imperative, so The Hymn, right now, does not get in his way, does not bring up those lines again for a while. Use this time to organize those syllables (six words? one? it wasn't told) into something Orrin can understand. It doesn't want to confuse and madden Orrin into a random killing rampage. And it doesn't want to fail, either. "Put Your Shoulder to the Wheel" has a good record so far and botching Orrin would be disastrous to its reputation. The Higher Ups might not use it again. Might think that it is outdated. But what can it do, with the kind of information it was given? It can try.

The Hymn will bide its time, playing music deep in Orrin's mind, maybe scraping up a little strength now and then, without his knowing, just to help him out. Let him become acquainted with his new "self," as he calls it. That will be enough for now. Make it clear to him that it's okay. Not only okay, it's obligatory. Help bring about a reconciliation. Help him see that sometimes, killing is what must be done. A time to kill, turn, turn. And this is one of those times. It can't come right out and tell him in so many words that he is an agent of The Lord, just like his great-granduncle. That's evident, or should be, and he must acknowledge it himself. The Hymn can push him toward it, but Orrin must make the leap.

Orrin's rounded the butte by now, heading for the base of the Flint Trail. The cliff looms two-thousand feet up out of sand and rock, trees on top, and stretches continuously for a hundred miles, either way. There's only one break in it, one trail up, and Orrin's watching for it carefully, can't afford to miss it. Something shining in the sun up ahead, too far away to make out what it is, but Orrin's got a gruesome hunch. As he approaches, he's proven right. Three buzzards and a flock of ravens flutter up, wait on the rocks nearby. Her father's Jeepster is on its side at the bottom of the cliff, bashed, dented, crumpled, even the sturdy roll bar is squashed. He came down quite a ways.

Laura's father is bloated, held in by his seatbelt, dismembered, partly by the tumble down the cliff, partly by the scavengers. The fall probably tore that arm off, left his head dangling, but it did not pluck out his eyes. Orrin looks up at the birds. They stare back at him, patient, hungry, black and, suddenly, hideous, though he's known all his life they are not wicked, cannot be—they are only birds. He returns one big buzzard's stare and says to it: "You are as of now an ag no stop ou los." He grins and unclips his semi-automatic .22 rifle from its snug position behind the seats. If you live in the West, you carry a rifle in your Jeep or pick-up when you drive in the back country. If you live on a ranch, you always carry it. It's part of living in the West, and if you search other vehicles you'll find bigger hardware than Orrin carries—not those sniveling lever-action carbines you see on TV, either. 30.06s and 7mm magnums are standard equipment. And don't get Orrin wrong. He's a Westerner. Grew up hunting and shooting guns, just never could hit what he shot at; nor did he wish to.

But so many things have changed that Orrin figures maybe now he'll shoot straight. He has no love, though admittedly, little hatred for that bird. He'd just as soon not kill it. He works the action to get the first round in the chamber and, leaning over the hood of his Jeep for stability, takes dead aim at the big bird's breast. Then, just before he squeezes off his shot, he hears himself chirp, "Wheat!" in his high-pitched voice that he tries not to use, but sometimes does when he's excited or angry. But he's neither of those now, and he misses. The bullet ricochets off the cliff ten feet above and at least two feet to the left of the buzzard. The birds don't even acknowledge the shot. They remain as patient and as hungry looking as before. Orrin doesn't have to search his memory long for the source of the word "Wheat." He's uncertain of its meaning, but he says it again, this time before he aims, so it won't take him by surprise, cause him to flinch and, therefore, he thinks, miss.

He squeezes off another perfectly aimed shot; the bird just sits there. Another, off the cliff somewhere. Another, misses again. Before he can squeeze off the next shot, that surge, that tidal wave he waited for beneath his Jeep, fills him with love, compassion, kindness, and he doesn't shoot at the buzzard again. Doesn't want to. He's glad he missed, wishes he hadn't shot at all. That bird to isn't an ag, and saying it is can't make it so. "I'm not a wanton killer," Orrin thinks, with relief. "I'm to kill one thing, whatever it is, and that's it. As for the other living things on God's Green Earth, I shall never kill!" He feels very good about that, but wonders if he shouldn't test his marksmanship objectively, see if he can hit an inanimate target.

If he's supposed to kill something, a gun's the best tool he can think of, and apparently his love for living things doesn't include an ag, so that won't ruin his aim when he finds an ag and shoots at it. Orrin takes a careful shot at Laura's father's spotlight, up the cliff about a hundred feet—misses completely. He must face the facts. He's a rotten shot. It's not his love for other creatures that causes him to miss. He just can't shoot. Can't hit his ass with both hands. Standing there, Orrin doesn't believe it. Anybody can shoot, he says, with a little training, and I've had more training than most soldiers. He takes another shot at the spotlight; misses again.

Cruising through the upperclassmen's parking lots, seeking an open slot, remembering the ordeal of shooting, Orrin can't understand why he made such a big deal out of it. He knows now it is not that important. He can't shoot; that's all there is to it. But then, then he saw it as absurd, illogical. A principle was involved, and he could see no reason why he shouldn't be able to shoot at least as well as the next man. He had no fear of guns, didn't jerk the trigger, aimed with both eyes open, as only the best marksmen do, had a steady, rock-solid stance. But he missed, even with a shotgun, he missed. He empties his gun at the spotlight, missing every time, and is still not satisfied. But there are more important things to do right now. He must get out of here. And to do that, to get up the Flint Trail, he's going to need a winch. He's sure Laura's father won't mind. Sure that he'd insist. He returns his rifle to its clips and hauls out his tool box.

Laura's dad is ripe. Ah, God, so ripe, but he must overcome, ignore the stench and get to work. Maybe he should bury him. No. The coyotes would just dig him up again. It'd be a waste of time. He was a good man, Orrin thinks. Good, and I liked him a lot. Have to see if I can't get him baptized, too. Then he gets down to work, thinking how handy it is that the Jeepster's on its side. He doesn't have to jack it up.

No empty slots, but a car's backing out of one right now. There's a Volkswagen, coming from the other direction, waiting, ready to whip in there before the car's completely out. Working in the hot sun, with vultures and ravens staring down his throat, and the smell of his lover's father choking him isn't easy. He has to rest and drink often. But he gets the job done, transfers the winch to his Jeep, before sunset. The bug's no competition for his Jeep though, if the car gives him a break and backs out toward the V.W., throwing, more or less, a brief but sufficient block. It does; the Jeep whips in before the bug can budge.

He finds some cans of food and water that aren't busted open, drives away from the stench, eats, drinks, sleeps as well as he could expect to sleep. Turns the Jeep off, pockets his keys, grabs his books from the back, and leaves, heading off across the massive parking lot toward his class, slowly coming back to where he is. Time, he thinks, is strange. A twenty-minute drive enables me to go over so much of my past, so many of the crucial moments of my life, a drive that seems much longer because of all the memories I recovered.

He stops, looks around, looks down at the asphalt and talks to himself so loudly that he attracts the attention of a buxom coed. "Memory?!" he says. "Raspberries! I swear it never happened till I remembered it."

"Isn't that called *Deja vu?*" the coed coos. Sheer, sky blue kimono, no bra, wooden shoes, and long, blonde hair. Big lips, straight white teeth, clear, blue eyes.

Embarrassed by his lust for her, Orrin mumbles, "No. The opposite of that." and shuffles off, humming The Hymn.

Chapter 6

Research in the New Library

If Lake Bonneville had not remained at a certain high level for centuries, the University of Utah, Fort Douglas, and some high-class homes would not have that flat, high bench (once beach) to sit on and look down smugly from clean air at the smoggy city. On bad days, temperature inversion days, there is no city to be seen. The entire valley from the Wasatch Front, where Orrin stands, to the Oquirrh (Native Ute for Shining) Mountains looks like a mud puddle, a sea of smoke, a soft, dirty, polyurethane cushion. When the temperature inversion lasts a couple weeks, people die, the bench is also engulfed, and to see the sun, to breathe, you must go higher, climb the mountains (thank God for the mountains), and from the top of

Germania ski lift at Alta, you can look down, way down at the murk.

However, a day of temperature inversion this is not. If Orrin looked, he could see the buildings, the busy highways of the valley through a thin veil of smoke. He would see the capitol, high on a hill itself, yet still below him; Temple Square and Welfare Square; and across the valley he would see Kennecott Copper Corporation's smoke stacks at the base of the Shining Mountains. He would see all that and more, if he'd look, but Orrin doesn't look out at the valley. He looks at the ground, at the new buildings going up, at the half-naked coeds. He would never do anything with any of them, because of his love for Laura, but he cannot help looking.

He was not like this before. If he would just look out at the valley, at the shimmering lake. How joyously it reflects the sunshine! It is a piteous drop in the Great Basin compared to Lake Bonneville, but the Great Salt Lake would cheer him, cleanse his mind. He could look at it, remember facts about it, forget the girls. He would not be so horny if he had not remembered Laura, if he had not been confronted by that blonde, with her sexy *deja vu*. But, still, Orrin could recall, for instance, if he would look out at the slivery body, hot and subtly curved, with islands jutting up, like dry breasts, that no one's ever drowned in the Great Salt Lake. Many a careless wader, boater, rafter, inner tuber, crashed pilot, many people in the lake for reasons of their own have strangled, choked, and gaged to death, but none have drowned, the brine will not allow it.

They have sacrificed themselves for naught. He won't look at the lake, will not recall them. He continues in his cheerless lust toward the building where his first class started a half hour ago, and his route takes him by the new library. The year that it was completed, the new library was the largest university library completed that year. Large, clean, white, with few and narrow windows, the library is mostly empty, as planned. If everything goes according to the projected growth of the university, the country, and the world, the library will be comfortably full two hundred years from now. Then, according to the interior architect's design, the existing and seemingly stationary shelves can be shifted, new shelves added, aisles narrowed, resulting in twice the original book capacity. When that new design is filled to capacity, it can be adjusted, re-configured again. And again, whenever necessary, as many times as necessary. Forever. This, plus the use of microfilm and other, anticipated, information storage technology, make the new library's capacity limitless.

Twenty-five stories above the ground, three beneath. From the ground floor to the top an open shaft the size of the entire central lobby creates twenty-five rectangular balconies. When a graduate student dives, everybody understands. The temptation start's about the tenth floor. From there up, one looks down the shaft at the busy lobby and hears music, and the carpet and the depth say "Come on down. Jump." Everybody hears it.

As Orrin passes near the new library some music of his own strikes up:

Yes, agree to Tony's deal,
Get him Secrets.
They are open, anyway,

Get the secrets.
I have my work;
I will not shirk.
Yes, agree to Tony's deal.

His mind's made up, and he is late for class, anyway. No sense going in late. Where has he heard that verse before? He wonders. It seems familiar. He turns into the library, through the two sets of double doors, and The Drone is on him. The Drone that in the summer must be the air conditioning and in winter must surely be the heating system. The Drone. The Drone of a massive library, the drone of empty space, of empty shafts. You only notice it as you enter and as you leave. Immediate drowsiness as the library drone assimilates and Orrin no longer hears it.

All around him, at the long tables, in the carrels, the scholars study, arms folded over open books, heads down, mouths relaxed. Orrin yawns and gives his head one quick shake to throw off sleep. His hair flows smoothly across his face. He flicks it into place, along his shoulders, down his back.

Where to find something Tony would accept as secret Mormon mind control techniques? Orrin figures there are many secrets in this place, safe, yet there for anyone who cares to dig them up. The Hymn says that they are open, anyway. Open to anyone who can stay awake, who can read between the lines and in the margins, who can worm his way through a maze of different styles of annotation and cross references.

Orrin doesn't work that way, never has. "Where can I find..." he starts to ask the buxom, braless, young blonde in the sheer, blue kimono, who is now stationed at the information desk reading what appears to be a paperback novel. She looks up and cuts him off, as though she knows what he's going to ask, and he's being redundant. "Sub three, section two, aisle thirty-seven, first, second, third and fourth shelves." Before Orrin can ask how she...she winks at him suggestively, jiggles her breasts, and returns to her book.

He holds yellow legal pads in front of his crotch as he hitches over to the elevator. Down into the bowels, alone, confused, determined. Okay, okay, he says to the empty elevator, so she was on her way to work when I saw her in the parking lot. Nothing wrong with that. He flicks his hair back into place, though it isn't out. A twitch, a tic, jerks across his face. The Hymn surges up out of his mind's ear to his lips. He hums it. Calms down. Sinks down. Shrinks. Descends. Three stories below the ground, sub three. The lobby's also shrunk. Cold. Closed in. Unlike the openness and light, the glass walls of the main lobby, this lobby is surrounded by four concrete walls with doors.

There is an illuminated sign above each door. He walks over to SECTION TWO. The door knob's cold. A Xerox machine glows in the dimness along the wall. It's even darker inside Section Two. He feels up and down around the corner inside the door, finds a row of switches, flicks them all. Fluorescent squares of ceiling flicker on above each aisle and continue flickering, soft and weak. Orrin tries to get his eyes blinking in time with the flickering lights, but it is hopeless. Maddening. So he turns them off, yawns uncontrollably, as he waits for his eyes to open up. It's dim, but he can read the signs. Small signs with aisle numbers and Dewey Decimal System numbers.

He hugs the wall, following the decreasing aisle numbers into a far corner. The aisle numbers are still high, and he's walked further than the library is long, unless...the subterranean dimensions are greater. He isn't worried, though; he's hugged the wall and all he has to do is turn around and follow it back to the door. But now he's in a corner and there's only one way around it, so he turns. He turns and there is no more wall: aisles on either side, shelves, long and sparsely filled, extending deep into the dimness of sub three. The numbers still decrease, so Orrin continues, humming The Hymn, for company. He feels he is never truly alone. Feels The Hymn is more than just a song. For him it is a being, not necessarily human, but it has a definite personality, and seems to have a mind of its own.

Aisle thirty-seven looks much the same as any other. Orrin thumbs through a couple of thick volumes—histories, not much good, nice old books, though, with ribs across the spine. Browsing along, squinting to read titles, he works his way to the fourth and final shelf. And there...There a book like no other he has squinted at attracts his hand. It is a strange book, with strange binding material. Evident strangeness of production processes involved. It is too heavy for its size. And...the book has a palpable vibe. Its title: *Prewar History Review Rejects, Vols. 1-5*.

It falls open in his hands to the copyright page of Vol. 1, No.1, copyrighted 4760, by SIAPHE, the Society of the International Association of Prewar Historians Expellees. On the same page, Orrin discovers that the founder of SIAPHE is the founder, publisher, and editor of *Prewar History Review Rejects*.

There, too, is a short statement of Policy and Purpose.

The policy of *Prewar History Review Rejects,* such an apt though negative title, which is yet more descriptive phrase than name, is to publish in a manner and a format befitting scholars, uncensored, and without condescension, the best short prewar history being written in our time, which unfortunately is, as our title states, being rejected by the Prewar History Review, simply because it is not about Islam. Further, our aim is to provide a professional home for our colleagues who, through speaking out, interpreting the past as they see it, and otherwise challenging the stodgy aristocracy of IAPH, are expelled from that once great but sadly now myopic association. To put it simply, we are the new and coming breed of prewar historians, who understand that there is more to prewar history than the Muslim Conquests, and our policy is to live, to grow, to offer an alternative—and, yes, to rebel, but intellectually. Our purpose is to contribute substantially to postwar man's knowledge and understanding of prewar man, thus enabling him to better understand himself.

Orrin digests this glop and looks around to see if there is anybody watching him, to point at him and laugh. But he is alone. No one is there, observing. But he assumes it is a prank. 4760! Raspberries! All they had to do was set the type. But, still... He fingers several pages. Still, the paper (can he call it paper?) has a quality and texture he has never touched before, and the type is either specially designed to prank him...or...it's truly of another time. How can he describe it? Futuristic? (That's playing right into it, but still...it's accurate!) Oriental? It's certainly not set in traditional Chinese characters. It's not the Japanese kanji or kana, but still...it's got that oriental touch. Like the lettering on a Chung King label. To be sure, it's English, he can read it, but the type face is strangely futuristic and oriental. And the paper—can he even call it paper? And it's bound in...rubber? plastic? Plastic, some kind of plastic would be the closest he could guess, but it seems to be beyond plastics...something very strange. He looks around again, this time walking, looking up and down several aisles. It's got to be a prank. It is an expensive prank, and there's nobody here to see my response, he thinks. But still....

Searching for pranksters, Orrin comes across a lonely row of carrels hugging a cold, dark concrete wall. Utilitarian, expensive, up-to-date, it is a pity these carrels go unused, being, as they are, down here where hardly anybody comes. But these, too, will come into use, eventually. Sub three, like all the floors, will be crammed with books and students, sometime in the future. The future, yes, that's what it is. He has the future, or the history of the future, written in a book, right here in his hands. Orrin doesn't know that he believes in the simultaneous existence of the past, the present, and the future. Yet. He sits down at the carrel, yellow pads to one side, the book in front of him unopened, turns on the built-in desk lamp—not fluorescent, thank God. *Prewar History Review Rejects*. That's what is says. It's got to be a prank...but, still...

Who on this campus, in this city, in this world, even, would go to the trouble to make this book and then hide it down here, where no one is likely to find it? Who could make this book? Now? Even if they wanted to? Sure, anybody could make up dates and set historical treatises in the post-apocalyptic future. Lots of writers have used that device. But who could *make* this book? This book on the desk in front of me. Orrin is no metallurgy, materials science, or chemical engineering major, but he is a cutting-edge consumer, and he knows that these materials are not available to manufacturers today. He would have heard about and, probably, would have purchased something made of these materials. Everyone would've heard about the stuff this book is bound in, if it existed now. And its vibe is so inviting. Orrin's never before felt a vibe off a book, just holding it. Not even off the *Book of Mormon.*

Orrin wants to *have* this book, as a matter of fact, no matter what the contents offer. He thinks he'll just take it home and put it on his book shelf. Steal this book, he thinks, rebelliously. But The Hymn reminds Orrin of his mission:

You're not here to collect books.

Get some secrets.

Get some secrets from the book.

You need secrets.

I have my work.

I will not shirk.

You're not here to collect books.

****

Reluctantly, Orrin opens the book to look for secrets of Mormon mind control. As it happens, the first article, Vol. 1, No. 1, is of particular interest, or promises to be. The author's name looks familiar and Orrin checks it against the copyright page to find that it is the founder's name—the founder of the whole shebang: the magazine, SIAPHE, the rebellion itself. He turns back to the article and reads, with what starts as curiosity but soon turns to astonishment.

An Interesting Case of Vandalism In Salt Lake City[1]

Although religion was a world-wide phenomenon in the centuries before the war, Salt Lake City stood virtually alone in that it was founded and controlled by an obscure religious sect known as the Mormons.[2] Basically a cultic organization, the Mormon Church placed rigid prohibitions on the behavior and ideas of its members but was careful to provide an intricate structure of activities that kept them occupied from early childhood until death. Many of the activities consisted of working for the church itself. "The Mormon services lacked a good deal of the pomp and ceremony usually associated with religious gatherings. Indeed, they were more of a quasi-religious business meeting designed to inspire each and every member to work harder at fulfilling his responsibility to the church, thereby assuring and achieving spiritual fulfillment."[3] The average Mormon was satisfied with the life plan supplied by his Church, and therefore the institution prospered greatly and, for a cult of its size, became extremely wealthy. Taken in this context, the acts of vandalism committed by one Heber Nephi Smith in the spring of 1971 become an interesting and meaningful footnote not only to the history of prewar religion, but to the history of prewar mankind.

Born to Mormon parents in Salt Lake City on June 4, 1953,[4] young Heber became, predictably, a devout Mormon himself. He attended one hundred percent of the meetings designed for his particular age group and performed his appointed tasks with excellence.[5] His nonreligious interests were not well-rounded, however, but limited to an almost fanatical dedication to rock climbing, which cost him a broken leg at fifteen, and chemistry, particularly explosives.[6] Having been instilled with patriotism, Heber "signed up" for the National Guard at seventeen, with the permission of his parents, and was sworn in immediately after graduating high school. It was in the National Guard that he received training in demolitions and had access to large quantities of various types of explosives and detonators.[7] It is not known to this historian when Heber Nephi Smith first desired to disfigure or destroy a Mormon monument, but the first record of any such desire is in Heber's diary (a small lockable and largely unused ten-year diary which allotted three lines for recording the activities and thoughts of each day, given to him with love by his "Aunt Lydia") under August 17, 1968: "Today I thought it would be fun to blow the pointing arm and head of Brigham Young."[8] An indication of the torment this idea caused is found in what Heber scribbled in his diary three days later on August 20: "I must be nuts."

There are no records of his consulting a psychoanalyst or casually mentioning his problem to his bishop, his parents, or anyone else, but one must assume that Heber did deeply doubt his sanity; that he truly believed, for many long and torturous months, that he was mentally, spiritually, and socially unbalanced; and that he was some-variety of perverted, heathen misfit. An overabundance of shame, combined with his relentless urge, undoubtedly forced Heber Nephi Smith to keep his secret. He knew full well that talking about it would not only embarrass himself and his parents, but would also jeopardize any chance he might have of performing the act. Keeping in mind that a fierce battle was raging in the conscience of the boy, a battle that pitted firmly entrenched morals and heavily fortified respect for his church against the ruthless, frenzied onslaught of mystical, rebellious impulse, the bald statements "I want to, but I know I shouldn't," and "I don't know what to do," which appear almost illegibly in his diary under September 3, and September 17, 1970, respectively, communicate, to us, though we be of the forty-eighth century, the inner turmoil a man must suffer when he is forced to choose between what his culture values as normal, moral behavior and what he himself, as an individual, wants to do.

This historian perhaps understands and appreciates Heber Nephi's dilemma more than most, because when first attracted to the idea of doing a paper on Heber and his vandalism, he (this historian) was faced with much the same kind of opposition. He knew, for instance, that the International Association of Prewar Historians would not readily, if ever, accept the subject as pertinent, because it was not about the Muslim Conquests. But, even though a part of him agreed with the IAPH, another part of him, a less rational, perhaps, yet more sensitive part, felt strongly that Heber Nephi Smith and his story were very pertinent indeed. For months the part of this historian that said a paper on Heber would bring disaster to his career and disgrace to his profession seemed to overwhelm his desire to pursue the project. But, after repeatedly laying the idea aside only to have it wake him during the night with excitement, this historian decided that, no matter what misfortune it might bring, he would do what he thought was right. As in Heber's case, it was a matter of personal conviction winning out over cultural pressure. Yet there is a subtle difference in the manner of Heber Nephi's winning out that reveals certain truths not only about Heber and the extent to which he was influenced by his faith, but also about the important nations of the prewar world and their incorrigible attachment to particular political philosophies.

The difference is that Heber Nephi Smith drew the courage he needed to do what he wanted to do from the very faith that told him he should not do it, just as the leaders of powerful prewar nations managed to find justification in their political philosophies for actions those philosophies explicitly forbade, by confusing the issues and misnaming what they did so cleverly that they could proceed with righteous fervor. In essence, it did not matter to a prewar individual (or nation) what he (it) did so long as he (it) could devise a way of making it seem to be compatible with whatever religious belief (political philosophy) was ingrained in his (its) conscience, and, to do so, he (it) was free to twist and warp his belief (its philosophy), not to mention the mother tongue, as much as necessary and then deceive himself (itself) about the very nature of his (its) deed. But this historian in no way distorted the original concept of his project in an attempt to comply with the standards so completely impressed upon him by the International Association of Prewar Historians. He neither interpreted the standards to falsely embrace his subject, nor endowed his subject with enough chimerical importance to raise it to the standards. He, unlike Heber Nephi Smith and the nations of the prewar world, drew his courage from within. This historian recognized that what he wished to do was outside the IAPH standards, and he broke away, rather than compromise he personal integrity.

Nevertheless, in asking the god in which he "believed" for advice, Heber Nephi Smith did not demean himself, and one should not think of him as having been weak-minded, for that reason alone. He was, as prewar determinism would have it, an innocent victim of his environment, an environment he did not choose, yet had to live in. Will any of us dare say we would have acted with greater honesty if we lived in that hostile, hypocritical, prewar world? Diary entries for almost every day from October 21,1970, to March 17,1971, read either, "Last night I asked God what I should do," or "I'm going to ask again tonight," indicating the utter dependency upon a supernatural being that characterized religious peoples of prewar eras. But the dependency was not of the sort it first appears to have been. Indeed, Heber did not want God to tell him what to do. He had already decided what he was going to do. He needed to pretend God had decided in order to avoid taking responsibility for his decision.

In the following diary entry of Monday, March 15, 1971, one perceives how Heber Nephi Smith managed, at least to his satisfaction, to remain perfectly pious while justifying, with no possibility of experiencing guilt, his rebellion, which he refused to accept as rebellion: "Last night God came to me in a blinding flash and said, 'My son, it is your mission in this life to use explosives on the monuments of your church to the best of your ability.'"

Sometime between two and four a.m. on March 16, 1971, Heber Nephi Smith expertly molded plastic explosive material—stolen from the National Guard during the previous summer camp, which act may indicate premeditation—around the icy neck and right shoulder of the statue of Brigham Young atop the "This is the Place" monument. At six-seventeen, a.m., just as the sun was rising above the mountains behind the monument, Heber's stolen detonator set off a blast that was heard around the Mormon world, a blast that marked the beginning of what would be called by Salt Lake City police and Mormon church officials, "an insane rampage, an atrocious blastphemy." (*sic*).[9]

An article in the evening newspaper described the "job" as "professional" and said that police investigations were proceeding. It was accompanied by an editorial claiming that the "vandal" was "sick" and calling for legislation imposing the death penalty for such "wanton attacks on our proud heritage."[10]

When his father brought the subject up at dinner, deploring the act as an outrage against every decent Mormon that ever lived, Heber—who that morning had slipped out of the house and back in again unnoticed—possessed enough poise to agree wholeheartedly, adding that they should search every cheap hotel and alley in the city till they found the miserable scum of the Earth and make an example of him—let others like him know that they can't mutilate a Mormon monument and expect to live. Though pleased with his son's impressive display of devotion, Heber's father argued for less drastic measures. It was doubtful that the vandal would ever be captured, the police being what they are, but if he were caught, a sentence of ten years at hard labor to finance the replacement of the statue would cure him of his vandalistic ways and put a damper on the hopes anyone else might have of doing something similar.

Later, in the seclusion of his room, Heber began a journal (a five-hundred-page spiral notebook with JOURNAL printed in bold capital letters on the cover) in which he described the day's events, including the conversation with his father, and stressed the "satisfaction" and "sense of accomplishment" derived from them. It is perhaps difficult to understand why Heber Nephi Smith was compelled to write about himself in a diary and then, for want of more space, in a journal, but only until it is remembered that he lived in an age of astonishing egocentricity. The capacity for brutality, dishonesty, and apathy displayed by prewar man has long been accounted for by his egocentric nature, but few historians recognize that it also accounts for the vast majority of the minutely detailed and carefully preserved descriptions of prewar civilization upon which they rely so completely. This historian, however, readily acknowledges the salience of Heber Nephi's egocentrically motivated writings to this work. Indeed, he finds it impossible to over-emphasize their capacity to reveal the true personal history of the events, a history that is all too frequently, and in this particular instance would have been assuredly, garbled out existence by more accessible sources of information. Only by going beyond the usual computer archives, The Tunnels, the museums, the libraries of records and published volumes, only by searching out the honest jottings of the individual responsible for what seemed to be a minor historical event, was this historian able to perceive that what he was dealing with was not *minor* in any derogative sense of the word, but merely in the sense that it was not a *major* historical event. It is clearly not in the same category with The War. But the vandalism in Salt Lake City in the Spring of 1971, is indubitably an interesting and meaningful footnote not only to the history of prewar religion, but to the history of prewar mankind.

General conference, a meeting held each spring in the tabernacle on Temple Square that brought Mormons from around the world to Salt Lake City to hear the messages of their prophet and other church officials, was scheduled for April eighth, ninth, tenth, and eleventh in 1971. It pushed Heber's first act of vandalism out of the spotlight of attention and furnished the potential for a climactic final gesture of discontent.

The golden Angel Moroni, perched on the front center and highest spire of the Mormon Temple with his beautifully long and golden horn to his lips, would be blown from that sacred, lofty (slightly more than 64m. off the ground) station on Sunday April 11, 1971—the last day of general conference. As Heber tells it in his journal, the idea came to him in a moment of inspiration—he calls them "flashes"—on Sunday, March 28, while driving past the temple en route to his grandmother's house for dinner. "I looked up at the angel and I knew right then what I had to do and when I had to do it."

Later that same evening Heber stopped to look at the temple as he had never looked at it before. From a block, away he studied Moroni and his roost with binoculars, finding that a ladder extended up the backside of the tower from the main roof of the temple to the base of the spire and that, extending from there to the very feet of the angel, there was something that appeared to be a cable—something onto which he could hold. A closer inspection revealed another stout wire, somewhat concealed from the casual eye behind the protrusion of the southwest corner tower (the temple had six towers, three in front, three in the rear, all with steeples), stretching from the ground, where it appeared to be embedded, to the main roof. As Heber wrote, in conclusion to the section of the journal entry just paraphrased, "It looked like the temple had been designed with my mission in mind."

Partly because of the relative ease with which he would be able to dethrone the angel and partly, no doubt, because of certain prewar aesthetic sensibilities involving units of three, Heber Nephi Smith felt, as he left Temple Square that evening, that something had to come before the angel, something had come between the beginning and the end—there had to be a middle. What he had done and was about to do would not be a whole without it. Left empty, the temporal, not to mention the spatial gap between the "This is the Place" monument explosion on March 16, and Moroni on April 11, would deprive both acts of meaning, significance, and beauty. With nothing to connect them, they would stand alone and formless. Heber had parked his car on the street immediately south of Temple Square, a street appropriately named South Temple Street, and, as he approached it, he happened to glance at the monument "in honor of Brigham Young and the pioneers" that dominated the intersection of South Temple and Main Streets (not to be confused with the monument in the foothills), discovering, in another moment of inspiration, another "flash," what would come between. To destroy this monument and cause no damage to the surrounding buildings was indeed a challenge, a challenge Heber Nephi Smith accepted. He spent the next six days and nights (how he stayed awake we do not know) toiling over calculations" and detailing plans for destroying the monument and dethroning the angel, necessarily concentrating, for the time being, on the monument.

At one-thirty a.m. on Sunday, April 4, 1971, Heber rose from sleepless contemplation (after all that time awake, he could not sleep!), climbed out his bedroom window, coasted his automobile for a block with the lights off before starting it, and drove to the gulley where he stored his stolen explosives in a sealed metal drum under an innocently natural looking pile of rocks. With the aid of a pocket flashlight, he transferred most of his supply to a gym bag, leaving what he needed for the angel, and drove into downtown Salt Lake City, where he parked only meters from the monument. The intersection and the monument itself were brightly lighted, in the unobstructed view of any passerby—be it drunkard or policeman. In three nervous hours of watching, running, hiding, and working in sporadic bursts, Heber compiled just an hour's honest labor on the monument, but that was all he needed.

At five-thirty a.m. Heber had just climbed into bed when he heard the blast, actually several skillfully placed charges detonated simultaneously, that reduced the monument to rubble and disappointingly enough, sent fragments of bronze and concrete smashing through windows and gouging ugly scars in the adjacent buildings, not to mention the crater in the street and the mangled gas and water lines. But no one was injured, and Heber felt that, although he had fallen short of his goal, he had not completely failed, for the monument was gone, and his acts would now be whole—there was, however tarnished with imperfection, a middle to precede the end.

News of the monument's destruction was broadcast over radio only minutes after the explosion, which, reportedly, awakened many people, including the Church president and his wife, who occupied a floor of the hotel on the corner of South Temple and Main Streets and awoke to find the bronze head of Brigham Young in bed with them. When Heber's mother came to wake him at seven-fifteen so he could be ready for priesthood meeting at eight, there was a special news bulletin on TV with on-the-spot coverage showing a fire truck standing by and investigators sifting through the result of Heber's efforts. As Heber tells it in his journal, the on-the-spot TV reporter, still half asleep, offered his opinion that it "must have been done by a demoniacal demolitions expert. Police were investigating possibility of a connection between this blast and the blast that blew the head an arm off the statue of Brigham Young in the foothills two weeks ago." Shocked and infuriated, Heber's parents watched the bulletin in silence but commented immediately afterwards, extensively upon the horror of the deed and the depravity of the perpetrator. Heber spontaneously agreed with everything they said as he devoured his breakfast of hot cereal and orange juice adding now and then a note of vengeance or hostility which he punctuated dramatically with his spoon, thrust upward into the air, a spoon turned weapon, a sword, perhaps, held not daintily but with a clenched and venous fist.

According to Heber's journal, every church meeting he attended, starting with priesthood meeting in the morning and ending with sacrament meeting in the evening, revolved, rather improvisationally, around what he had done in downtown Salt Lake City. "That's all anybody talked about," to quote Heber directly. It is only logical to assume that the event permeated Mormon meetings throughout the valley to the same extent, for the ones Heber attended were typical and may be relied upon as accurate indicators of the general Mormon reaction to the destruction of the monument, a reaction that would not die quickly, a reaction that would add immensely to the effectiveness of Heber's final expression of rebellion.

His nocturnal activities were still front page news the next day, and, along with value judgments (quoted earlier, see note #9) from both Salt Lake City police and Mormon church officials, was the police Chief's solemn promise that "All available personnel and equipment are on the case around the clock and will continue to be until the person or persons responsible are arrested and enough evidence to assure conviction is obtained."[11] This promise, designed of course to appease the population, roused little fear in the heart of Heber Nephi Smith, for it was highly improbable that they would apprehend him before April 11, if at all, and he knew it.

Germane to the entire body of prewar history is the most important contribution to Heber's assurance that he would achieve success and never be arrested (aside and noticeably different from the fact that there were very few clues with which the police could work). Heber, like prewar nations (including most notably, the Islamic nations) engaged in the numerous and frequent demi-wars, believed that God was, as popular jargon put it, on his side. With such a talented, versatile ally it was impossible for any of them to fail, lose, or be in the wrong. As Heber himself phrased it, "Why should I get paranoid? God told me what to do, and He'll watch over me."

During the first week in April, Heber worked and reworked the elaborate calculations and refined the strategy involved with separating Angel Moroni from the temple. The safety of thousands of fellow church members, his "brothers and sisters," who would be in the immediate vicinity was, of course, Heber's prime secondary concern. His objective, then, was two-fold. 1) to blow the angel off the temple on the last day of general conference, and 2) to inflict no injuries upon a mass of innocent bystanders—quite an impressively difficult challenge indeed, and noticeably different from the goals of the prewar Muslim suicide bombers. Heber was more symbolic and artistic than murderous.

The gates to Temple Square—an entire block (perimeter: one- half mile, approximately 16.08 km.) in the center of Salt Lake City, completely encompassed by a high stone and concrete wall— were opened at six o'clock each morning and closed and locked at eleven o'clock each night. A night watchman spent most of his time in the information booth at the north entrance but made at least three rounds, one when he came on duty at eleven, one at approximately two-thirty a.m., and one at six, as he unlocked the gates, where, during conference and the peak tourist season, crowds were eagerly awaiting him. If anyone scaled the wall or one of the gates in the night, a rather archaic yet effective alarm system alerted the watchman, and he phoned for police assistance, which was promptly supplied in the form of a ten-man SWAT team, two dogs with their handlers, and an armored van. By carefully observing the watchman's behavior and doing a little research on a previous incident at Temple Square (in which three harmless teenage pranksters, who wished only to wade nude in the Sea Gull Fountain, were taken into custody by the aforementioned forces) Heber was able to take these important elements into consideration when he devised his plan. He had perfected the theoretical aspect of his "mission" by Friday, April 9, and the following statement, concluding that night's journal entry, implies his intense anticipation: "All that remains is waiting till tomorrow night."

Although the slim, lightweight "fanny pack" strapped to his waist when he entered Temple Square at ten-thirty p.m. on Saturday, April 10, 1971, was designed by its manufacturer to rest on the small of one's back—permitting the kind of free movement necessary for activities such as rock climbing—Heber had deemed that position too conspicuous and decided to wear it in front, disguising the plastic explosives, the detonator, the pair of heavy leather gloves, and the short rope it contained as a protruding stomach, or, as he described it, "a spare tire." The fine, cold rain that had been falling all evening, tremendously increasing the element of danger

149

involved in ascending and descending the temple, justified the corduroy car coat that aptly concealed Heber's paunch and stylishly coordinated with his Levis[12] and low-topped, lightweight, lug-soled climbing shoes—shoes that would serve him admirably in the early hours of Sunday, April 11. A Nylon windbreaker beneath the coat, which was far too bulky to wear while climbing, would protect Heber sufficiently from the predawn chill yet cause no hindrance to his movement.

For twenty minutes Heber Nephi Smith strolled around the Temple Grounds, consciously yet unnoticeably working his way into the dimly lighted southeast corner, where he waited, standing flush against the rear of a restored, Mormon pioneer's log cabin, while the night watchman made his rounds. After allowing time for the watchman to get settled in the information booth, Heber slipped into the cabin and sat down in the darkest corner to wait, to contemplate. It was dryer in the cabin and slightly-warmer—"not uncomfortable at all," as Heber noted later in his journal.

When the watchman emerged from the information booth at two-thirty to check the gates and, to quote Heber's journal again, "have a quick look around," Heber watched him from the cabin, seeing in his mechanical, routine movements a camaraderie Heber felt "glowing in there with the fear and excitement." As soon as the watchman re-entered his booth, Heber removed his corduroy coat, shifted the slim "fanny pack" to the small of his back, where it belonged, and embarked on the most dangerous part of his "mission"—dangerous because of the recent rain, the height and steepness of the Temple, and because once on the roof of the brightly lighted Temple, Heber would be conspicuous and trapped. There was no escaping. The police would merely wait for him to descend. Heber had to hope that anyone who happened to see him would think he belonged on the temple, on that spire, at the feet of that angel; for he could do nothing about his obviousness, except, as he put it, "hustle and act like I owned the place."

There is no doubt in the mind of this historian that Heber Nephi Smith did indeed "hustle" up that spire, continued to "hustle" as he sat straddling Moroni's roost, tied to the angel with a short rope, carefully molding the explosives, and inserting the detonator, and "hustled" back down again, resting only when he was safely hidden. As for acting as though he "owned the place," this historian can only assume that he did.

At five-thirty a.m. on Sunday, April 11, 1971, Heber returned to the rear of the pioneer's cabin, waited while the watchman, whom he considered his friend, now, unlocked the gates and buildings. When Temple Square was once more crowded, Orrin walked casually to the nearest gate and left. He stopped en route to his suburban home and removed the pack and windbreaker, hiding them in the trunk of his automobile.

When he arrived, his parents were up and full of questions. He had told them that he was taking a new girl, the cousin of one of his buddies from the National Guard, to dinner and a movie, and, naturally, they wanted to know where he had been all night. Heber Nephi Smith sadly confessed that he had sinned, that lust had overwhelmed them both in the

151

middle of their pizza, and that they had spent the night in a motel as Mr. & Mrs. Jones. Now, he was sick to his stomach. His soul ached; now he wanted to repent. He began to weep and sob about how sorry he was that he had done such a thing, that he had "violated the Temple of God." His mother, wilting on the sofa, blankly stared into space and hummed a hymn; his father, embracing Heber about the shoulders, understood. He could discuss the matter with the bishop that very day and free his soul of the tremendous burden, for it was apparent that he was truly repentant. When his father suggested that he take a hot bath and prepare for a day of watching conference on television[13] and Heber said that he was awfully tired and could use some sleep because he hadn't got much during the night, his mother groaned and stared further into space.

While Heber slept, the final conference meetings proceeded as though he did not exist, as though he had not visited the temple the night before, as though Angel Moroni would stand safe atop the front center spire forever. Heber's mother, somewhat resigned to the cold (fictitious) facts, woke him at five o'clock p.m., and, after a solemn bath and solemn dinner, Heber drove to his bishop's home to keep the appointment his father had made earlier. The bishop had known Heber since he was a small boy, knew that he was basically a fine, morally decent young man, and perceived that his was truly a compunctious soul; unlike most young men in his situation, Heber Nephi Smith was sincere in his repentance. There was a short silence, between the discussion of Heber's recent sinning and consequent contrition and the bishop's asking if he had decided to fulfill his obligation to the church by serving as a missionary.[14] It was time to start thinking seriously about it, for he was nearing his nineteenth birthday. Heber, repressing his amusement at the bishop's unintentional implication that he had not already completed his mission, retained his sorrowful countenance and said he didn't think he should go on a mission for the church. The bishop, momentarily disconcerted, apologized for mentioning the subject at a time when Heber entertained such a poor opinion of himself and said they would discuss the matter again in little while, when he was back to normal. Heber agreed but added that he probably wouldn't change his mind.

After a refreshing cup of hot chocolate, Heber thanked the bishop for everything and went home to work on his journal. He spoke with his parents briefly "so they wouldn't feel neglected," then withdrew to his room, where he wrote, with a blue ball-point pen, in silence, filling seven pages with clear, precise print before eleven o'clock. At eleven he set the pen aside, closed his journal, and stared at the face of his clock radio, seeing there no dials or hands but an empty Temple Square and his friend, the night watchman, locking the gates, the buildings, and returning safely to his booth. Then, he saw Angel Moroni with explosives at his feet, waited several seconds, heard the blast, and saw the golden angel fall. Only after this extraordinary vision did he see the face of his clock-radio, at which he had been staring all the while.

Heber switched on the radio, and tuned in the station with the most alert news facilities to wait for the announcement of his achievement. He heard a record shop's advertisement, two popular songs, and half of a third—three in a row—before the "disc jockey" interrupted with an initial report that had been an explosion at Temple Square just a few minutes ago (details would be broadcast as they came in from the station's newsman on the scene). Heber switched the radio off, content to wait for one of the later, regular newscasts to find out how well he had performed his task. He was not to be disappointed; for Angel Moroni now stood on his golden head (imbedded in the lawn) sixty-four meters directly below his once proud pedestal, his precious, silent horn safely parallel with the Earth, appearing as though he had decided to commit suicide and gracefully dived to his death. Justifiably pleased with the quality of his work, Heber finally put his journal away at two o'clock and listened to one more news report before going to bed. While sleeping, he received a second message from God. It is recorded in the journal entry of April 13. "My son, you have completed your mission. Now, cool it." (Note God's use of the vernacular.) Heber would soon realize how sound the advice had been.

Heber Nephi Smith had expected to create a disturbance, but he had not anticipated the maelstrom of retaliation that ensued. When "The Committee of Concerned Citizens" (10,000 bitter citizens) mobbed the Hall of Justice, presenting electronically amplified demands for action, threatening to "take the law into our (their) own hands if something isn't done, and done now, about these heinous crimes,"[15] Heber became, in his own words, "extremely grateful for the second revelation." While the majority of the citizens were merely talking about "taking the law into their own hands," others were doing it. "In the interest of Justice and the Future Security of The Church" a group of Mormon Elders organized, with neither public permission nor public opposition from the Mormon Church, a regiment of secret police and immediately began their own search for the "enemies of all respectable, God-fearing people in this Valley."[16]

Heber could not join the Guardians of The Faith because he was not yet an elder, but he promised his father, who had taken an administrative position, that he would keep his eyes and ears open and report any clues he might come across. On Wednesday, April 14, 1971, Heber's father informed him that the Guardians of The Faith had compiled a list of thirty-eight "suspects," each known to be "the type who would do something like that." Heber noted in his journal that he didn't have to ask what they were going to do with their suspects. But on Thursday, April 15, before the Guardians could do anything with their "suspects" the Salt Lake City Police arrested a suspect of their own. Manuel Gonzalez, alias Juan Martinez, age forty-six, was apprehended on the West Side at 2 a.m., with explosives, detonators, and blueprints of several Mormon edifices in his truck. He gave no address.[17]

Heber was insulted, insulted yet relieved. He wrote, "That old drunkard couldn't climb out of the gutter, let alone climb up to Angel Moroni! And if he ever had a stick of dynamite in his life, he'd hawk (*sic*) it for a drink. But, anyway, the heat's off me now, and he's got a warm, dry place to sleep." Four days later the chief police announced that a signed confession, detailing each of the three crimes, had been obtained from Gonzalez, just hours before he died of natural causes.[18]

The population of Salt Lake City was satisfied that justice had been done; the Guardians of the Faith was officially dissolved; and Heber Nephi Smith, having expressed his rebellion, having completed his "mission," returned to the activities assigned by his culture, and left Salt Lake City for Jerusalem with the rest of the Mormons in 2015. Thus, he illustrates an archetype prevalent in prewar civilizations, i.e., the "young rebel," who viciously, though briefly, attacked the aspects of his society that displeased him, then, satisfied with his efforts, though nothing came of them, accepted his appointed role and did what was expected of him for the rest of his life. In this respect, Heber Nephi Smith and the acts of vandalism he committed in the spring of 1971 are an exceptionally interesting and meaningful footnote not only to the history of prewar religion, but to the history of prewar man.

1 A city on the shores of a salt water lake in the North American Great Basin, first discovered by Dr. P.R. Dihogo in 3650. The capital of Utah, one of the ancient, prewar, United States of America, deserted en masse in 2015 when two Mormon (see note #2) missionaries (see note # 15) were killed, along with 34 others, by a Palestinian suicide bomber in Jerusalem. This was interpreted as the long-anticipated sign that The End of The World, or Judgment Day, was near, i.e., two Mormon missionaries dead in the streets of Jerusalem. See my article, "The Pilgrimage of the Mormons," in the January, 4754 issue of *The Prewar History Review.* (This historian was still a member in good standing of IAPH, at that time,

and the paper touched on Islam and the Muslim Conquests, which evolved into The War.)

2. The Church of Jesus Christ of Latter-day Saints was the formal name of the institution, and its members preferred to call themselves Latter-Day Saints, or LDS. Founded in New York State, in 1830, by a plagiarist named Joseph Smith, in much the same way that Islam was founded, the cult experienced difficulty being accepted by its neighbors. After being run out of cities in the East and Midwest, the early Mormons decided to go out into the then unsettled Mexican Territory and establish their own Domain, which they called Zion. Therefore, they became the first North American Zionists. Salt Lake City was the first and became the largest and most important of the several Mormon settlements in this western Zion.

3. Dr. T.S. Oniki, *Prewar Religions of the Western Hemisphere* (New Tokyo: Akiyama's Sons, 4746) p. 569.

4. Genealogical Records of the Church of Jesus Christ of Latter-day Saints (The Tunnels, no. 28046S58.) The Mormons were most industrious record-keepers, and thanks to their air-tight Tunnels, drilled into solid granite, we are provided with a store of information on prewar man unequaled anywhere for sheer vastness and quality of preservation. No fewer than seven monographs have grown out of these fertile files already, among them, mine on the thesis that all prewar man, whether they knew it or not, were Mormons, if not while they lived, then now most certainly. There is ample documentation, and the Mormons had the theological machinery to see to it, i.e., baptism

after death, a practice, which until understood, led us to believe the living body of the church to be much larger than it ever was, including all the heads of every state, Popes, Rabbis, even Muslim Clerics, one could go on forever, but this is just a note. My monograph, *Posthumous Converts: Freedom Of the Soul?* will be published soon by SIAPHE.

5. Attendance and performance records, Highland Park Ward of Salt Lake City, Utah (The Tunnels, Little Cottonwood Canyon, Utah) File 26403, reel no. 51897H35.

6. Heber Nephi Smith, "My Favorite Hobbies" (English Theme, Highland High School, Salt Lake City, Utah, 1965) *pp.* 3-4.

7. National Guard Records (Utah National Guard Headquarters, Salt Lake City). These files were an utter mess, but documentation was possible after piecing Heber's files together and having them restored. Finding them took three weeks of rummaging through the ruins! Indeed, one is softened by The Tunnels.

8. Heber was referring not to the man, who was then long dead, but to the statue of Brigham Young atop the "This is the Place" monument in the foothills overlooking the city. It was supposed to be on the exact spot where, extremely weak, ill and tired of the long, jarring wagon ride, Brigham Young, the Lion of The Lord, second prophet and president of the Mormon church, pointed to the barren desert and said, "This is the place." It was not quite so dramatic as it sounds. An advance party of several men, led by one Orrin Porter Rockwell, the Avenging Angel, trail scout and horse thief, had been in the valley of the Great Salt

Lake for days, planting crops, diverting streams, and erecting crude shelters.

9. *Deseret News* (Salt Lake City) March 30, 1971, p. A2. (The Tunnels, Little Cottonwood Canyon, Utah) File 64824, reel no. 65839D2l. The *Deseret News* a Mormon church-owned newspaper, was preserved in The Tunnels on microfilm and is the best-preserved newspaper, though undoubtedly not the best newspaper, from the prewar cultures.

10. *Deseret News* (Salt Lake City) March 16, 1971, p. B5; A16. (The Tunnels, Little Cottonwood Canyon, Utah) File 64824, reel no. 65839D21. It is interesting to note that in a rectangle at the head of the editorial column of the *Deseret News* there appears the following: "We stand for the Constitution of the United States as having been divinely inspired." Similar admixtures of religion and politics were not uncommon in many prewar cultures and, as Dr. Sukoshi Isamuno points out in his excellent *Prewar Civilizations,* were prime catalytic agents of distrust and hatred between several nations.

11. *Deseret News* (Salt Lake City) April 5, 1971, p. A2. (The Tunnels, Little Cottonwood Canyon, Utah) File 64824, reel no. 65839D21.

12. The trademark and brand name of close-fitting, low-waisted trousers made of denim with copper rivets at the strain points. Levis were extremely popular among the young Americans of that era and were accepted as proper attire for most casual occasions. Heber chose these trousers wisely, for they were rugged enough for any activity, including climbing (this historian was

fortunate enough to locate the hermetically sealed canister in which Heber had preserved, for antiquity, the pair of Levis he wore when he climbed the temple, which will soon be on display, hopefully, in the Takakama institute's museum of prewar history, and he can attest to their obvious durability), and did not set him apart from the casually dressed young tourists and pilgrims.

13. Most Salt Lake City Mormons forfeited the privilege of attending General Conference in person to their out-of-state brothers and sisters.

14. It was customary among the Mormons for nineteen-year-old males to embark on brief (usually two-year) proselytizing missions, to convert members to the cult. Serving as a "missionary" endowed one with certain status. "Returned missionaries" were highly prized as husbands by young Mormon women and recognized as experienced, seasoned, salesmen by insurance companies and automobile dealerships.

15. *Deseret News* (Salt Lake City) April 13, 1971 3 p. A3. (The Tunnels, Little Cottonwood Canyon, Utah) File .648243 reel no. 65839D21.

16. Charter, Guardians of The Faith, Para. 1. (The Tunnels, Little Cottonwood Canyon, Utah) File 84735, reel no. 5.40171\112. Though neither opposition nor permission were public on the part of the official church, it may be assumed, because the charter of the group is in The Tunnels, that there was at least tacit approval of that charter.

17. *Deseret News* (Salt Lake City) April 15, 1971, p. Al (The Tunnels, Little Cottonwood Canyon, Utah) File 64824~ reel no.65839D21.

18. *Deseret News* (Salt Lake City) April 19, 1971, p. C 12 (The Tunnels, Little Cottonwood Canyon, Utah) File 64824~ reel no.65839D21.

Chapter 7

There's Something Happening Here.

Whatever doubts Orrin had had about the volume's authenticity that were not erased by its appearance and its vibe are gone by the time he finishes reading the first article. His own Patriarchal Blessing foretells his passing from this world into the next without dying. He will be translated into heaven, which can only mean that the End of The World will occur during his lifetime. It also means that he is one of the righteous, one who does not have to experience physical death. Orrin isn't the only one of his generation with that in store. The frequency of such Patriarchal Blessings has made the approximate date of the End of The World common knowledge among Mormons. They await the death of two missionaries in the streets of Jerusalem, and prepare for the exodus and The End.

How can Orrin not believe that there will be a few survivors of "The War," survivors who will raise another fallen, human civilization, dig up our ruins, write articles. It all exists already in God's mind— Orrin, SIAPHE, the past, present, future, all are one and perfect. And this article has come into his hands as a sign. Quickly, he scans the table of contents for another interesting title, but no others seem directed at him, at his narrow interests. He has found what he came for, part of it at least. More than he was looking for, actually. It will serve a larger purpose than satisfying Tony. What more could Tony want? The Ultimate Secret of Mormon Mind control: Divine Injunction. Even Mormons of the highest order do not know that there is new prophet in their Church, a prophet who is not the president of the Church, a prophet who articulates his message with explosives.

As much as Orrin dislikes what Heber Nephi Smith will do next spring, he cannot argue with Divine Injunction. Is he not, himself, a prophet who must perform an even more distasteful act? He is. And would he listen to any arguments? He would not. Not even his own arguments. But if Heber Nephi Smith came to him and asked assistance of some sort that he could render without endangering himself or his mission, he would give it willingly. And he thinks that Heber will give him a bomb.

In his elation Orrin springs from the carrel, book in hand, ready to look up Heber (who will, he feels, somehow recognize and trust him as a fellow prophet on sight) and then to present Tony with what he feels, in his elation, to be astounding information. But The Hymn reminds Orrin with its melody that, perhaps, this information is not tactical enough for Tony, and that he must give Tony what he wants, if he is to enjoy free, unwatched mobility. He knows from observation of the freaks in the Student Union, that the police can inject relentless paranoia and impose limitations that Orrin could not live with. Everyone becomes a "narc," watching you and waiting for the bust. As he walks through, they catch his eye, seeing what they take to be a drug-induced intensity, and they bob their heads in unshared camaraderie and overestimated understanding, stoned out of their gourds, spaced, but not so spaced that they are actually untouchable, unbustable, and this knowledge works into their drug experience, demands and gets equal time with more pleasant sensations. He can see it as they bob their heads at him. Their faces squirm with dread that grows upon itself out of proportion. He can see it. He may have long hair, longer than some of them have, and he may have wild eyes, but he is free...free from fear...free to move about. He stops right there, mid-stream, and doubts that thought, harder than he doubted it at the ellipses. Are the campus heads the only ones who mistake him for one of them? Are his hair and eyes as signal fires to those who watch and wait?

"No," he whispers loudly, "that's not what I meant at all." He is talking, he pretends, to someone just like himself, someone who will understand, achieving freedom in conversation. What a character! But it is not, he finds, true, spontaneous dialogue, and so will not work as well, will not work at all. The Hymn is right. He has made a great discovery, but it is not what he came for. That sometimes happens. Searching for silver, one finds gold. Searching for open secrets, Orrin finds a prophet who will help him kill Agnew. A trusting, kindred, if more devious soul, who will not ask why he wants a bomb, will not inquire of its use, but will give him better than he could ever make himself. "Must I dig those grubby secrets now? Before I get a bomb?" Orrin whines silently, asking, in reality, The Hymn.

The Hymn stolidly repeats the stanza that ended Orrin's dream, a dream recurring at least a thousand times last night but unremembered—unremembered as a decision-making process, though the decision remains firm, re-enforced by a thousand unremembered smotherings. So he goes about his work, thinking, first things first. I cannot use a bomb if I'm hounded by Dan Watersman and his minions. He goes about his work oblivious to time, to classes missed, gleaning from the useless-looking volumes on the shelves half a yellow legal pad of mind control techniques used by the Mormons, none of which are uniquely Mormon, and all of which Tony could have found himself. The deepest secrets would not, he thinks, be here in a library for any patient scholar to discover. They would be someplace else, someplace nearly inaccessible, like The Maze, or in the spiritual realm, not in books or in the hands of human beings. But the Hymn says that the secrets are open secrets. Open secrets. Ah, ha. These secrets are not in books. It is not mind control "technique" at all. It is revelation. Revealed mind control. The Mormon Church doesn't control the minds of its members. God controls our minds through revelation, revealing what He wants us to know when He wants us to know it, and telling us what to do. Tony's not going to like this.

Orrin emerges from the elevator on the main floor sometime in the afternoon with writers' cramp and a knotted, growling, angry stomach. The fatigue that comes only from long hours of research at the bottom of a vast library hangs on him—literary, something he must drag across the central lobby to the check-out counter. As he crosses that carpeted expanse he cannot help looking upward, up the shaft, soaring empty twenty-five stories above him, cannot help it any more than the people up there can help looking down, watching him and others move across the lobby. They are only heads, necks, shoulders, upper torsos, increasingly small, of people peering over railings. They could be mannequins, for all he knows, as he could be a robot, moving far beneath them in some other, separate, smaller world.

He slides the book, together with his student ID, across the counter, where it is functionally plopped open by a different young, braless coed. She is wearing a tight, purple, ribbed tank top. It is cool in the library, and her nipples are erect. Orrin notices immediately that her breasts are lovely. Now, again, added this time to the scholar-fatigue and hunger, comes his blood-hard lust. She is so beautiful, standing there giggling...giggling? So beautiful and tasty, soft, and I could eat her, melt into her, lose myself in her...ah...giggling?

He hears her saying something now. Her tone tells him she's repeating it. "(giggle) You want to (giggle) check *this book* out?" She slaps it voluptuously. Still, he'd love to touch her. Her giggle breaks into full laughter, her lovely breasts are bouncing with her laugh. She leans against the counter, closer, weak with uncontrolled laughter, beautiful. Oh, baby, baby, baby. She leans on her forearms, so her head almost touches Orrin's stomach. He reaches out, laying a tender hand upon her head.

"What is it about this book?" he says, as though he's telling her that he loves her.

She brings her laughter slowly to a smile, then looks up, directly into his eyes, for the first time seeing the innate wildness, softened with honest lust, yet wild just the same. As she raises her head, Orrin allows his hand to glide down her hair. Short, brunette. She tilts her head slightly into his hand, like a cat, but more subtly, though he feels the pressure and knows it is not an accident. She smiles a different smile, caught by his piercing eyes—eyes that with a glance have shut the mouths of longhair-hating truck drivers twice his size. They pierce the braless girl the same way, but, of course, they carry a different message to her soul. Neither can say how long they stand there without talking. Both think it to be an extraordinarily long time after a few seconds, and the girl tears her eyes away. She returns to the book, shutting it, turning it, plopping it open again, as if it'd just been slid to her. Performing this routine enables her to say routinely, "Oh, I'm sorry. This book is not in circulation at this time." Fingering his student ID, turning it to read his name, "And, besides...Orrin..." she cannot help herself, she must give a little laugh here, "besides that, it's empty, blank!" She fans the pages in a gesture of proof.

Orrin inspects the fanning pages, seeing strange, blurred, futuristic print, and realizes that the girl is teasing him. But why? Is she flirting? Can she see his bulging crotch from where she is across the counter? He knows she feels something, even if she can't see his crotch. But she's not flirting. She is avoiding his eyes, looking down. He touches her chin lightly, raises her head. "And tell me," he says in a knowing, easy tone, "why is this blank book in the library at all, and how did it get here?" More an invitation to elaborate her silly lie than a confrontation, his words fill the girl with hilarity. But she is uncomfortable in his gaze. His passion is confounding. Her hilarity is trapped, and his hand is solid beneath her chin, gentle, unmovable.

Orrin thinks her silence is an affirmation of the old adage about the difficulty of lying while looking the recipient of your lie in the eye. But he is as wrong as the old adage. The poor girl knows the story behind the book. It is a library legend that any member of the staff could relate to him. She could tell him what she's heard, but not like this, like this she couldn't verbalize her name.

Assured now that whatever leaves her lips will be untrue, Orrin drops his hand, releases the girl from his stare. She begins immediately, the words are scripted; the story, handed down.

"You found it on Sub three, right?"

Orrin nods, but she isn't asking him, and doesn't pause for a nod. "Well, this book belongs there and must stay there. You see, when this library was opened, which wasn't long ago, Mr. Brandywine—he's the chief—started an all-out campaign to bring in books. There were *entire floors* completely empty—not a volume—just rows and rows of shelves, like skeletons. His budget was—and is—minuscule compared to this (she waves a hand), so he requested donations—went begging for books, as he says. He wrote to publishers in New York, to University Presses across the land, pleading for unsalable, old, or otherwise useless books they might have in costly storage. He enclosed ghastly photos of the empty shelves and stressed the tax deduction they could take if they gave us books.

"Well, sure enough, about nine months after the letters went out, crates of free books started arriving—novels, biographies of forgotten men, scholarly books on next to nothing, unexciting exposes, archaic etiquettes, old textbooks on theology, psychology, junk like that—we didn't look too closely. These books were only fillers. But Mr.

Brandywine rationalized that they might serve someone, sometime, and had them spread among the empty shelves. It was disappointing—the shelves looked worse with little clusters or one lonely book on them. "Anyway, this book," she pats it lovingly, "was among those castoffs we received. In Processing we discovered that it is blank. Mr. Brandywine was notified. His secretary says he thought it was, ironically, the most appropriate thing that could have happened. He laughed out loud, she says, and slapped his knee. He found the binding material interesting and the paper strange, so he gave the go-ahead, and it was processed and shelved in Section two, Sub three. We've had a few people mention it before, but you're the first one who's tried to check it out.

"If you'll notice, it is a reference book, and, therefore it cannot leave the library. All Sub three is reference material—*esoteric* reference material."

She pauses, looks briefly up at him for the first time since she started talking—at him but not into his eyes. "I'm glad you did. I've never seen it." She places her hand upon it lightly, as though taking an oath. "I wasn't laughing at you, honest. It's just that I've heard about this book—the funny stories—and then you show up with it and..." She breaks up again.

"Why don't you just give it to me, then? Just let me take it home. I kinda like it. If it's so worthless, the library won't care."

"Oh, I can't give it to you. And if you tried to steal it, you'd never get out the double doors."

"May I use it here?" Orrin asks.

"Oh, oh, oh," she is laughing, holding her ribs now, "Oh, yes...yes, certainly."

Orrin slides the book from the counter, turns, heads across the lobby looking for a Xerox machine. He glances upward. Crowds have gathered at the railings. Theater in the pit! His lust has shrunk; he is sullen, vaguely angry. "A likely story," he thinks, looking back at her. She is talking to another pretty girl and pointing hysterically at him.

****

The cafeteria in the Student Union is closed. It is vast and straight and closed by the time Orrin hauls his hunger to its doors. The Snack Bar is open, though. Open and, as always, full of freaks. Buffalo Springfield's "For What It's Worth," is booming from the jukebox. They've spotted him. Already their heads are bobbing at him. Crowded. Orrin stands on the periphery, looking for an empty table. A place to take his sustenance in peace. He has been hungrier before, perhaps, but still it gnaws, forces him to bear the music, brave the freaks. Seven at each four-place table. Crowded. Greasy hamburgers or the ambiguous, prepackaged sandwiches—which would be the greater insult? Standing in the line for food he spots a table, off beside the jukebox in a corner, empty, a cardboard pup-tent sign on it: RESERVED.

He sits there, opens one of the sandwiches and a carton of milk, begins. But a short-tempered, self-righteous, aproned woman emerges from behind the scenes, stands over him, working hands on retired hips. "Listen, you no good hippie, this table's ours! We gotta have a place to sit an' eat. We get two ten-minute breaks. No lunch. We gotta eat and relax, just like anybody else, and we finally got this table, here, reserved, so move on."

He looks up at her, finishing his mouthful before he speaks.

By then, his eyes have done more than necessary, and she has retreated to her drudgery.

Some of the freaks were watching. They bring their chairs.

Orrin eats, head down, ignoring them. His books, legal pads, and his typescript of the SIAPHE article are on the table to one side, safe, within his head-bent view. A fat, powerful hand enters that view, grabs the typescript with nail-less fingers, slides it across the table. Orrin follows it with his eyes, and then levels them at the large, grizzly-bear-like, hippie thief. But the culprit's reading, chortling, interjecting a subdued "Wow!" Then he adds, "The Muslims. Yeah, that's probably right. They just about killed off all the Buddhists, once. But Buddhists come back. Even the enlightened ones. Bodhisattvas. Tulkus. I Met one in London. The eleventh reincarnation of.... "

In one quick move Orrin drops the sandwich and snatches back the precious typescript, which he pounded out on a dime-consuming electronic typewriter after three Xerox machines refused to re-produce the futuristic print of *Prewar History Review Rejects*.

"Uptight, huh?" The de-clawed Grizzly Bear observes, bobbing his head, puffing out his cheeks, apparently unaffected by Orrin's flat-out stare.

Orrin thinks maybe his eyes are just tired and weak. He returns to his food, but the sandwich has lost appeal. He feels their bobbing heads, their uninhibited presence, their unjustified joy, surrounding him. One is beating on the table to the music, loud, irreverent. They're all talking to him, too.

171

"I've been strung out bad before," one is saying.

"Just ride it out," another, says, "You'll get your head together."

"I'm not strung out," Orrin lets them know. "I'm hungry."

"That's good. Eat." from yet another; they're all around.

"I can't, with you harassing me."

In a tone that takes Orrin's last comment as proof, one of them says, "You're strung out."

Another says, "You're crashin' hard."

Another, "Your eyes, man!"

Another, "Wow! Your eyes, man. Your eyes look like Rasputin's!"

"My eyes are tired, and I'm hungry. Otherwise, I'm my normal self. Do you ever wonder about your freedom? Doubt it, I mean, fundamental freedom."

"Oh, wow, every day."

"Oppression, persecution..."

"The Combine!"

"Yeah, right. I doubt it," a philosophically inclined freak says. "Bracket it and doubt it."

"Freedom?" says the Grizzly, and carves brackets in the air around it. "I doubt it every day."

"No. No. That's not what I mean, I don't think. This is freedom of the soul, or mind, or self, something like that. Not political freedom. It's hard to describe. I mean do you feel like you don't get to make any decisions?"

"You mean Free will," a freak suggests.

"Yeah, right," another Freak agrees.

"We got into that in one of my classes. Free will Vs. Determinism."

"Erasmus Vs. Luther."

"We've got free will."

"Who's we?" Orrin breaks in.

"People," the freaks respond in harmony.

"That seems too general. Couldn't some have it and some not have it. Free will, I mean. If that's what you want to call it. I don't have free will. No. And I think that maybe the Devil has blinded you guys and made you think that you are alive and well and have free will. Sure, the Church says we have Free Agency, that we can choose, but I don't think so. I think the Church is wrong. For instance, there is The Hymn. What about The Hymn?"

At least some of them ask: "The Hymn?"

"It tells me what to do. I can't shut it up. I feel like a robot. And, when I "remember" something, I swear, it's happening for the first time. I feel like I was born yesterday, you know?"

"You're whacked out of your skull," one freak observes.

"Did you get some of that orange sunshine?" another one asks.

"I had some of that," another answers.

"I've been there." They are all talking over one another.

"Real bummer."

"You doubt everything."

"Something as basic as free will...you doubt it."

"I thought my life was a dream, someone else's dream. Doubted my flesh. Thought I was pure spirit, pure thought, a figment of imagination. But I got my head together."

Orrin cuts in, "I don't dream. I have nightmares, now and then. But I don't dream, usually. The Hymn's no dream. I know that. I can hear it now. It's always there. Have you ever done something you didn't want to do? That's not free will. Have you ever wanted to do something or not do something, decided against it, for it, to just think about it for a while, then...in the morning.... I don't know. And my shooting...it's absurd. I can't hit my ass with both hands."

They all recoil, "Shooting?!?"

****

Now, Orrin is walking across the campus toward the lot in which he parked his Jeep. He has forgotten the conversation in the Snack Bar (and so should you). He is walking past the football practice field.

Look up Heber Nephi Smith,
Get a bomb.
You can blow Agnew to Hell
With a bomb.
I have my work;
I will not shirk.
Look up Heber Nephi Smith.

He is thinking along those lines when a loose ball—poorly kicked or badly thrown—wobbles to a stop in front of him. He hears, "little help!" bends one knee, stretches the other leg out in back of him, grasps the ball, and flicks it, sidearm, in a perfect spiral to the coach—some sixty yards across the field.

The coach is not expecting it, so his good assistants shout, "Heads up, coach!" He turns, looking, and gets drilled in the face.

Orrin sees the coach take it, shake it off, then wave at him. He waves back, glad the coach is all right, but continues on his way, surprised that he

174

threw the ball so far, but not sharing the coach's enthusiasm.

Walking along, seeing in his mind's eye, Agnew blown to bits, he feels an urgent grip on his arm, whirls to defend himself. The coach, a smoker, is out of breath. "Don't look at me that way, son. I want to help you. We can help each other. You throw for me. I'll see that you get the world at your feet. What year are you? A Freshman? (He hopes, but he can see that Orrin isn't interested). You like Corvettes? How about some swingin' clothes? Girls? We can get ya all the girls ya want! And you won't get hurt.

"Listen… You'll be safe. No danger involved for the quarterback on this team. Just stand back there, behind that Samoan line of mine, and throw the bomb. I got these colored boys at split end. They are fast, and they have got moves…and hands. Goddamn! The touchdowns! You *were* throwing at me?"

Orrin nods.

"You're *great*, kid! The pros will draft you. You'll put the U of U on the football map." He looks Orrin over. "You play ball in high school?"

"Does the word linebacker have anything to do with ball?" Orrin says. But he is still hung up on one of the coach's earlier phrases. "I *didn't* know I could throw like that."

"They had you playin' linebacker?! With that arm! You didn't know? You're shittin' me! Come on. You knew. You turned hippie. Listen… You won't have to cut your hair. That'll make great press. It's a *personal* statement, a good touch. You'll make Joe Namath look like a crew-cut square. How're your knees? You're not a junkie, are ya? Little grass now and then,

175

that's ok. None of that hard shit, though. No acid. No shrooms. Booze is ok. Little booze now and then."

"I'm no hippie, coach. And if I throw the bomb for anybody, it'll be for Brigham Young." The coach is supposed to think and does think he means arch rival BYU, but Orrin means Brigham Young.

He's got it figured out, now, Orrin does. The chain of command from **Brigham Young** (Most certainly God of his own planet, somewhere, with, nonetheless, interest in this planet.), through **Orrin Porter Rockwell** (Brigham's loyal servant, now as then.)**, two ways,** through the lineage, the **DNA** (inherited characteristics, name) and through the **Anointing** in The Maze. So, if he throws the bomb, and he thinks that he will, it will be for Brigham Young.

"What? Are you a Mormon?"

"More so than most."

"Well, fuck a duck!" The coach lets go of Orrin's arm in despair. But quickly, for he is an optimist, a coach, "Listen…. Listen, son, I'll cut those niggers. I'll get some local talent, just like BYU, some ex-Marines. I'll import Slavs. I'll…." Orrin turns and walks.

"Hey, listen, son, anything you want…."

****

Returned to the exact spot (he's sure of it, though the lot is vast) Orrin finds his CJ5 not there. Instead, a mud-spattered, tan Land Rover 88 with two white dogs in it and a spare tire mounted on the hood. The dogs (looking to him like a matched pair of Samoyeds) are friendly enough (no growls or barks), but they don't make up for his Jeep's being gone.

Just as Orrin is about to climb up on the spare tire and survey the lot, the dogs become agitated. A figure in blue (Levis and work shirt) is bouncing across the lot toward them. Bouncing—walking, rocking with each step high onto the balls of his feet, wasting energy. And he leans—from the ankles or waist it is impossible to tell—leans forward as he bounce-walks, precariously oblique, as though he'll fall on his nose. He nods, and their brown eyes meet. "Lose something?"

His inflection implies that he knows damn well Orrin has lost something, maybe even what and how.

"Might lose my mind soon. Now it's just my Jeep that's missing. Did you see one here? In this space?"

Long hair swirls, a smile cracks, as the Land Rover driver shakes his head. "It was empty."

"Hmmm."

"Look, if you need a ride somewhere...to the fort...or someplace, anywhere..."

"The fort..." Orrin repeats it softly, trying to reconstruct the morning. But that involves most of what he knows to be his life, and he can't separate them now.

"Okay, sure, the fort. Hop in." It is a friendly order. He opens the door. "Blizzard, Nepha, in back." The dogs obey cheerfully, making room for Orrin, who doesn't know why he should obey but can think of no reason why he shouldn't.

"It's a mess," the driver points out as he lights a cigarette, and he is right. White dog fur all over, cigarette butts spilling out of the ash tray, squashed, empty packs, papers, different wrappers, caked mud on the floorboards, on the gear shift knobs, doors, on the Springfield 1911 that is securely holstered to the front of the bench seat platform, below the cushion, on the drivers' side, where the driver can reach it between his legs. Glancing over his shoulder, Orrin sees the back is worse. There, a muddy shovel, muddy jack, muddy clothes, boots, sleeping bag, an ax, and boxes force the dogs up onto the seats that run back along either side.

"Over in the Book Cliffs a couple weeks ago," the driver explains. "Had her down one of those little no-name tributaries of the Green. Skirting a beaver pond, and the bottom fell out. Sunk in mud up past the doors. Had to crawl out the window. Tried to dig 'er out. Shoved rocks and logs under the wheels. No way in hell." He looks both ways then jolts the Land Rover out of the lot into traffic. "Walked, oh, fifteen miles to the reservation. Indian there had a pick-up with a winch. He pulled me out for twenty bucks. Haven't had a chance to clean 'er up, yet. Been workin' on a novel."

Orrin thinks he might be grateful for the ride, though he doesn't know why, but that doesn't mean he has to be friendly with or listen to this slob. Silently, he clutches his books and his typescript in his lap. The traffic is dense, slow-moving. He glances over at the driver, who is at that moment glancing at him.

"You know," the driver says, "I'm as surprised by this as you are." He looks away at the traffic briefly, then, back. "Or, perhaps, you're just bewildered." Back to watching the traffic, he talks to the windshield. "I'm surprised. You're bewildered. And I don't blame you, either. Anyone in your position has a right...no...not a right.... Anyone in your position cannot escape bewilderment. Accept it,

Orrin, and don't be too rough on the narrator. I mean, don't criticize your existence too much, okay. Don't abuse the freedom you find in dialogue. And don't give me that innocent look. You've found it."

There are no sentries at the entrance to the fort. It is being phased out, almost is phased out, and it needs no guards. They haven't driven far into the fort when Orrin spots his Jeep in front of a row of three-story, red brick buildings. He shifts his books and the typescript to the middle of the bench seat, readying himself for action.

"Is that your Jeep?"

"Yeah!"

The driver swerves toward it, bounces over a curb, across the parade grounds, past the flag pole, off a curb on the other side, and Orrin has the door open and is half out before the Land Rover stops.

****

His Jeep is abandoned, its wires hanging down beneath the dash like the entrails of a gut-shot deer. While the Land Rover pulls away and leaves the fort, while McKinstry emerges from the bushes that hug the red brick buildings, while Agnew is briefed on what to do and say, what to accomplish in the Mountain States (And for God's sake, Ted, don't call Moss a radical-liberal. Even if he is. He's a Mormon. He got cigarettes off TV. They like you, Ted, but don't force yourself between them and one of their own), while Tony meets a truck full of produce boxes up from southern Arizona (the contents of the boxes, up from Cuba via Puerto Barrios, Guatemala, and Mexico), while a freshman on work-study returns the empty book to Section two, Sub three, Orrin reconnects the wires properly and stuffs them back where they belong. Luckily, they are color-coded.

Lookit him concentratin' on that mother like she was alive. More alive than me. McKinstry leans against the Jeep waiting for Orrin to notice him and maybe say something. *Just say something, peppergut.* Broiling for a fight *I'll bust you open like a hot tamale.* For combat. *Spill the juice all over this fuckin' lovely vehicle.*

McKinstry, if you're interested, reports to his commanding officer, who isn't in and isn't expecting him, anyway, whose sergeant is asleep and doesn't wake when McKinstry shouts, "I'm here, Goddamn it, a year or so late, but I'm fuckin' here", billets himself into a vast, empty building that had housed the Selective Service Board and still houses the history of the fort in dusty volumes and, pictorially, on the walls, makes himself a home, and relaxes with Volume I of the History of Fort Douglas. If he can't get it goin' with the fuckin' people at the fort, Goddamnit, he'll get it goin' with the fuckin' fort itself. Poor fucker, he can tell by lookin', it is down the tubes. Damn good fort, too. Good location, good high ground. Kinda beauteous, McKinstry thinks, with that valley stretched out there below and the mountains in back. Poor fucker...Served your fuckin' purpose, huh? And now, now you're dyin' slow. Naw, you're already gone, just rottin' away completely now. And that, that uni-fuckin'-versity is eatin' up the remains. I saw it. All them longhaired shits strollin' through converted fort.

He reads slowly, ponderously, accustomed to Army Prose, but not used to reading. He reads and smokes and naps, looks out the windows, and when he hears the first vehicle he's heard all day, he is up and out into the bushes.

Come on, you enchalada, I know you know I'm here. Orrin doesn't know it, not until McKinstry grabs his hair and yanks his head back to greet him face to fuckin' face. "Thanks for the ride boy. Thanks. When the gooks get here, maybe you'll think twice, huh? Maybe you'll..."

Startled by the move, not frightened, perhaps, not even startled, or surprised, perhaps just more bewildered momentarily, Orrin listens till McKinsty falters. Then he swings out of the Jeep, knocking the hand from his hair and clenching the wrist desperately for a few pulses, before he drops it. That's enough. No need, no reason, no motivation to beat him to a pulp. He's sad to look at. Sorrowfully insane. *Should have taken him to the V.A. hospital like I planned.*

"All you fuckers back here in the world think the gooks are playin' games. Think they're just like anybody else. Sittin' over here with your heads in your ass thinkin' everybody's Jesus Christ himself." He is moved to tears. Not by his speech. He's preached this countless times, but always to the deaf. Orrin, though, is standing there, listening. "And this fort," he pans the fort with his gaze, "this poor, fuckin' fort. They've conned the Army into thinkin' there's no need for it no more. But I know about those Mormons. They got horns and twenty wives each. They're more communist than the Communists. They ain't Christians. They ain't Americans. They hate the U.S. government and the Army. They fuckin' fought the U.S. Army! That's why this fort is here. So, if you know any Mormons, boy, you tell 'em Stephen B.

181

McKinstry IS the Army, and he knows what they're doin'. And he's here now."

"Yes, sir." He's crazy. Orrin isn't going to argue.

"They're as bad as gooks. Worse. They're just as sneaky, just as low, but worse because they're fuckin' *here,* right here in our country. Wormin' their way into our government. Actin' like they love it. Like bygones is bygones, and now there's no need for a fort to watch 'em. At least you spics know where you're better off, and you're grateful, right?"

"Oh, yes, sir."

"Hmm. Well, most of 'em are, anyway. The onlyest thing wrong with spics is they're a little cocky, like a nigger, sometimes. But they're good fighters. Fuckin' drink and fight, that's what they like. Most of 'em are clean, too, considerin' and allowin' for the grease. Few longhairs, though, like you, ruin everything for the others. You're one of them…Chihuahuas…or chico…whatever they call themselves. You're one of them, aren't you, boy? Causin' trouble every chance you git, bringin' the county down."

"You mean, 'Chicano,' sir. And, no, I'm not a 'Chicano.' I'm a Mexican." Orrin says, reminding himself of the way Tony had stated it, with pride. "And, listen, sir, I'm sorry about this morning. I had a lot on my mind. But I'd be glad to give you a lift now. There's a place not far from here where you'll be appreciated, where you'll find others like yourself to talk to. Come on, it's not far."

McKinstry contemplates the offer carefully; for spics, like gooks and Mormons, are a sneaky bunch. *Proly settin' me up for an ambush! Git me off the fort, up there in he hills where his buddies are awaitin' to slit my throat.*

"Sorry, kid, I got my orders. I'll stay right here an' keep an eye on that Mormon stronghold down below. Keep the peace, you know. Harass 'em a little, make 'em show their cards. The Army will see what they're up to and send me reinforcements, get this old fort back in shape."

A tape-recorded bugle sounds over loudspeakers, calling the fort's token personnel to mess.

"Ah, well," McKinstry says, "I'd best go see what I've got to work with. See ya, boy. Cut your hair."

****

Orrin starts his Jeep and gets back to what he was doing before the intrusion of that minor character from his past. Why, he wonders, does this morning seem so long ago. But a stanza of The Hymn gets his mind off time and back to events. Events that must take place. He must visit Tony, first, The Hymn reminds him. Give him the secret Mormon mind control information and find out when Agnew is coming to town, get his schedule. Then, look up Heber Nephi Smith. With his schedule set, Orrin looks at the empty passenger seat. The information....

After cruising through parking lots for a little while, Orrin spots the Land Rover, clear across the campus from where it was before, slyly parked behind the heating plant, out of view from the arteries of traffic. There are no empty parking slots nearby. No matter. Orrin stops behind it, peers in the driver's side window. His books, he thinks, are there, and maybe his legal pads. But the inside's such a mess. The dogs are on the front seat, and the window's dirty. Orrin starts to open the door, which isn't locked, and the dogs (all smiles till now) are suddenly all low growls and rolled-back lips and laid-back ears. "Hmmm…Good doggies," Orrin soothes, "I just want my books, now, calm down. That's good dogs." But the dogs aren't soothed. He'd give them one of his withering stares and melt their courage, but they won't look him in the eye. They're watching him, be sure of that, but their eyes will not meet his, no matter how he shifts, trying to arrange it.

"Raspberries," he sighs and rubs his forehead. Maybe, if he had some food, he could bribe them, but he doubts that. A sudden, ugly thought wrenches through him: "I could shoot them." (His .22 is still in the Jeep.) "Couldn't miss at this range." But now that his hand is off the handle, the dogs are all smiles again. No. He wouldn't think of killing them. And he stands there wondering where that thought came from. It wasn't in a Hymn stanza, seemed to be an ordinary thought. But, again, *he* wouldn't think of it. He knows he's not responsible for that thought. He had it, he admits that, or at least he admits that he experienced it. It's more like the awful thought passed through him. That's a better image. The thought came from without, passed through his mind, and he rejected it. Partially satisfied with that rationalization, and wanting to leave the dogs before anymore murderous ideas bombard him, Orrin sets off in search of their master.

And their master is right where he expects him to be. He looks up at Orrin from his seat at a table in the Student Union Snack Bar.

"Oh, Hi, Orrin, grab a chair." He isn't glad to see him. "For What It's Worth" is on the jukebox. It seems to Orrin as though "For What It's Worth" is always on the jukebox, and this time he picks up a few of the words.

"There's somethin' happenin' here,
What it is ain't exactly clear."

Orrin agrees with that sentiment and likes the rhythm of the song, but he snaps out of its trance.

"I'm kinda in a hurry. Thanks." Orrin recognizes some of the freaks at the table. The Grizzly Bear is there, and the Table-Drummer, and there are no chairs to grab. "I left some things in your Land Rover, and I'd like to get them now, if you don't mind."

"Oh, sure, go ahead, it's..."

"I know where it is."

"Well, it's not locked. Help yourself."

"Yeah, I know it's unlocked. But the dogs."

And everybody but Orrin smiles.

"Those dogs won't hurt you, go ahead."

"I don't believe that," Orrin says as politely as possible. "Why don't you just come with me."

"Yeah, well, ya see, I was right in the middle of an important conversation here, and..."

Orrin places a hand on the guy's shoulder, locks eyes with him. Brown eyes, like his. "Come on. My Jeep's outside. We can ride over to your Land Rover. Won't take long."

"Okay, okay, you are persuasive. Your eyes are great. But why don't we save ourselves a little action here. I'll admit I took the story, okay. Now we don't have to..."

"What story? You mean that article. What'd you do with it? What about the legal pads?"

The Land Rover guy holds up his hands. "Everything else is there. When I ran into you, I was going home to get a story for my fiction workshop. Supposed to write a story a week. So I saw your stuff there and looked through it. I know who you are. I looked through your stuff and found that story. I saved myself a trip home, that's all. You'll get it back, I swear."

"Oh, I'll get it back, all right! Who'd you give it to?"

"Look, Orrin, you can't go after it. You're all wrong. I mean, you shouldn't even be talking to me. We shouldn't be talking to each other in front of...."

Orrin looks around at the freaks for some help here. The Grizzly appears to have something to say. Orrin waits.

"Ah, wow, he thinks—we were rappin' on it before you came—ah, he says you remind him a hell of a lot of this character in his novel. He thinks maybe you are that character. Which means that, if he can see you, you know, and touch you and talk to you, *in public*... If *we* can see you and talk... then, if you are a character in his novel, so are we. Wow. And so is *he*. But I don't dig his premise. I mean, I *know* I'm not a character in his novel. And I'm almost positive these other dudes aren't."

Orrin looks from The Grizzly to the Land Rover driver, who is watching The Grizzly, listening, making sure he gets it right.

"But, ah," The Grizzly Bear continues, "It gets heavier than that."

"Who teaches that workshop he was talking about?" Orrin interrupts involuntarily. It comes out like a hiccup.

"Must be Dilayett," The Grizzly answers before he thinks. "Dr. Dilayett."

Orrin leaves. And just in time. He thinks the freaks are out of their minds, especially the Land Rover guy.

****

The English Department. Offices on either side of an empty corridor. Orrin stops at one with an open door. It is no more than six feet to the desk. Two steps. Orrin checks the card on the door. It is not Dilayett's office. So, down the hall he goes, past the bulletin boards, posters, closed office doors, reading cards.

Henry G.R.W. Dilayett, PhD.
Professor of English
Will be around this quarter for:
English 618 M.F. 2:00-5:00
English 2001 T.Th 1:00-4:00
Office Hours:
"Any time you feel down hearted."

The door is not open, but it is unlocked. It swings only a few degrees before a bookcase, parallel with the corridor, stops it. Orrin slides through, closing the door behind him. The place is lit by a source-less light. A little sign tacked to the bookcase: "Behold, this is the hole of the tarantula."

He finds he is in a corridor formed by the bookcase and a wall. At one end, the bookcase and wall are flush, but at the other...at the other is space enough to slide around the bookcase into... another even narrower aisle formed by another bookcase. There is a sign on this new bookcase, too: "The future already exists." Orrin has to walk to the other end of this aisle for passage around...into another. But this time there is a sign on the wall, to read as he's rounding the bookcase. "Drink deep, or taste not the Pierian spring." And having rounded the case into a new aisle: "Walking in the midst of others, one returns alone." The line stops Orrin short. He reads it again. Remembers The Maze, Laura (ah, God, sweet Laura), and her dad. Walking in their midst. Wonders if whoever wrote that line...if he ever had something happen...if he actually knew what it means...or if he just had a way with words. Close by, as if to answer, another sign: "My bowels are torn with sorrow." And near it, in this narrowest of aisles so far, is a break in the bookshelf, another aisle curving off to the left. Curving? Orrin looks. Yes, it curves, bookshelves on each side. He cannot see where it goes without committing himself to it. But he will not. He will follow the straight aisle He can see where it goes...to the wall, though the wall looks further away than it should. If he follows to the wall, and everything is true to form, there will be a passage into the next or to Dilayett's desk. Orrin thinks, these offices are too small for all this. His desk must be on the other side of this bookshelf, if all the room is not taken up with books.

At the wall there is passage around and a sign: "What could be more stupid than to persist?" Orrin agrees, but he must retrieve the article. However, once around the shelf, the aisle begins to curve back on itself...or so it seems to Orrin. And he thinks it is the same curving aisle he saw before. Simply a half-circle designed to turn students around and get rid of them. His theory gains weight as the curving aisle empties into the middle of a long, straight aisle near a sign that reads: "My bowels are torn with sorrow."

Right back—not quite where he started from but—where he's been before. Now, because he suspected something like this, Orrin kept a careful watch for corridors—secret, hidden, narrow—taking off from the curving aisle But there were none. So, resolved, despite this setback, he proceeds backtracking down the aisle, deciding to call upon the professor at his home, for obviously his office is no office but a labyrinth of books and random quotes. When the next sign, the one that so touched him earlier, comes in view, he reads it, thinking it will bear rereading. But he finds it bears much more...more words to begin with. Now it reads: "Walking in the midst of others, one returns alone, and so follows the right way."

All of which brings up at least two questions, one immediate, one of greater import. The immediate and obvious question is, in two parts: Has someone changed this sign since I was here last? Or was I never here before? But more importantly (thinking, as before, of The Maze, Laura, her father, returning alone): Am I following the right way? The author of the quote never intended it to mean that killing Agnew is right. But what else can it mean to Orrin? To Orrin, what other message is there in the words?

Orrin continues to walk as he ponders and upon rounding the book case, bumps his thigh on something sharp. The corner of a desk. Orrin makes no sound. Behind the desk is what he takes to be Dilayett. With his back to Orrin and his feet on the windowsill, he appears to be asleep. Orrin scans the office for his article. No need to wake the man. Except for the window (and there are bookshelves below it) the desk is walled in by books, and little signs. One that is close enough to read: "Oh, I should never, never have come to Utah."

On the desk, Orrin spots a paper with a word that looks like it might be "Heber" on it. He snatches it and reads:

Hebephrenic Lecture

Too much of anything's never enough.
Sorry, Pal, you can't get there from here.
Because, you see, it's all in the wrist.
Nothing's impossible. Nothing is
People. And just like anybody else,
You can't start over again, you can't.

You can't. Start over again? You can't.
Too much of anything's never enough,
'cause you're just like anybody else.
Go on, try, you won't get there from here.
Nothing's impossible. Nothing is
When you know that it's all in the wrist.

When you know that it's all in the wrist
You can't start over again. You can't.
Living's impossible. Living is
Too much of everything and never enough.
Give up, Pal, you can't get there from here.
People are just like anybody else.

People are just like anybody else,
If you know that it's all in the wrist.
Sorry, Pal, you can't get there from here,
And you can't start over again, can't
Do much of anything, never enough.

Nothing's impossible. Nothing is

Someone's impossible dream. Truth is,
People are just like anybody else—
Too much of something but never enough.
Look, here, notice. It's all in the wrist
Why you can't start over again, can't
Make it. No, you can't get there from here.

It's sad you can't get there from here
When nothing's impossible. Why is
It you can't start over again? Can't
People be just like anybody else?
The answers, they're all in the wrist.
Too much of anything's never enough

To take you from here. Anybody else
Would say nothing is hidden in the wrist.
But then, why can't nothing be enough?

Hand-written, to the right and below the poem:
"Hybrid Sestina/Villanelle—A+"

The professor snorts in his sleep, stirs, and Orrin
looks at him—balding, heavily shouldered, probably
tall, nervous, smokes a lot. And, probably, not from
around here. Back East, somewhere, more than likely.
Orrin slinks around the desk for a look at the man's
face. Surprisingly young and sensitive, open, boyish,
the face does not quite go with the rest of him. And,
though he has never heard of this man, Orrin knows
he is a poet.

He holds Orrin's typescript in his lap, having
read, it appears, either the entirety or no more than

the first page. Thinking he can take it, if he's careful, Orrin tries to remove the article from the professor's sleepy grasp. His movements are gentle, smooth, and slow. But as he touches the paper, the professor stirs again, begins to wake. Or is he waking? Orrin tries again, more carefully. The professor stirs more dramatically. Now it's clear he's waking up, so Orrin scoots into the proper position for a student calling upon a professor in his office. He clears his throat to help the professor along, and to make him think that is what awakened him. Dilayett lowers his feet from the sill, and as he swivels the chair around, Orrin says, "Excuse me, Dr. Dilayett. I'm sorry I woke you up, but..."

Dilayett looks up at him with drowsy eyes, not yet awake, and says: "'I wake to sleep and take my waking slow.'"

Thinking, I knew he was a poet, Orrin says, "I'm sorry, I hope it isn't serious, I mean... All I want is..."

"'It sounds as if somebody intends to fill in the blank,'" Dilayett says sleepily, "'What is all this nonsense about?'" Then with little pity he says, "'You can't always get what you want.'"

"But it's mine! I need it. He had no business giving it to you!"

"'He who goes about as a talebearer,'" Dilayett begins, pointing at Orrin's nose with the typescript, "'reveals secrets.'"

"Yeah, I know." Orrin grabs at it, but Dilayett is quick. "I've no choice in the matter," Orrin admits. "I wish..."

"'If wishes were thrushes, beggars would eat birds. And to act faithfully is a matter of your own choice.'"

Orrin is silent, put down, but thinking "I don't make any choices."

"'I have read it,'" Dilayett cracks it like a whip, reaches for a pack of cigarettes on his desk. "'...a disconnected manuscript...'" He knocks one out and lets it dangle from his mouth. "'A touch of parody gave its theme the comic relief of life,'" he says around the cigarette, "'but in a cosmos that may be purely imaginary no absolute truth can be known, for everything depends upon the point of view,' 'and they have lost the capacity to release themselves from the actual and to see things in their true perspective.' 'As flies to wanton boys are we to the gods.' 'Man is flung backwards on stage from right wing.'" Dilayett lights the cigarette, snaps his lighter briskly shut. He exhales profoundly, watching the smoke. "'Sometimes...' 'I fear I am not in my perfect mind.' 'Where was I...' 'Ah, yes,'" he does a two-word impersonation of W.C. Fields. "'...a disconnected manuscript.'"

"May I have it?"

"'Not by beginning but at the last man's end.'"

Twenty are not that many quotations, but they are too many when they come one upon the next one, one two three four five six seven eight nine ten eleven twelve thirteen fourteen fifteen sixteen seventeen eighteen nineteen twenty, strung on temporal thread like so many borrowed beads. Orrin knows. There's no denying what his grandpa once said: "Git too much learnin', too much readin' books—fancy-ass poetry and fairy tales—can't think your own thoughts no more." Grandpa actually said that, exactly, Orrin recalls to his own amazement. And more: "Gits to where you say somethin' and you're using other people's words, and you don't sound like yourself.

But you don't care, 'cause you don't remember what you sound like, anyway, and you think it's showin' how smart you are, but it ain't."

"You've got nearly the same kind of problem I've got with The Hymn, then, don't you?" Orrin says before anything can be done about it.

"'It was not exactly consistent, but bugaboo, buddy-boy, as Ralph Waldo Emerson meant to say,'" Dilayett answers quickly (as though talking to someone else, someone in the ceiling), so quickly that nothing can be done about *it*, either.

"Now, see, that sounds too polished, too light and witty to be thought up in spontaneous dialogue—conversation like this," Orrin begins, and talks on like a speed freak, thinking, daring to presume that it is being written.

****

Now, Orrin is walking quietly toward his Jeep. The typescript of the article from the distant future about an act of vandalism that will occur about six months from now is under his arm; his mouth is shut; his mind, occupied by this stanza of The Hymn:

Look up Heber Nephi Smith,
Get a bomb.
You can blow Agnew to Hell
With a bomb.
I have my work;
I will not shirk.
Look up Heber Nephi Smith.

There is nothing else, nothing to distract him. There is no one for him to talk to. No passersby. No one for him to corral, corner, throw down, pin to the ground and talk to. He is alone, walking.

"'Are you quite all right?'"

It's the professor. I remember him. I imagine him saying something like that. I remember his office and why I came back, but it feels different, the whole thing. I feel different.

"No, not really," I say because it is true. "Do you believe in the Devil, or evil forces?" I don't wait for him to answer. I don't care what he believes, and, besides, he's fading. I have to keep thinking him or he goes. I don't let him go completely. But I do glance over my shoulder at a place where I haven't been thinking 'bookshelves' and see the bleakest kind of hole. I think the bookshelves back immediately, but I can't forget that hole. There was *nothing* there. I mean NOTHING! Not just nothing in the foreground, with something in the background, not just a hole in the wall through which I could see outside, not just the absence of bookshelves, nothing. It scared me and I probably put too much strength into replacing the bookshelves. I feel weaker.

"I've just fought him off," I say, looking only at the professor, keeping him just barely there, concentrating the rest of my strength on what I have to say. "He's been trying to possess my spirit. He's taken over my mind. Controlled my thoughts, dictated actions. Darkness. Darkness all around me. I saw what I was told I saw. The rest was darkness. I've thrown it off. I've cast it from me. I feel light and weak. But I see what I think I see." And saying it, I know. I shut my eyes, forget Dilayett and his bookshelves, think of Laura. No. The preposition is maisleading. I think Laura. I think her with all the strength I have.

I open my eyes again and she's here. Laura. I reach out for her, I think she reaches for me, and she does. She fills my eyes so I have to think of nothing else. It is an extreme close up. I'm holding Laura in my arms, kissing her all over. I never would have suspected, but I should have known it would be like this. I must think constantly of details, or she for example quits breathing. I am weak and ill-prepared. But she moves only when I think a movement for her. Talks when I think words for her, not now. I can only think tears for myself. I feel what I think I feel. And I can feel them down my cheek. At least I know she didn't die out there in the Maze. I know I love her. But she's gone. There's nothing now. As far as I can see in all directions. No, there aren't any directions. I must think of something. Anything I want.

Chapter 8

Personal Recognizance

Orrin Porter Rockwell Christianson wakes thinking only of Heber Nephi Smith. He's had a restful night with good dreams, a series of successes, no nightmares to remember. His head is clear, he feels fine and strong. The sun has barely risen. Everything is bright and effortlessly seen. Humming The Hymn, he prepares and enjoys his breakfast. His bowels move smoothly—well-formed, healthy, floating stool. He knows what he'll do: he'll press explosive plastic into the joints of the podium, blow Agnew to pieces in the middle of his speech. The detonator will depend on what kind of information he gets from Tony. And if he can trust that information. If it is accurate and detailed, if he knows exactly when Agnew will begin, when he will finish, he can use a timing device. That is if he can trust Tony's information. It may be better to plan on a remote control electronic impulse wavelength intensifier detonator. He doesn't really know. He'll have to see what Heber thinks, and what he has available. If he knew how much, exactly how much Agnew will weigh in the tabernacle, shoes included, he could rig a mine. A mine that would explode when and only when Agnew put his full weight on it. No one else could make it work, unless...

He's excited by the possibilities of explosives, but he will not rely on them completely—primarily but not completely. He will be there, waiting in the audience, applauding so as not to draw attention to himself. Waiting, with a poison needle in the finger of his glove, spring-loaded, if the bomb doesn't do the job, with a cleaver just in case, a hammer if he needs it, a garrote if it comes to that, his bare hands, if all else fails. Too bad I can't shoot, he thinks. A sniper rifle would be the best weapon. Tony's gonna tell me where he'll be. I'd set up a thousand yards away and....

He'll have all those other things backing up the bomb, but more importantly (the surest weapon in the world) he'll have the assurance of his convictions. He will kill Agnew with his teeth if he has to. It is not that he will not accept failure, but truly that failure is impossible, and he knows it. He's come to the realization that some slowly dying men come to: the inevitable will happen. Simple, frightening, not easy to admit, or live with, the tautology is privately denied by most for their entire lives. Readers of fiction and philosophy are familiar with this problem. Orrin doesn't have it anymore. It is solved by the coming together of a man's concept of his existence and his existence. Orrin is no longer fooling himself. Agnew doesn't have a chance.

He remembers his grandpa's telling him that yesterday morning. Grandpa used different words, talked about Destroying Angels and how there's no stopping them, but he meant the same thing. "The Angel, the Destroying Angel that is in me but is not me, is going to kill him. The Destroying Angel and The Hymn." Orrin is certain, there is a Destroying Angel in him. All the evidence indicates that it's been there at least since The Maze and probably, according to his grandpa, since he was born. Maybe it was in him as an embryo. It must have been; for it was surely in him as a fetus. Something swerved that bullet from its path and saved his fragile body from its concussive power. If Grandpa is right, and there is no reason to doubt his testimony, that "something" was the Destroying Angel. And he was saved for one reason. Agnew doesn't have a chance.

Orrin's really getting into it now. Or, if you like, out of it, which is closer to being the case. But we must all withdraw. We must all, somehow (we find the ways and means), remove ourselves sometimes from what we do. In order, of course, that we might do it. And avoid deciding not to do it, which may be the natural decision, but sticking by that decision is sometimes more difficult and unpleasant than doing something we do not want to do. Free will has nothing to do with it and all of this is unimportant, off the point, and not at all what Orrin is about.

Orrin is about to leave for the high school Heber attends. He could look in the book for Heber's home phone number, but he doesn't know Heber's father's first name. There are twenty pages of "Smiths" in the Salt Lake City phone book. He could call the school and ask them for the number, but they would not give it to him, and besides, he doesn't want to talk to Heber on the phone. He wants to meet him in person, shake his hand, look at him as they talk. He is leaving. But Tony's Chevy blocks the private roadway, and there is no other way out of the court. Orrin pulls his Jeep right up to it and lays on the horn.

The old army blanket nailed up to the window as drapery is raised from one corner. Tony's head appears. Orrin signals with his hand: "Get out here and move it." Tony signals with his finger: "Come inside, Cousin, and we will talk about important things." Well, Orrin's not getting into anymore unnecessary conversations, not after what happened in the last chapter, so he jumps out of the Jeep, ready to move the car himself. But the doors are locked, all four of them. And he can see that the car is in gear, first gear, and that the hand brake is pulled. Why it is so, is difficult to say. Tony doesn't seem to be the type of person to pull the hand break, roll up his windows, and lock his doors. But that's the way it is.

Orrin feels forced—perhaps by Tony's well-laid plan, perhaps by something else—but he feels forced into a confrontation. A confrontation for which he is not ready. He simply does not move for a stretch of time. Then, grumbling something about there being more that one way to move a car, he locks his hubs and jumps back into the Jeep, shifts it into low range, four-wheel drive—the Jeep sounds and moves like a vehicle four times its size. Slowly, powerfully, the winch crushes into the grille, which buckles and retreats into the radiator until the bumpers of the two machines meet—the top of he Chevy's bumper meets the bottom of the Jeep's bumper and brush guard. The Chevy's bumper retreats, crumpling the fenders along with it, but soon all is up against the frame, the engine and the transmission, driveline, differential, wheels. Orrin keeps the pressure slow and steady, but all four wheels begin to spin in the ruts of the unpaved private roadway, so he depresses the clutch. The Jeep rolls back about six inches. Tony watches from the window, lighting a cigar, picking up the phone. Orrin looks at him and screams, "Raspberries to you!" Tony turns a deaf ear toward him and gestures: "Try again."

Which Orrin intends to do. He revs the engine and slams into the Chevy's mangled front end. Nothing. Not immediately, nothing except a rocking of the body on the springs. But again Orrin keeps the pressure steady, sings his Hymn out loud:

(Put your shoulder to the wheel,

Push alo-ong.

Do your duty with a heart full of so-ong.

We all have work;

Let no one shirk.

Put your shoulder to the wheel.),

and after a straining, cracking snap that is all but imperceptible over the Jeep's growling duel exhausts, the Chevy grudgingly begins to roll. The crumpled fenders peel the front tires. The rear brakes, engaged by hand, burn.

Orrin is desperately exhilarated as he pushes the car out into the street and backs away from it: a man who's just looked death in the face and got away, escaped untouched; a man who's raced and barely beat the freight train to the crossing; a man caught on the face of a cliff during rain who's felt the rock to which he clings grow slippery and cold, who's just now saved himself from sliding off into nothing by driving one numb finger, like a piton... Hell. It's not like that at all. If anything, he feels like a man who's just bulldozed his way out of a wet paper bag, when all he had to do was ask, and the bag would've been opened for him. Actually, all similes aside, he feels that he's just successfully avoided something that needn't have been avoided, will have to be arranged soon, and could possibly do his cause some good. He

201

also feels he's wrecked a poor man's only car. But he had his reasons, and he cannot feel sorry.

Orrin, in his desperate exhilaration, is not thinking about how he feels, he's feeling it and thinking about other things as he turns his hubs to the free position. He's thinking that after all that, he is finally going to see Heber and get that ever-loving, sweet-exploding bomb. He's finished turning hubs and shifting knobs, performing the ritual that translates the Jeep back into a street machine. He's finished that, and he's ready to go see Heber, talk to him about being prophets, using bombs, and how the Church would never understand them. He's pulling away, but...there are screeching tires and a tail-spinning black and white right in front of him! *A cop! Police officer. Be polite. Don't, for God's sake, say anything. Pretend to be asleep. ZZZZZ No. He won't go for it.*

The police officer reaches for his clip-board and ticket book, turns on the whirling lights, puts on his hat. Symbolically, the Jeep's engine sputters and dies. Orrin's palms are sponges that drench him when he clamps his hands into fists with which to beat his forehead. It seems to Orrin's body that he's been transferred to the tropics, and it is responding accordingly. Pores, like mountain springs, are gushing sweat, gushes flowing together in the low spots forming rivers of nervous sweat. His long hair sticks to his forehead. His long hair sticks to the back of his neck, touching off a tingle that zips down his backbone, turns cold, streaks back up to the base of his brain and is distributed throughout his body. He pees his pants. His knees tremble against each other. His fingers are numb and useless, his lips quiver. Now his pores, truly like mountain springs, gush cold.

Just be calm and polite and careful. Just nod or shake your head. Get your license out. He'll want your license. Have it ready. Don't aggravate him. Don't...

Besides trying to think, Orrin is instinctively humming The Hymn, but it sounds like a deaf-mute's drone. Orrin is only trying to please the officer, trying to make a good first impression so he'll get off easy and not let this stupid incident bring about the failure of his mission. He is only reaching for his wallet. But he makes the move too nervously, with too much of a sudden jerk, a frenzied rush that connotes danger to the cop. Orrin hears a booming, "Freeze!" yelled with all possible authority. He freezes and looks through the windshield at a pistol, a heavy cop revolver, a Smith & Wesson Highway Patrolman .357 magnum, more than likely, held in both hands, resting steady on the roof of the cop car, pointed straight at his head. Behind it, a deadly serious cop. Orrin looks at the cop and his gun, and he knows he is superior. He wants to laugh—not hysterically—a deep and satisfying laugh. He feels it growing, lets it come. Oh, ho, ho, oh, yeah. Laughs at the silly, serious man and his gun. He laughs, also, at himself as he had been a few moments ago, at what he did. A stupid thing. Almost, but not quite, as stupid as pulling a gun on him. Just like a cop. Ha ha ha ha. He knows, now, his reaction to the sudden appearance of the police car was as much embarrassment as fear. A good deal more embarrassment. But fear was there, fear that he would be detained for some reason while Agnew makes his visit. Or that he might, during questioning, let some hint drop that would tip them off. All this, all this nervousness and possible botching of the most important thing in his life, just because of one stupid, thoughtless, cowardly, escapist act. No, Orrin thinks, it wasn't the act. It was the cop. It would not have been so bad, if he'd not been caught. Now, and only now does he remember Tony in the window, dialing.

And, not because he thought of him, remembered him, Tony shows up, walks into the street just as the officer tells Orrin to get out of the Jeep slowly, with his hands on his head. "You'd better stand back," the cop yells at Tony, nodding at Orrin as an explanation.

"Yes, sir," Tony makes it sound like love.

"You the one who reported the accident?" Orrin can tell he's being talked around.

"Yes, sir," Tony says in his sycophant-peon voice.

"Do you know this man?"

"Yes, sir. He is my neighbor. He is not dangerous. I think he hit his head."

"Could be," the cop allows, but he's making sure. He gets Orrin spread out on the ground, searches him, looks at his license.

"May I stand up now?" Orrin asks, knowing immediately he should've kept his mouth shut.

"Don't move!" The cop searches the Jeep. In the back, under the folded 8'x12' waterproof canvas tarp that is weighted down in one corner by Orrin's toolbox—there is no back seat—the cop finds Orrin's Ruger 10/22 carbine. The chamber's empty, but the magazine is full.

"What's this for?" the officer wants to know.

"Rabbit hunting."

"You were going for it!" The cop announces.

Making it sound too much like an explanation for a child, Orrin says, "No. I was reaching for my wallet.

My license is, or was, in my wallet. I wanted to get it out for you."

With no verbal response or warning, the cop handcuffs Orrin, stuffs him into the back seat of the squad car, and radios for help. Salt Lake City cops cruise alone, but the regulations say that it takes two to bring in a suspect. Facing Orrin now through expanded metal from the front seat, the officer begins, "You have the right to remain silent."

"The right, huh?! I have the right to remain silent!? Did you hear that, Tony? I have the right to remain silent!" Orrin's shouting. Orrin's sounding quite mad.

"Shut up."

"Enforcing my right?"

"Anything you say can and will..." the officer continues, finishes.

But Orrin doesn't hear or pretends he doesn't hear. Makes it seem that he is ignoring the officer by singing The Hymn at the top of his lungs, the standard version.

"Do you understand these rights as I have described them?"

"Nope. Not a word. Would you please explain?"

"Which one?"

"All of them. I don't understand any of them. Not a word."

Not knowing what else to do, the officer begins again, reads the words he's been given to read. Orrin only hums The Hymn this time, while an Agnew verse reels off in his head.

"Do you understand these rights as I have explained them to you?"

"You didn't explain! If anything, you muddled. You call it a right. That's an excellent example of equivocation. I mean, are you serious? I don't have any rights. I'm silent because I'm forced. And only when I'm forced. If I weren't forced to be silent, I'd talk your ear off. But every time I talk to someone, every time a conversation starts picking up a little meaning for me, gets around to what I want to talk about, WHAM!"

"Wham?" The cop inquires.

"Yeah. WHAM! ZAP! BINGO! I'm someplace else, not talking. It's no fun," Orrin tells him. "Why do you think I did it? Huh? To avoid a conversation. Why do I want to avoid a conversation? I don't!"

"I see." The cop sounds nice enough, but he's getting all this down on his note pad.

"You don't see anything! You're told you see things. Have you ever looked over your shoulder and seen nothing? I mean nothing. A void. A vast, infinite void. Gray from the absence of all color. Have you ever stood in the middle of it? Huh? Have you?"

"No."

"Well, then, don't talk to me about rights!"

"Okay," the officer agrees as his help arrives. He gets out to confer, leaving Orrin to regret having opened his mouth, wasting it all on the cop.

"He's crazy," Orrin overhears. "Committed this here 308; was about to make it a 45-70, when I arrived. He made a furtive gesture, and I found this in his vehicle." The arresting officer holds up Orrin's Ruger.

"Concealed?" assisting officer number one officers inquires.

"Yeah. Legal, though. I know he went for it. He was so scared he pissed his pants. And then he started laughing. I think we've got more than a 308 here."

"Maybe," assisting officer number two concedes. "Read him his rights?"

"Shit. I read 'em to him twice.

"Smart ass, huh?" number one.

"No. I think he's crazy.

"Yeah, well, we got a lotta paper work," number two points out. "You want me to take care of this?" He looks over at Tony, who is standing silently, waiting. "He the victim?"

"Yeah. Could ya handle that? We'll take this nut downtown."

****

"Sir, what do you mean he's being held without bail?" Tony asks the man. He had expected none of this, least of all no bail. What he had expected was a ticket for Orrin, a hassle maybe. He'd talk to Orrin when it was over and the cops and the tow truck went away. He left his car blocking the roadway, locked and in gear with the hand brake pulled to stop Orrin so he could talk to him, see if he had any information for him, and, whether he did or not, to tell him Agnew is due in Salt Lake tomorrow afternoon—a last minute change in the campaign schedule.

"I mean ya ain't gonna bail him outta jail so he can rape and kill again, that's what I mean."

Tony sees in the man's eyes that it's no use explaining that Orrin is neither a rapist nor a murderer, because the man is doing his job. So, instead of wasting his time, Tony leaves the jail and goes to the main desk of the Police Department,

207

which is adjacent to the jail, asks to see Captain Dan Watersman, gives the officer his code name. The officer calls Watersman and then buzzes Tony through the security door. Tony goes upstairs and walks right into Captain Watersman's office, without knocking.

"Oh, Hi, Tony." The Captain twirls a confiscated joint in his fingers, as a drummer twirls a drum stick. "Que Pasa?"

They each take a toke, settle into it, establish their stoned-mind connection. Tony tells him that in order to bust Cervantes (a marijuana kingpin) he needs to get Orrin out of jail.

Captain Watersman nods, makes a phone call, finds out who's holding Orrin. Makes another call, asks a favor, complains, threatens, says to Tony when it's over: "God, Tony, you know I've got to bust Cervantes."

"I know, Captain. That's why I figured you would help."

"Yeah. Yeah. I can get him out... But..."

"A 'but,' huh?"

"A Goddamn big 'but.' They haven't finished interrogating your man yet. Don't know what to charge him with."

"Que? Charge him? It was an accident. No one was hurt."

"Shit. I've always said there's no cooperation between departments. They'll let him out. But, simultaneously, they're issuing a warrant for his arrest."

"Okay. I'll make sure he doesn't run any red lights."

"That's half the 'but'."

"What's the other half?"

"Surveillance. A tail. Wiretap. And they'll bust your man if he farts."

"Can you tell me what they think he has done or might do?"

"Aw, I couldn't get it straight from 'em, Tony. I don't think they know. They were gonna put a 72-hour psychiatric hold on him."

"Well, I will tell you straight, Captain. Whatever it is, it's a fabricated lie. It has no basis in reality. He is clean. And he is not crazy."

"I'd like to believe that, Tony, but..."

"A blue drew down on him. I think he's making up excuses."

"Oh, is that it?"

"You should have seen it, Captain."

"You were there?"

"I reported the accident. He hit my car. He is my cousin."

"A patrolman investigating an automobile accident drew his weapon, huh?"

"Yes. And then made up some story, I do not know what, to justify it. Are you sure you can't tell me why they want him followed?"

"It's got nothing to do with narcotics, Tony."

"You know that such surveillance could blow the whole Cervantes bust."

"Ah. I know. But under the circumstances. You'll just have to do the best ya can, Tony."

"Yeah. Well, thanks a lot, Captain. See ya."

Before Tony gets to the door, Watersman asks casually, "Oh, say, Tony, what'd ya know about a bomb, or bombs, or just the makin's?"

"Me? Nothing. Nada. Squat. I'm into dope."

"Okay, just wondering. See ya."

Back at the jail again, the man is processing Orrin out. "Personal recognizance, my ass. Big man with friends upstairs?" he snarls at Tony.

"I know one person," Tony admits with humility.

"Yeah, well, just remember, no matter how many friends ya got, no matter how many strings ya can pull, you're still a spic."

He turns to Orrin, who is passively waiting for his personal things, his fingers black, his mug-shot taken. "Don't look so smug. You'll be back. Personal recognizance, my ass. I know your kind. Worthless sewage. A waste of taxpayers' money."

"Amigo," Tony interrupts, "his father pays more in taxes every year than you'll earn in your entire happy life. Enough to pay for his visit here."

"Spoiled brat," the jailer mumbles as he finishes his work. "Never worked a day in his life. Got no values." Like the crazy man talking to himself on the street. You've seen him.

****

"What did you tell them, Cousin?" Tony asks once they are in the fully-leathered cab of the lowered, cherried-out '52 GMC pick-up he borrowed for the occasion. "Dan asked me about bombs. Did you talk to them of bombs?"

"No. I haven't said a word since that little speech I made in the squad car."

Tony raps the steering wheel, yells out the window to an annoying motorist, "C'mon, move it!"

"Why'd you get me out?"

"We're cousins." He laughs. "What are cousins for?"

They drive a block without exchanging words, then Tony tells how they were holding him without bail and how he got him out. He tells Orrin everything, except he doesn't tell him about the warrant and the surveillance.

"Hmmm," Orrin ponders. "He just asked about bombs out of the blue?"

"Yeah. I thought it had something to do with you and why you had no bail set. But I guess not."

"Ah, God, I wish I could be sure it didn't."

"Well, if you did not tell them, and you weren't carrying ..."

"Yeah. That sounds right. But people have a way of knowing things about me that I don't tell them or indicate or hint or anything. I don't know."

"Is there any reason they'd be watching you, tapping your phone, investigating you, surveilling you? You're not a public radical, I hope."

"You know I'm not. It's not that. It's.... How did you know all you knew about me? How'd that luscious girl in the library know what I was going to ask before I asked? How'd that guy with the dogs know so much? Answer that and you'll know how the cops know about the bomb. If it was me they were talking about," he adds.

"You've got a bomb?"

"No."

"Are you going to get a bomb?"

"No."

"Then it doesn't matter if they know about it or not."

More silent driving through downtown Salt Lake City. They drive past the new seventy-eight-story LDS church office building directly opposite and dwarfing the Temple, the two graphically illustrating which has priority in the minds and hearts of Mormons—God or mammon.

Tony breaks the silence as they enter the West Side. "Have you had a chance to get anything for me yet, Cousin?"

"Yes. I have it hidden at home. It's yours, part of it, anyway, when we get there."

"Part of it?"

"I could explain, but I won't right now. The other part you can look at. But I'd like to keep it. You can copy it if you want. I don't care."

"Okay, Cousin. Good. Because I've got some news for you, too. News that should make you happy and excited, for reasons of your own."

Orrin knows that when Tony uses the phrase, "for reasons of your own," he's talking about Agnew. At least he thinks he is. The way he says it gives Orrin the feeling that he's talking about Agnew, implying that he knows but isn't saying, because it's supposed to be a secret, a secret they, as cousins, share. Like using "you know who" in place of a the name of a person you want to talk about in front of children. Orrin has to remind himself that Tony may very well *not* know. That phrase could imply knowledge of a multitude of plans, an all-purpose, heavy-duty phrase one could use and, if applied properly, make people think he knew everything. Orrin decides to test, it.

"Is the news about Agnew?" he asks as Tony down-shifts to take a corner.

"As a matter of fact..." Tony glances into the rear-view mirror too obviously, and Orrin looks out the back window at his tail, not recognizing it as such, however, because it is a V.W. dune buggy.

"As a matter of fact what?" Orrin pushes.

"Yes."

"Hmmm. I don't suppose you'd give me the news before I give you the secrets of Mormon mind control?"

Tony laughs.

****

"Ours is not purely a business arrangement, Cousin," Tony announces when Orrin comes over with the secrets. "We may not be friends, but we are close."

"So?" Orrin isn't feeling particularly close to him now. Tony's house makes him nervous. He looks around at the icons to see if they are alive.

"So, I want to know why you killed my Chevy. They had to tow it to the junk yard. They impounded your Jeep. We can liberate it later. But right now I want to know why did you killed my Chevy?"

"Killed?!" Orrin collapses in the chair as though Tony's neatly cut his hamstrings.

"Figuratively, Cousin. You put it out of commission, wrecked it. Why?"

"You sound like a little kid—why? why? why?"

"I am only twenty-three, Cousin, still young enough to ask. Are you such an old man that you cannot answer?"

Suddenly and with a dramatic release of tension that would lead an observer to think Tony has been grilling him for hours, Orrin spurts, "I was scared! Scared of talking to you. To anyone. Okay? I'm sorry about your car, but I was scared."

Tony respects that answer and believes it. He bobs his head, smacks and sucks his lips. "Okay. Shall we get down to business?"

"Don't you want to know why I was scared?"

"No."

"Good. Okay. I've got two sets of information here. This one," he flaps the typescript, "I typed, so I want it back. It won't give you any technical knowledge of the church's methods. But it does reveal the essence of Mormon mind control, without which the techniques are meaningless. It talks about Divine Injunction. Revelation. It might also convince you that what you're planning, your revolution, is unnecessary and probably too late. The end of the world is at hand, Tony. The Muslim Conquests and a really big War are going to destroy civilization as we know it."

Tony takes it, looks it over, flipping the pages, then starts reading at the beginning. He reads only long enough to have finished the first few sentences. Then he chucks it back into Orrin's face.

"You think I'm a fool!?! You should be scared to talk to me, if this is your secret information. Holy Mary Mother of God! I ought to slit your throat."

"You didn't read it. How can you judge?"

"It has no meaning for me. That I know. Without reading it. If I want to read fairy tales," Tony growls, stooping for something, on the floor, "I read this." He waves a *Zap* comic book in Orrin's face. "It is, at least, realistic."

"Oh. I see." Orrin sounds like a psychiatrist. "You think it's not true. Of course, I didn't explain." Before Tony can slit his throat, Orrin explains how he came across the article, describes the Sub three level of the new University of Utah library, tells about the futuristic strangeness of the book, the *Prewar History Review Rejects*, about its vibe, about his own doubts, about the Xerox copies coming off blank, about the girl behind the counter, and the people on the soaring balconies. At first Tony thinks he'll laugh. Then he becomes disturbed and solemn. "It's got to be true," Orrin begins to wrap it up, "you see, because I'm going to talk to Heber Nephi Smith and he's going to give me a bomb. And The Hymn keeps telling me that, and The Hymn is never wrong." Only after he's said it does Orrin think about it and, too late, clamp a hand over his mouth.

"So. You think you're going to look up this...this character of fiction, and get from him a real bomb to kill a real man?"

Orrin starts to point something out.

"Shut up, Cousin. You've talked enough." Tony goes into the bedroom, rummages through cardboard boxes, re-enters. "Here," he snaps and tosses a manual into Orrin's lap, "if you want to know about bombs, read that."

Orrin doesn't even have to open it to see it's in Spanish. "This is meaningless to me," Orrin says and throws it back at Tony, much as Tony threw his article back at him. "I can't read Spanish."

"A disgrace to your race. If you'd open it, you'd see it has the translation on the opposite page." Tony opens the manual and shows him.

"Well, I don't need it, anyway. I know this article is accurate, even if you don't."

Tony snorts his doubt.

"I have reasons of my own for believing it, that you could never know about."

"You also have, supposedly, more information for me. In return for my news."

"Yeah. And this is probably the mundane, materialistic, tactical sort of stuff you wanted." Orrin hands the yellow legal pads to Tony.

"Let us hope so, Cousin."

****

Tony looks at Orrin's handwritten, scribbled, notes, scanning the pages, reading only when something interesting catches his eye.

Every Mormon completely and fully believes that Mormonism is the only true way. Mormons believe that they are elite, better than non-Mormons, whom they call Gentiles. Mormons strive for moral and physical purity, because they know that the world will soon end. Mormons follow a long list of rigid rules and do not have access to material that would lead them away from the group.

Tony looks up at Orrin. "I knew this already. What I want to know is why? Why do they believe they have the only way? And why are they willing to follow all those rules? Does the church have some machine or drug or behavior modification trick, some operation, like circumcision of the brain, or something that is easier than an imposing an entire lifestyle?"

"I already told you what we have. It's Divine Injunction. Revelation. God controls Mind. All minds, not just the Mormon mind."

"Shut up, Cousin." Tony goes back to scanning Orrin's notes.

Temple recommend interviews, interviewer represents Jesus Christ, should answer all questions as if talking to Jesus. Breaks down barriers, conditions the member to completely submit to church's authority.

Mormons are not allowed to research and produce their own curriculum to teach in a Mormon church. All lessons are pre-planned by the LDS Corporation and sent out to all Ward Houses. All Ward Members are taught the same thing in every class including Priesthood, Sunday School and Sacrament.

Naked touching

Temple washing and anointing ritual

Breaks down barriers, creates submission to church authority

New name, reassignment of identity.

Temple endowment experience is hypnotic, produces a relaxed, even sleepy alpha state for receptivity to church indoctrination, oaths, instruction, commitment. There are repetitive indoctrination sessions, where chanting, singing, and long periods of lecturing happen. The Mormons use secret signs, tokens, passwords to get into Mormon heaven. If one does not have this exclusive information, they will be denied access past certain angels along the way back to God's presence. This produces exclusivity.

Mormons are required to wear church approved underwear night and day

Special protections.

Strict tithing requirements. Yearly face to face confrontation with a high church authority to declare to him (as the lord's representative) how much money the member was able to give to the church. Encouraged to give everything that the lord blesses you with, even one's time, and talents to the building up of the LDS church. In addition to tithes, generous fast offerings are encouraged. Giving to other charities or worthy causes outside the church is heavily discouraged. The member intuitively knows that the tithing, fast offering, missionary funds and perpetual education funds must be donated to first... and only THEN should outside charities be considered. The member is even told that if the tithing is not "honest" they will literally burn up at the Lord's 2nd coming.

Outsiders not permitted to enter the Temple. Exclusivity.

Jesus literally walks the halls of the temples and no other buildings on earth receive this privilege.

Blatant Us vs. Them mentality. The LDS testimony conditions members to "know" based on feelings that they are the only ones on earth with the Truth or approved plan of God. Everyone else is wrong and must be saved or baptized into the LDS church. This doctrine goes so far as to maintain that every human who has ever lived in this earth must be baptized. While logically impossible, the doctrine is widely believed. God will figure it out. Members have been conditioned to never look at anti-Mormon material. Outside information is evil and has satanic origins. Anything that could potentially deprogram a Mormon is satanic. Family members, spouses, newspaper articles, radio, movies, poetry, literature, the Bible. Members are encouraged strongly to never look at "anti-Mormon" literature.

Purity. Bishop interviews are obsessed with sexual purity for youth and missionaries. Adults have been told which sexual acts are permissible and which are not.

No oral sex, no anal sex, no birth control.

"Petting is indecent and sinful, and the person who attempts to pet with you is himself both indecent and sinful and is likewise lustful... Is that what you want? **Will you not remember that in the category of crime, God says sex sin is next to murder?"** This young person (male or female) believes they are talking to Jesus Christ's representative in these interviews. Lying to the bishop is equated to lying to Jesus.

Missions. 80 hrs a week free labor (Missionary makes no money). Missionary pays largely for his own meals, lodging, transportation and clothing out of his own pocket. The missionary is told that the two years in service is a "tithing" of the first nineteen years of his life that God gave to him. When not working in the field, read scripture and pray constantly. Self-indoctrination and mass indoctrination at zone, district meetings.

Guilt tactics. If low recruit numbers are happening, the missionary is frequently blamed. Reasons for low recruit numbers are tied to reasons such as a lack of dedication or commitment to mission rules or even a suggestion that too many missionaries were masturbating too frequently in the past month. This is mind control.

Encouraged to frequently recite scripture and hymns, carry a prayer in ones heart at all times so as to fortify ones efforts to keep rules, remain "sanctified to the cause" and not have impure thoughts or masturbate. No outside influences, no TV, no radio. Must always be with companion except for showers and toilet. Confined to one area, not permitted to go outside geographic boundaries extremely limited contact with family, letters once a week, no phone call home but twice a year. Primary job is to recruit new members, give the prospect milk doctrine and no meat doctrine. Deception (by only telling the rewritten version of the church's history and doctrine) is encouraged. Every person met is sized up as potential recruit. Current members are badgered for referrals for new recruits, friends and neighbors.

Loaded language, acronyms. Outsiders cannot follow many regular LDS conversations.

Mormon church uses fear. If one ever leaves the church, they are told and conditioned to think they will be sent to outer darkness in the after life. There is a fear of imminent damnation if they leave the group. One man (the prophet figure) speaks for God. Members see this as extremely positive as they believe the prophet will never lead them astray. When confronted that prior prophets in history have been wrong or even preached harmful doctrine that was widely held up as God's word (racial discrimination) the member quickly dismisses this. This is supported by the perceived good works the church produces and the notion that Mormonism produces good people and strong families.

The Mormon concept of a Living Prophet is one possible reason the Mormon Church commands such unquestioned loyalty and control over its otherwise normal followers.

Tony looks up at Orrin again. "So, this 'revelation' theory is not something you made up?"

But Orrin is off in his own story, about him and Laura, living happily ever after, and doesn't respond quickly enough for Tony, who goes back to Orrin's scribbled notes.

"When Brother Joseph Smith lived, he was our Prophet, our Seer, and Revelator; he was our dictator in the things of God, and it was for us to listen to him and do just as he told us....

"Brother Joseph is gone and now Brother Brigham Young, the Governor of the Territory of Utah, is our Prophet, our leader, our Revelator; and it is for me and you to listen to him with all diligence, the same as we would listen to Joseph were he alive.

"Brother Brigham is his successor, his word is sacred; and if you do not observe it, it will not be well. And there is where I fear for you, brethren, because it will go hard with you if you disobey his advice. There will many of you turn from the faith. You will turn your backs to us, and some will be guilty of shedding innocent blood, if you are not aware. This will be the result of apostasy." (Journal of Discourses, Vol. 2, p. 106-07).

Mormons are taught that Satan wins a great victory when he can get members of the Church to speak against their leaders and to "do their own thinking."

Once someone accepts the "true and living prophet" script, the stage is set for mind control. The only difference becomes which prophet is pulling the strings.

****

Tony puts the legal pads down. He can finish reading them another time. "That's more like it,

Cousin." Tony says. "Maybe, we can use that living prophet script."

Orrin looks up, thinking of something else. He hears only a sound from Tony, no understandable words.

"Can we transcend our circumstances
By the proper exercise of will?"

Tony has to think a moment. Orrin's question, Orrin himself, is out of context and getting more so.

"No." Tony decides. "We change them, but we cannot transcend them. Are you all right? Que pasa?

"Everything that is
around us is,
Therefore I am.
Would you consider
That a poem?"

"No." Tony doesn't even have to think about it.

"I am
And think.
Therefore,
Everything around us
Is?"

"What's the matter, Cousin? Are you sick?"

"I've made, I think, another
Stab at poetry—
About a girl I loved."

"You haven't brought any girls to your house. I have kept a careful watch."

"She's from my past,
Before I moved
To Salt Lake City.
All I know of her is memory."

"Yes. But, listen. About the mind control techniques of the Mormon Church. Your information is extremely general. I could have discovered it myself. Don't you have anything more confidential? I mean, how do these 'Prophets' convince the people that they are 'Prophets'? I see how that plan could work, but you've got to get them to believe that you're a prophet, first."

"They just *are* prophets.

They don't chose to be,

They just are.

And people recognize them."

"That's no help, Cousin. Are you sure I can't chose to be a prophet?"

"I lived when I remembered her.

Then I brought her back and died.

I died and now I'm back.

It seems I'm back.

Tony, is there life after death?

Is there even life and death?

As we know them?

Or conceive them so to be?

I don't want to kill a man!

I don't want to kill a rabbit.

I don't want to kill a man

Named Agnew, in the Temple,

Tomorrow afternoon."

"Rosita!" Tony calls, "Bring tequila. No. Bring us coffee. No. Never mind. Stay where you are, Rosita." Tony rips the cord out of the television set nearby— the big, old-fashioned one with antiquated knobs. Not out of the wall, out of the set, exposing copper wires. Two strands. He peels them apart. Places one on each of Orrin's temples.

"Laura...." Orrin whispers as his electrons shift, or whatever the theory of electricity demands of them.

****

There are wire-shaped burns on Orrin's temples. Tony can't remove the wires, and it is several seconds before he thinks of kicking the plug out of the wall. Tony watches Orrin on the floor, knowing he isn't dead only by his faint heartbeat, his pulse.

"Bring tequila now, Rosita."

Rosita brings tequila and almost drops the bottle when she looks down at Orrin. Little Jesus crawls after her, and when he reaches Orrin, he crawls all over him like a big ant, playing with his ears, his hair, sticking his fingers one by one in to Orrin's nose.

"Don't worry," Tony says as he opens the bottle. He downs a hot mouthful, squints, exhales. "He's okay."

Rosita accepts Tony's judgment, but nonetheless—okay or not—she snatches Jesus from Orrin's belly, where he's just begun to bounce, and takes him on her hip back into the kitchen. Tony sips tequila and scans the rest of Orrin's information, glancing briefly now and then down at Orrin. Speed reading through Orrin's scribbled notes, Tony picks up main ideas.

Angels deliver messages from God. Give instruction.

Joseph Smith and Muhammad had this experience and each produced a book and started a religion. Islam and Mormonism use the same mind control techniques.

Music—Hymns—keep the mind on track.

Bloodlines—Mind Control is in the DNA. Genealogy is important.

Revelation. Divine Injunction. Prophets.

Control their activities.

Control their finances. Good jobs to good Mormons. Tithe.

Tony is more interested in the Tequila than he is in these scribbled notes. He looks down at Orrin as if he were an imbecile lying peacefully on the floor, thinking, the poor fool must believe it. Tony doesn't doubt the reality of Mormon mind control or any of the other, material aspects of Mormon power. But he trusts his Urban Guerrilla Tactics Manual. He knows the Catholic Church, with mind control techniques of its own, is bigger than the Mormon Church. The world isn't going to end. World without end, Amen. The world is going to change. It is going to be changed by the Revolution. Life is good now. He's making good money from the narcotics squad, and the Revolution keeps him busy. When you work for the Revolution, there's always the opportunity, the necessity to take your living expenses from the revolutionary funds. But you, of course, must raise the revolutionary funds yourself, with fund-raising activities like the Zion's First National Bank fund raising robbery tomorrow afternoon, when everybody and his cop will be over at Temple Square watching this madman try to kill Agnew and/or trying to stop him. Taking revolutionary funds from a Mormon bank is, Tony thinks, an appropriate gesture.

Orrin begins to jerk and throw his limbs around on the floor like a restless epileptic. Tony watches him for a moment, worried, then thinks, "A snapper!" He rummages through some boxes in the bedroom and returns with an Amyl nitrite "snapper." He kneels, breaks the aluminum foil open under Orrin's nose. It works. Orrin wakes up, looks around, unable to focus well on anything and untroubled by it. Fully awake, his once weak heart beat is now obtrusive, his mind streaking nowhere—phrases, phonemes, no conclusions. He glances down at his chest, expecting to see his shirt throbbing, then checks himself. It's too fast to see. Checkmate. He looks up at the shape that must be Tony. Tony looks back into Orrin's scrambled eyes, eyes in no shape to frighten anyone, unless they feared for Orrin's health.

"Are you okay, Cousin? I didn't think a little 110 would hurt you." Orrin doesn't answer. He has shut his eyes, trying to reprogram, trying to teach himself to think again.

"Try some tequila. It will help." Orrin pushes it away and opens his eyes. They are only slightly less scrambled, but he tries to say something anyway.

"You're the only friend I've got.
But we're of one mind, design,
And I don't like you.
It's true we need each other,
And that's it. That's why
You're the only friend I've got.
But I had no voice in it.
I have had no choice of friends,
And I don't like you.
My predicament is also yours.
Please help me, Tony!
You're the only friend I've got.
We can control our own lives!
But I've tried it by myself,
And failed miserably.

I'm stuck where I'm most
Useful, helpless, dead.
You're the only friend I've got,
And I don't like you."

"You're not the most likeable person in the world, either, Cousin. But what you say is true, though you cheated on a line. We need each other. And, now that you've kept your part of the bargain, I think I should tell you about Agnew."

Orrin sees that his poetry has been wasted. Tony doesn't understand. But Orrin's feeling better, so he tries another approach. "Tony," he says, "don't tell me." He holds up his hands. "Just don't tell me, okay. It doesn't matter. I'll get the information. Even if you don't tell me. If I don't look at any media at all. If I crawl into bed and hide my head under a pillow, I'll find out anyway. Don't you see?"

"The media will announce his visit tomorrow. But it won't give the details I that I am about to tell you."

"No. That's not it. Don't tell me. I'll explain it. I wouldn't know in the sense of something learned. Something found out, say, from you. But I'd **be** there. See?" Tony doesn't see.

"Well," Orrin searches his not yet entirely unscrambled mind, forcing hunches into articulated thoughts, though they resist him. "Hold it, Tony. Don't tell me. Hold it back."

"But, Cousin, we made a deal. I can't fink out on a deal with my own Cousin."

"Tony, tell me about it. Describe the urge you have to tell me about Agnew's visit. Talk about it."

Tony pauses, takes more tequila. Orrin's stranger than ever, he thinks. Describe the urge? He's almost talking dirty.

"Cousin, I want you to know. For reasons of my own. For your own reasons, too. I just want you to know. That's all."

"Yeah, okay, right, right. But is there something forcing you to tell me? Something pushing up the words?"

"Honor. And I want the Revolution to succeed. In your own way, indirectly, you will help that happen if you know what I'm going to tell you right now. Agnew arrives at two p.m. tomorrow. There's a motorcade from the airport to Hotel Utah. News conference limited to the press. Phony talks with church officials. His only public appearance is a speech in the Tabernacle at four-fifteen. It'll last till four fifty-six. His plane leaves at five-forty."

"Do you know," Orrin begins, wrapped up in it in spite of himself, "do you know what route he is taking from the hotel to the Tabernacle?"

"Yes. Sidewalk. Unless there seems to be a threat of danger. The sidewalk from the hotel's south entrance to the south gate of Temple Square. Then straight into the Tabernacle. If there is a threat, they'll use the tunnels. But, Cousin, do not worry. There will be no threats. The streets for three blocks around will be blocked off, however. And, of course, there will be guards.

"What about the demonstrators?"

"They'll be at the north gate of Temple Square, where I told them Agnew would enter. My informants among them have already convinced authorities that the demonstration, though possibly loud and emotional, does not warrant taking Agnew underground. Also, the demonstration will be contained on the northern side, not allowed into or around to the other sides of the temple grounds. They have a permit, for Christ's sake. They pose no threat.

"What time does Agnew leave the hotel for the Tabernacle?" Orrin, it seems to Tony, anyway, is testing him by pushing for details.

"Exactly seven minutes after four. Allowing eight minutes for a slow walk, handshakes, waves to the crowd, kissing babies. Eight minutes."

"He will shake hands, then?"

"He will, but not with you, Cousin."

"Ah, ha!" Orrin shouts. He jumps up, embraces Tony. "See! See! How'd you know that, huh? You're no prophet. But you knew, didn't you? Right then, when you said it, you knew. It may change, now, of course. We can't trust anything. But you do see, don't you?"

Tony struggles just to talk in Orrin's arms. "I see you're stronger than you think." Orrin loosens his grip. "Whooo. Say five Hail Marys, Cousin. You could have killed me without knowing it, I think."

"Was I squeezing that hard?"

"I'll be bruised tomorrow, if you want to come by and see."

"No. Tomorrow I'll be busy. I've got a busy day ahead of me yet today. But listen, Tony. Have you ever thought of something and had it be, because you thought it?"

Tony starts to say something. Orrin clamps a strong handover his mouth, catching the back of Tony's head on his other forearm. Immediately, Tony sinks his teeth into Orrin's hand, hangs on like a bull dog. "Think, Tony! Think! The Devil possesses both of us. Cast the Devil out and think. Make the world the way you want it, Tony, with your mind."

Tony has worked his right hand down between them to Orrin's crotch. When Tony grabs and squeezes Orrin's balls, Orrin throws him against the wall, then doubles up on the floor.

"You fool! El Diablo probably does possess you. As for me, my soul is in the hands of our Creator, and I have no time for conjuring up my own solipsistic world." Orrin raises his head to speak in defense of, or to clarify his position, but Tony raises his foot and with a quick flick of his knee, kicks Orrin in the throat.

Chapter 9

Explosives

Sitting in his liberated Jeep in the high school parking lot, Orrin remembers his good old high school days and thinks of an approach. He rubs his throat. Tony can surely kick. His voice is hampered now. It's difficult for him to talk. There are certain words he cannot say at all. He sounds like a man, no not a man, a boy, a boy who's had his throat kicked, or operated on for cancer. His voice is now constantly a high-pitched rasp. High, he thinks, just like old Port's. The thought of the similarity makes him nervous, makes it difficult to sit. He can think just as well on his feet, he thinks, so he swings out and walks toward the building.

Into the administrative offices, hands down on the counter, waiting for one of the busy women. "I have to talk," Orrin begins to say to the lady in a printed dress who approaches him; he coughs, rubs his throat. "I have to talk with one of your students."

"What about, sir?" She eyeballs him suspiciously. The toe mark on his throat looks to her like a monkey bite, and the teeth marks on his hand, to her, are ominous. His general appearance—hair, eyes, love/battle scars—makes her distrustful. "We have strict rules," she tells him. "A student cannot be summoned from class except for unusually important purposes. Are you related to the student? Is the student male or female?"

"Ah, he's male. And, ah, yes. I'm his cousin... His mother sent me. We, my parents and I, just arrived in town. We're staying at his house. His mother sent me over to get him. See, my dad, his uncle, is in very bad shape. About to die, I think. We had a wreck on the freeway coming in. And..." All this in a squeaky, difficult voice. The woman's pulling faces, raising her eyebrows and nodding, mocking him. "And Heber's his favorite Nephite, I mean nephew. I'm very upset. Please..."

"Well, I can see you're upset, all right."

"I hurt my throat in the wreck. The shoulder harness slipped up around my neck, see, while I was asleep. We'd been on the road all night from Moab, and I was asleep, with the harness around my neck, when this guy just stopped in front of us. His engine had fallen out, we discovered, but he just stopped in the middle of the freeway. My dad was only going seventy-five but couldn't stop in time, because he was tired and didn't expect it and we'd just topped a rise, so we slammed into this guy in the middle of the freeway with his engine fallen out, see. And the harness about took my head off. I find it hard to talk, so please..."

Orrin rubs his throat again. The woman asks him to wait a moment and goes into an inner office. Soon Orrin hears Heber summoned to the office over the intercom. Rather dramatic, Orrin thinks, and embarrassing. Raspberries! Why couldn't they just send a courier, a girl wearing boots and a mini-skirt, who would enter the classroom silently, slip a note to the teacher, who would deliver it, with dignity, to Heber.

Orrin walks out before the woman returns. He'll catch Heber in the hall. They'll go outside, cruise around maybe. Head for the hills, up some Jeep trail, talk. They can't talk in here, with those women around. Someone walking briskly down the polished hall. Orrin recognizes Heber before he can make out any of his features. That mountain-climber's walk. Orrin walks to meet him. "Heber?"

"Yeah," Heber answers. "Who are you? I'm in Chemistry now. Are you why they called me down?"

"Heber... Don't you recognize me?"

"Of course not. Who are you? What do you want?"

"Ah, you don't know me..."

"You're damned right, brother, and I don't want to."

Heber turns on his heel, anxious to return to Chemistry, remembering not to talk to strangers. But Orrin grabs his arm and jerks him around so he's facing him again."

"But I know you, Heber Nephi Smith. We have a lot in common, and I'd like to talk to you about it."

Orrin's eyes have recovered from the 110-volt scrambling enough to help his grip and his words convince. Convincing—that's a sweet description of the pure fanaticism in Orrin's eyes. Orrin holds on to Heber's arm till they get to his Jeep. A canyon wind sweeping down from the east whips Orrin's hair into his eyes and mouth, but he uses his left hand, not his right which holds Heber, to brush it away.

"What do you want?" Heber tries to sound tough, but he's scared and his voice betrays him.

"I want a bomb," Orrin tells him straight and, before Heber can protest, Orrin tells him just a bit of what he knows, but not how he knows it.

"Okay. So I like explosives. I've made a few bombs, a rocket. Blew up a garbage can once, but I don't make them all the time. And I don't make them for people I don't know. And I'm not actually active in the National Guard, yet, I'm still in high school."

"But you've got a bomb that you'll give me, right? Some kind of homemade job. Anything. Look..." And Orrin tells him more of what he knows about him, about the monuments he will blow up next spring. About The Hymn's promise.

"*You're crazy!*" I would never blow up Brigham Young. And if you want a bomb for anything like that, anything remotely like it, you're not getting it from me." And with that Heber breaks free and bolts.

Orrin doesn't bother chasing him. He's made a fool of himself. Fairly well botched things up. At least the bomb part. He gets into his Jeep. How could he make such a mistake, he wonders, and looks over the steering wheel at Heber—a safe distance away, jotting down his license plate number.

"Raspberries!" Orrin's cussing more and more. A sign of many things—ineffectualness, frustration. The happy, effectual assassin seldom cusses. Now it seems every other word out of Orrin is "raspberries." He can't imagine it. He understands Heber's surprise, his denial. Orrin himself, before The Maze, would not believe it, if someone told him then, what he is going to do tomorrow. He can barely believe it today. He looks again, and Heber's gone.

At least Heber is real. I met him. My timing was lousy, but Tony was wrong. I didn't get a bomb, but the article is true. Maybe Heber would not blow up those monuments next spring, unless I told him when he is going to do it. Orrin chastises himself as he pulls out of the lot and, as it is the middle of a class period and he is in the student lot from which no cars should be leaving, he notices a dune buggy pull out of the lot shortly after he does.

Down the hill from the school at a traffic light, Orrin glances in the center mirror at a V.W. dune buggy, the same dune buggy that followed him out of the lot. The same dune buggy he now recalls that he saw behind them earlier, coming home from jail with Tony. The same V.W. dune buggy, and it has a long, whip radio antenna. The mark of many unmarked cars. Orrin chuckles to himself at the originality of using a dune buggy as cop car. Probably seized it from some drug dealer. But his forehead's twitching with excitement. A cop is following me. Raspberies. Has been since I left jail. Will be for how long?

Orrin turns right, up that street to a gas station. He tells the boy to fill both tanks. And while the boy is doing it, Orrin drags the air hose around to each tire, checking the pressure, and deftly, locking in the hubs. He pays, pulls out, and passes the dune buggy, parallel parked down the street. It pulls into traffic a respectable four or five cars behind. Orrin tries buzzing through a few yellow lights, one of which turns quite red before he enters the intersection, buzzing through lights and making sneaky turns while the cop's back there waiting for the light, but he doesn't really think that kind of driving is going lose him, and it doesn't, so he hangs loose after the first few lights, just drives like he's going home, till he gets to State Street.

Then, he heads up State Street toward the Capitol, around the Capitol, up into the foothills of the Wasatch Mountains. The dune buggy's still back there, no cars between them now, but hanging back for some reason anyway.

Orrin finds the gravel road that switchbacks up to the Union Pacific microwave station, throwing stones, keeping up the speed, keeping up the dust. Let the man eat dust. Hanging in around the switchbacks. Young lovers drive their parents' station wagons up this road at night when the weather's good, not quite as fast as this, but this road's no sweat. Glancing over the lip of the hill at the road below, Orrin sees the dune buggy, still back there, down there, coming through the dust. Hope he's self-reliant enough, cocksure enough not to call for help. Hope he's just made a report and is not expected to make another for awhile. Hope he thinks the dune buggy is a mountain goat. Some people do. Hope this policeman does.

Orrin tops the ridge, passes the microwave stations, heads on down the other side, still pushing it, still on fairly good dirt road. No more gravel, no more grading past the radar stations. Down across the face of the foothills, now down a gully, shifting into four-wheel drive, make it easily up the other side, top it and swerve off the road to the right, following a pair of tracks, a Jeep trail, up the ridge. The dune buggy will make it up out of the gully with a fast run down the approach. It's not that long a pull. It'll build his confidence. Orrin tears up the ridge faster than he really should, spinning in the loose dirt, to where it flattens slightly. Then he stops.

The dune buggy shoots up out of the gully, speeds down the road, missing, as Orrin hoped, the turn he took. But he knows the cop will realize his mistake, come back, and probably force the buggy up the ridge. It'll make it if the driver's any good. Orrin takes off, heading for the top of the foothills, where they merge with the northerly ridge of one of the major canyons of the Wasatch Front.

Off to the left and down, the dune buggy has turned around. Orrin can see it down there, streaking back to the subtle intersection. If the cop's got any pride at all, he'll do it on his own. Orrin's been careful; the trail is just rough enough to challenge a good dune buggy driver. For a couple miles. But up here a ways, near the top, along the ridge of City Creek Canyon, up there near the pink sandstone cliffs—get up there in a dune buggy and you'll learn it's not a mountain goat.

Orrin's got no problem with this trail in his Jeep. But the cop gets back to where he's sure Orrin must have turned and stops. He looks it over. Jesus. But he knows dune buggy's are good on hills. They have good traction, and this dune buggy has a six-cylinder Porsche engine. He turns toward it, backs across the main dirt road, past it as far as he dares, to get a good run at the hill. Takes a run at the hill in first. Pushes down on the gas so hard his calf knots up. Oh, come on, baby. One hand on the gear shift knob pushing it, holding it in gear, as it tries to jolt out. But the buggy's got power and good traction and the grade's leveling out a bit, still up but not so steep. Up for awhile, then down. Then up, more steeply. And coming down's no fun, either. A steep, roller-coaster trail that's never seen a blade. A pair of tire tracks, ruts and more ruts now as the grades get steeper. And the fuckin' Jeep's just toolin' along. Maybe I should just wait for him. Unless there's another way out of here. Or maybe he's meeting somebody up there. Shit.

He makes it up another hill. But the buggy complains and is heating faster than air can cool it. And the ruts and rocks—God, he thinks they'll tear the wheels off. Down the other side, looking where the wheel tracks will take him, he sees the Jeep scoot into some oak brush. Ha. Not so far ahead of me at that. Below, in front of him, is City Creek Canyon. The Jeep trail leads onto the ridge of that canyon, more roller-coaster. More up than down. The longest downhill stretch from here on out is right in front of the cop, and Orrin's down there in the oak brush. The policeman hesitates. He's twenty-nine years old, married, two kids, brave as any cop in the department, and he drives well. He's worked hard enough getting the dune buggy this far. There doesn't seem to be anyplace special for the Jeep to go. Two ways out of the little oak brush hollow down there: back this way; or keep going up.

Until he moves, I'm staying right here, the cop decides. He lets the dune buggy cool off. Orrin looks up through oak brush at the cop on the top of the hill. The cop, plainly clothed, in a heavily modified Volkswagen dune buggy, looks down at the patch of oak brush, wondering if he should call in. The suspect obviously knows he's being followed. But before the cop starts his call, before his hand moves for the radio, the Jeep emerges from the brush and starts up the opposite hill, one face of which is eroded down to pink sandstone.

The dune buggy makes its way slowly down the slope. It's rough, the ruts are deeply gouged by Jeeps and 4 x 4 trucks that tried to make it up the hill when the hill was muddy. The cop tries to straddle the ruts—a good strategy, but almost impossible on this trail through dense, high oak brush, brush that will tear your eyes out if you try to walk through it, brush that is trying to reclaim this trail through it, brush that will give no ground on either side, so the dune buggy must use the ruts. And its brakes. The slope is too steep and first gear not low enough to bring the bug down safely without the aid of torturous braking. The ruts are deep and the policeman grimaces each time he hears an ominous THUD and feels the buggy hit solid ground, or solid rock. Each time, he hopes that the frame took the blow. The brush reaches from either side for the buggy as it passes, scratching at it with the sound of fingernails. Now and then a stout branch will clout a mirror, knocking it off angle, loosening its pivot, then, as the car continues, another branch clouts the antenna, making it whip; a stout crotch traps the antenna now and then and is soon joined by other branches of clutching oak brush. The brush releases the antenna at great cost, and then the antenna takes some of the brush along to carry as a burden that bends it backwards.

The Jeep has topped the hill and is parked there, waiting. Orrin sits, thinking of nothing, his mind completely occupied with The Hymn and the circumstances at hand. There is no one to talk to, so he is silent. The dune buggy escapes the scrub-oak gauntlet, badly beaten and starts up the hill. This hill starts out no steeper than some of the others on the trail, but it is the longest and, near the top, just around a sharp curve to avoid a crag, the grade increases abruptly, and there the hill has turned back

Jeeps and monster trucks for many reasons. Something as simple as inadequate tread, or being in the wrong gear has done it. The hill around the crag is scarred from attempts of those who couldn't make it but wouldn't quit. There are also signs of those who lost control.

Orrin leaves his Jeep, walks down the hill and out on to the crag to watch. He's sure the cop won't make it past the curve. He sits, wraps his arms around his legs, rests his chin between his knees, and watches. Watches the dune buggy, with its antenna dangling, move agonizingly up the hill. The cop is too intent to notice Orrin on the crag, and Orrin knows he wouldn't hear his feeble, injured voice, if he tried to cry out a warning to him.

The dune buggy makes it through the curve and up the steeper grade about ten feet before the high-powered engine lugs out. It stays where it stalled for a heartbeat until the cop depresses the clutch to restart the engine or shift into reverse for greater control while backing down—it doesn't matter what he planned to do. The brakes cannot hold the car. It starts down backwards. The cop pushes harder on the brakes, locks them, lets the clutch out, thinking that'll stop it. But the buggy jerks out of gear, swerves off the trail at the curve, and balances, momentarily, sideways on a grade too steep to maneuver sideways, before it rolls down the long, steep hill, over and over, seventy times, into the bottom of a gully choked with oak brush. It rests not twenty feet from the grown-over, stripped and rusted carcass of a 4x4 pickup truck that met the same fate years ago. The same, except its driver was thrown out and died instantly. The undercover surveillance cop is belted in and is not dead yet, but the buggy and his body are broken, and his radio is out of order.

Orrin gambles that there is only cop assigned to follow him and drives straight home. The sun has just touched down on the horizon, directly in front of Orrin as he drives—huge, red-orange—and Orrin feels he could drive right into it. He'd like to, but he doesn't have time to try. He must get his stuff together and find a safe place to wait, to hide until tomorrow afternoon. If there isn't a cop watching his place already, it won't be long until there is, until they come knocking on or breaking down his door.

He's got to move, and he does. He pulls a suitcase out of the closet, puts down a layer of shirts for padding, then the weapons he's collected, then another layer of clothes. Shuts and locks the suitcase, hefts it, shakes it—quiet. Now.

Now, he's got to decide how to appear tomorrow, tonight, from now on. They'll be looking for him. And even if they weren't, he's always known he'll have to do something about his hair—they'll never let someone with hair as long as his near Agnew. He sits on his bed and looks into the mirror above his dresser. It is, of course, a stranger looking back at him. The eyes of the person in the mirror have the look sometimes seen in old photographs, the look caused back then by exploding powder. Wide open, fully illumined, stark, the pupils closed down to pin-sized spots, and it seems the eyes no longer take light in, but through those pin-sized openings, shoot out finely focused beams of madness. Orrin looks at them briefly, once, and not again.

He thinks he might dress as a girl, developing and using the cliché about not being able to tell the difference anymore because the boys wear their hair so long. But he dismisses that idea before he finishes thinking it. He never believed the cliché, and he doesn't think the people who say it believe it, either. No one ever mistook him for a girl, and he doubts if he could mislead them even to thinking he is a dike or an Amazon. No. He looks at his appearance and tries to think of alterations—quickly—that will keep him safe and allow him to approach Agnew.

He gathers his hair and pulls it up onto his head, holds it there, considers his appearance thus. Maybe. His appearance smiles. Orrin springs from the bed to the closet shelf. Way in back is the sweat-stained, sun-bleached, dust-darkened, true-to-life cowboy hat he used to wear every day at home on the ranch. He returns to the mirror, holds his hair up again and slips the hat on over it. It works. Yes, indeed. Orrin springs back to the shelf, ripping off his shirt on the way. From the back he drags a cowboy shirt, a working cowboy shirt, minus all the frills and sequins, a faded plaid, subdued by sun, dust, wind, sweat, washing. Long sleeved. He slips into it and returns to the mirror. He smiles broadly as he snaps the snaps, springs back to the closet shelf again, ripping off his Levis on the way, Levis he's worn only in Salt Lake City. He drags down from the back of the shelf the most beautifully faded pair of Levis you can imagine. He changes into them, and magically his legs are more obviously bowed. As if he's just dismounted. He's never stopped wearing his cowboy boots, so he's ready. One last look in the mirror. Dressed like this right-wing cowboy come to the big city to see his hero. Self-reliant, law-abiding, outspoken, down-to-earth, American cowboy come to see big Spiro

Agnew in person. Well, maybe he just happened to be out of work, probably wouldn't make the trip for a politician. But, that detail aside, Orrin thinks he can pull it off. He's not that far from being what he's dressed as. He can't really call it a disguise, except that his hair's up under his hat. And, if he stops to think of it, he's not any-wing. But he doesn't stop to think. That's too dangerous. The Hymn increases its volume. It's been there, soft and low, his own Muzak, while he dressed, now it's growing louder. Urging him to leave before the cops get here.

He grabs his suitcase, whirls into the middle of the living room-study, looks around. He'll miss his Mormon Tabernacle Choir tapes. He sighs, moves to the door, stops. He's hungry, hasn't eaten since breakfast, doesn't want to eat at some dark greasy spoon or show himself in a clean, well-lighted place. He'll eat quickly before he leaves. Perhaps his last meal. He's becoming melodramatic as the time approaches. He walks into the kitchen, flips on the light.

Two large, ripe avocados weigh down a note on the table.

Cousin,

(It is scrawled in soft, blunt pencil on the back of a cellophane-windowed envelope with the return address of Acme Collection Agency. It comes as no surprise to Orrin that Tony doesn't pay his bills.)

Accept these gifts along with my apologies. These beautiful avocados were delivered to me only yesterday. They are for the revolution, Cousin, but I'm sure you have good uses of your own for them. Handle them with care. Do not peel them, do not cut into them, do not pull the stems until you are ready for them to explode. They are not avocados. But always call them avocados. I know you did not find that fairy tale you went searching for today, so use these in good health. They are like the U.S. hand grenade. We use them the same way. But they are, oh, I guess, two to two and a half times more powerful. They are very good high-velocity explosives. Just pull the stem and count three, then throw it at the person or thing of your choice. If you come close, you'll wipe him out. I give you two because I don't know what will happen. So much for the gift. I apologize for kicking you. I don't know what came over me. I'm sorry. I also apologize for not telling you something. You are being followed by a plain-clothes cop in a dune buggy. He's not a narc. I did not double cross you. I am ashamed I didn't tell you right away. There is also a warrant out for your arrest. I thought I had my reasons, but now I am ashamed. Also I apologize for electrocuting you earlier. At the time I thought it was the only thing to do. Again I don't know what came over me. I didn't think it was the best thing. I didn't think at all. I just did it. I seldom just do something without thinking. I don't understand. But I think it had something to do with what you were saying. You were talking nonsense and something swelled up inside me, and I almost killed you. No. Nothing swelled up inside me. It wasn't that emotional or good. I just did it.

My limbs were not my own, no longer under the control of my own brain. I don't know what I'm saying. I think it's starting to sound like you. But enough apologies. I have things to do and so do you. I hope the avocados will be helpful. One thing I've always admired about you, Cousin, is your pride.

Remember, I said you weren't the most likeable person in the world? Well, you're not, but I admire your baseless pride. Don't swallow it for anybody. You'll die on the spot if you do, because it's poison. I have the feeling we will never see each other again. But I will remain forever

Your Cousin,

Commander Tony Archuleta

P.S. Destroy this note.

Orrin smiles, picks an avocado from the table. It is six-times heavier than any avocado its size could possibly be. He grows accustomed to its weight by tossing it up and catching it, rotating his arm with it in his hand. He goes through the motions of a few throws without releasing it just to get the feel. As he told the football coach, he will throw the bomb. He plays with them like that for much too long then puts them between the layers of clothes with his other tools. He eats, drinks down a quart of milk—no sense leaving it to spoil in the refrigerator. He shares Tony's feeling that they will never meet again, but also feels he'll never get back here, nor to the ranch, nor back to school...if he continues along those lines, he'll cry.

But The Hymn is doing its job, and Orrin stops thinking about what will be over forever soon and gets back to doing what he is doing. He leaves his dirty dishes on the table, uses the back door, makes his way through a vacant lot choked with sunflowers and weeds, trimmed and blown-off branches, pulled motors, and mounds of household garbage, to the chain-link fence that marks the Interstate's right of way. Everything in the suitcase is well-padded. He tosses it over the fence, then climbs after It. Through Salt Lake City, I-15 is elevated on man-made embankments of earth, over-grown with weeds and sunflowers. The fence is at the bottom. Orrin follows it in the dark, heading South. This is okay for a while, but soon he has to climb back over the fence and cross a street that goes under the Interstate. He's away from his house now, so he just walks the darkest streets to a cheap hotel near the Greyhound Bus Terminal. The Barth Hotel. He's Bill Jacobson, quiet boy, and he pays for a week.

Chapter Ten

The Celestial Kingdom

The crowds, the loyal and the loyal opposition, arrive at Temple Square early—the opposition having met even earlier for final briefings, distribution of signs and literature. Most of them carry signs saying, "Hooray For Our Side," and march up and down along the northern wall of Temple Square on the sidewalk and in North Temple Street. Others, stationed at the gate, distribute true broadsides about Agnew, his past, his fascism, his stupidity, handing them to anyone who will accept, risking racial slurs and bloodied, broken noses, broken teeth and other, worse abuses at the hands and feet of those who know another truth.

The loyal, having filled the tabernacle well before Agnew is due, cover every inch of pew, sit in the aisles, thumbing their law-and-order noses at the fire department's code, waving small American flags. They spill outside and fill Temple Square, perch on benches, on low walls surrounding flowerbeds and fountains, hoping just to see their hero as he passes. More arrive as the time approaches, among them Orrin.

He's been up since false dawn, preparing, waiting in his gray room at the Barth Hotel. He's had no thought of food. To eat this close to when his metabolism must have one goal, one purpose, would be foolish. He has no appetite, but if he had, he would not be able to slow down long enough to eat, and if he could slow down, he couldn't eat, couldn't force it down, but if he could, his stomach would toss it back. So he doesn't even think about it.

He paces, lies on the rickety, saggy bed and listens to The Hymn. It is so loud it gives him a headache, and it suggests that he arrange his weapons. The cleaver, the garrote, straight razor, the poison needle, and the five-pound ball-peen hammer have been concealed and made comfortable, practically unnoticeable by previous long hours of experimentation, re-adjusting. But the "avocados"— he smiles each time he thinks of Tony's "Always call them avocados"—the "avocados" must be fitted in somewhere. He spends the time, seeing where in his clothing, on his person, they will fit. He checks his appearance with a mirror that features scratches, pits, and years of filmy dirt on its surface and a worn amalgam backing that reduces the sharpness of the image but confers upon that image an eerie depth.

He wastes no time trying to acquaint himself with that stranger. He doesn't mind being told that he sees other things around him, other people, but he will not accept as himself or even as his appearance that thing he is told he sees in the mirror. A small, personal victory, he thinks, but it is nothing. He looks at that thing in the mirror, though, makes sure it has no weapons sticking out, but he will not look it in the eye.

He tries the "avocados" in his crotch. They bulge, make him look like the victim of some exotic venereal disease. They cramp his balls and inhibit his walk. He places them inside his shirt, which is better, but they're loose, they'd bounce around, and he'd have to fish for them, something he won't have time to do on Temple Square. Only the smaller ends will squeeze into the hip pockets of his Levis. And he can't walk around in a crowd with them in his hands, so he gets back to the first place he thought of: the breast pockets of his cowboy shirt. He unsnaps the turquoise snaps, lifts the pointed flaps and slips one "avocado" into each pocket. They fit snugly, but the flaps will snap shut again, to keep the "avocados" in when the going gets rough.

But his so-called appearance in the mirror, straight on or profile appears to have elongated, avocado-shaped boobs. Maybe he *should have* dressed as a girl. But no self-respecting girl would be seen in public with boobs like these. If she had them, God forbid, she'd hide them or cut them off. She would never take a gym class, never marry. She'd waste away in doctors' offices—hormones, plastic surgery. Only a girl like Laura could wear boobs like these, though she didn't, and get away with it.

Laura, Laura, Laura.

He solves the problem with a Levi jacket from his suitcase, checks the solution with the mirror, buttons the bottom two buttons, looks his so-called appearance in the eye for the first time, winks, and is about to say something but turns and leaves the fading room before he has a chance.

There are more people than he expected. Two blocks from where he has to be, the sidewalks and the barricaded streets are full of people. At least half of them are cops or secret service agents or FBI or

Army or CIA. At least half of them are out to get him, if not on sight, then certainly on his first move toward Agnew. The other half is unaware and in his way, antagonistic, pushing, bumping up against his cleaver—still unaware. It is hot, too hot to be wearing a jacket and gloves. It is a bright, hot, glaring day, and The Hymn booms inside his head, swelling it with pain till it seems to him it will burst his skull and cowboy hat and splatter his secret on the faces of the crowd. He pushes, sidles, bullies his way through. The noise of those around him—complaining mostly— the chants of the demonstrators on the other side, the chopping of the National Guard helicopter, a guardian angel, overhead—all these noises from the outside and The Hymn within. He wants to scream. He wants to whimper. He wants Agnew to show his face so he can kill him and get it over. One of the noises from the outside changes. Shouts of joy. Cheers. Orrin bounces up on his toes to see a the crowd opening up a corridor. They must have started from the hotel early. He left his hotel with plenty of time, still has time, but they've started. He thinks, Raspberries to you, Tony, and bounces high again. The corridor is moving through the crowd like a short snake, like a droplet of water, following the course Tony plotted for him yesterday. Orrin's fifty yards from the gate, and with the crowd so upset and excited, he'll never get close enough to touch him. He's being shoved and pushed from all sides, has no room to cock his arm back for a deep "avocado" pass.

Careful that his index finger doesn't touch anyone, he jostles people aside, muscles his way to the wall, scales it and stands, unsnapping one turquoise snap. He already feels the eyes of a dozen agents, cops, and body guards. Hears a bullet whistle past his ear, and as he pulls out the "avocado," hears the pistol. Looks quickly, briefly in the direction of the sound, sees an arm with a gun at the end of it whip up out of the crowd with the recoil of the next shot. Immediately it ricochets off the wall at his feet. And now there are whizzing bullets all around him, as if he's smashed a wasps' nest with a stick. Temple Square sounds like a firing range. Women are screaming. Men are shouting. Everyone is running somewhere, except those who are shooting at Orrin, and they have assumed positions as dead rock steady as statues for the sake of accuracy.

Agnew is running best he can toward the Tabernacle, his guards shielding him with their bodies, knocking his admirers brusquely to the ground. Watching them, timing their speed, estimating where they'll be, Orrin pulls the stem out of the "avocado," counts one and two silently, screeches three so loud his testicles withdraw, and throws. Follow it through the air. Arcing over the sea gull fountain thirty yards into Temple Square, glistening green in the bright autumnal sun, spiraling down, into the crowd; but look: Agnew and his guards are bursting through, running under it. It hits Agnew in the head, knocks him down and knocks him out, but bounces harmlessly into the crowd, which scatters as if it were a bomb.

Orrin doesn't wait to see if it explodes. He unsnaps the other turquoise snap, pulls out the other "avocado." But before he pulls the stem, a pair of powerful arms locks around his legs. Orrin goes down grudgingly, reaches toward the tackler, lightly touching the man's neck with his gloved index finger, triggering the needle. The arms release him, and he regains his feet, pulls the stem, spots the cluster of Secret Service Agents and medics moving and examining, caring for the still unconscious Spiro Agnew, trying to bring him around with smelling salts, and throws, having counted with his heart. The "avocado" is on target, but one of Agnew's guards, like a graceful cornerback, intercepts it and hurls it away. It explodes before it gets ten feet from him. Explodes in the air and people within a thirty-foot radius are flattened, many killed, all wounded, except for Agnew, who is protected by a blanket of human bodies. He crawls from under his dead and bleeding guards and hustles, crouched low, into the Tabernacle, soon joined by other agents who saw what happened.

Agnew is so scared he can't talk. Inside the Mormon Tabernacle with its famous acoustics, he hunkers silently against the wall. "Get that chopper down here!" one of his secret service agents growls coolly to a local cop who has a radio he is supposed to use for crowd control techniques he learned in a two-week seminar last summer, which the department wanted to show-off to the feds. But instead of crowd control, the tabernacle is an exhibition of panic and dread. The people gathered inside the Tabernacle know that there is something to fear outside and that what that thing is after just came in. They are hiding under pews. Some have crawled into the massive organ, others, brave or stupid, are approaching Agnew for his autograph, but most are yelling and running into each other trying to get out the doors on the other side.

Another secret service agent, a doctor, checks Agnew over, inspects the knot on the left side of his head, wipes his brow, confirms that the blood all over him is not his own, gives him an injection of morphine for the pain and sub lingual nitroglycerin for his heart. "Don't worry, they've got him by now," he's saying as Orrin leaps off the wall screaming like a baboon, hammer in his right hand, cleaver in his left, into a team of waiting captors.

His hat flies off; his hair falls loose about his shoulders. He tosses his head to get it all onto his back and roars his agony. The Hymn is so loud he's seeing it, and the pain can only be expressed with roars and screams. He sinks the cleaver into someone's back as that person slams his shoulder into him. Another one grabs that hand before Orrin pulls the cleaver out. He hits that guy with the hammer. But someone's on his back, trying to pull his head off. And somebody else clips him from behind. He goes down with a pile of them. Tries to stand again, but somebody's got his legs. He kicks and wiggles, rolls, scratches, bites, screams and cries.

Somebody's hitting him in the head with a pistol. It off-sets the pain of The Hymn, and allows Orrin to relax momentarily. And when he does, all the men on him prepare to get a better hold or reach for handcuffs, but just as they release and just before they grab again, Orrin explodes to his feet, bellowing, running toward the Tabernacle. They catch him and the pistol-whipper tries to let him have it again. Orrin takes it on the shoulder, hits the man in the stomach. They're swarming on him. He manages to stay on his feet a second, his arms locked in the embraces of separate men on either side. They wear shoulder-holstered Colt 1911s. The butt of one is slammed into his hand, and as they knock him down again, Orrin grips it just to have something to hold on to. It comes free and before he knows it, he's shouting, "Wheat! Wheat! Wheat!'!' and with each "Wheat!" he shoots someone at very close range. Most are thrown away, but some fall on him. He rolls them off and stands. The ones he hasn't shot are running away, drawing their guns and firing. The bullets whiz and whistle past. He turns. Behind him people are dropping dead and wounded from the bullets meant for him. "Just like Mom..." he starts to think, but a gust of wind swirls his hair into his face.

The chopping of a helicopter is growing louder. Orrin whisks his hair out of his eyes and looks up at the giant, descending—apparently to land in the space on this side of the tabernacle, where Orrin is standing. There isn't room for it on the other sides. "It's too late for a helicopter now! Laura's already gone!" He fires at it once, and there are no more bullets in the pistol. The government agents notice this and a few of the bravest ones run at him. But he drops that gun and looks around at the bodies nearby for another, finds one and shoots the closest agent, who is upon him, just to keep the others back. They turn back. And he empties this gun at the helicopter. He needn't have shot more than twice. It is faltering, spewing fuel, and falling faster after the second shot; but the helicopter seems to him more feathered vulture than sputtering machine. He shoots it, ejaculating "Wheat!" with each shot, even as it gives up flight and falls like scrap metal from the sky. He hits it every time, and he enjoys his marksmanship.

Spiro Agnew's rescue helicopter falls like scrap metal but crashes into the beautiful, domed, shining roof of the Mormon Tabernacle like a four-ton fire bomb. Crashes through the roof, breaks apart on the pews, explodes, and the Tabernacle—hand-made by pioneers with wooden pegs and leather thongs—the huge organ, the polished columns, the sophisticated equipment used to put its choir on the air and on tape—all of it is so much tinder.

****

Things are going so well on Temple Square that Tony and his comrades decide to rob another bank, right down the street. But, instead of robbing it, they just loot it. All of the bank's employees are gone, running toward Temple Square with tears, as if their tears will put the fire out. They leave the vault wide open.

Orrin looks around for another pistol, finds it and sprints past men shooting at him into the burning Tabernacle, to see if Agnew is still alive. He is. Orrin sees him led out another door on the same side just as he bursts in. He chases the group around to still another, smaller, metal door on the West end of the Tabernacle. The man leading them is a Presiding Bishop. He unlocks and opens the metal door, holds it open for Agnew and his guards. As he's about to follow them through the door and shut it, Orrin shoots him, and his body falls between the door and door jamb to hold the door open for him.

Down a steep stairway, lit only by the shaft coming through the open door—the Bishop was supposed to lead the way and turn on the lights—one of Agnew's guards starts back up to move the body, shut the door. Before he gets there, the shaft of light is blocked by Orrin's body. The stairway, deeper than anyone expected, echoes his rage and torment. There is an exchange of shots in the dark. Agnew's man squeezes off three quick shots; Orrin, one. Agnew's man catches the bullet in his chest, flies backward with it through the dark air, then, goes into an awkward backward somersault down the stairs. The body has just come to rest when Orrin reaches the bottom and hurdles it, landing in the mouth of an empty tunnel lit by dim, mesh-covered bulbs. Closed circuit TV cameras, mounted at overlapping intervals, go unmonitored in the chaos. There are, however, guards down in the tunnels under Temple Square. Agnew and his entourage meet one, armed with an M-16, and he tells them to keep going, safety is straight ahead, he'll stay behind and stop the attacker.

Running to keep pace with the tempo of The Hymn, screaming with its mind-consuming volume, Orrin hears his screams as low, barely audible moans. Agnew and his guards are so far ahead that the sloping, gently curving tunnel looks empty behind them, but they can hear Orrin's voice like an approaching train. His vision is blurred by pain, but Orrin can make out a fuzzy figure, standing in the middle of the tunnel up ahead. He hears only the first burst, like a swarm, go past him. The rest are drowned out by the cacophony of automatic fire in the tunnel. Orrin charges through the swarms, through the sound. But the guard stands his ground, snapping in another clip, prepared to stop the madman with his body. Pausing insensibly, mid-step, Orrin swipes the guard upside the head with his pistol and continues.

When they stop at the end of the lights to catch their breath and find (they hope) another light switch on the cold wall, one of the guards says, "Think we ought to try to negotiate with him?" They all laugh a short, uncomfortable laugh and, when the lights are on, discover they must make a choice. The tunnel forks. Each fork as well lit as the other, nothing to be seen at the end of either, both slope just as much or not at all—no criteria for choice, except that the guard had told them safety was straight ahead. "I wish we had that fucking Bishop with us," another guard says, looking over his shoulder at the empty tunnel, filled with the racket of the M-16 and then with Orrin's voice demonstrating the Doppler effect. "Goddamn! That fucker's still comin'! Gainin' on us, too! Let's just go this way for Christ's sake!" And he starts down the tunnel branching to the right. Agnew hasn't said a word. It is fine and good for these men to swear and joke around—nobody's after them. They all run down the tunnel to the right, following the first man's lead, as if he knows where he is going.

They are still within range when Orrin gets to the fork. He shouts "Wheat!" shoots into the group, and hits the man who made the joke. In order for his guards to shield him effectively, Agnew must stay in front of them, running faster than men much younger, stronger, and almost as scared as he, and he knows that the shoves and pushes he gets from behind are given as aid and out of loyalty. A second shot takes out another guard and his body trips still another, and he almost knocks Agnew down. But before Orrin shoots again, Agnew and his two remaining guards reach the end of this set of lights.

They keep running, without a thought, straight into utter darkness, fearing it less.

****

Heads down, arms stretched out in front of them like the sensitive antennae of insects, only not so sensitive, Agnew and his men walk quickly (how can they keep running?) through the dark tunnel. It seems endless to their panicked sense of time, till suddenly—everything that happens in the dark happens suddenly—they are enveloped in softness—velvet or velour. They swim around in it feeling for an opening, while every possibility flashes through their minds, leaving them with no idea at all of what they will see, where they will be, if they get through. The softness parts and there is light again. Blinking, squinting against the light, Agnew and his men pass through the curtain into—the last thing they expected. Nothing in their world could lead them to expect a room like this. They stop just inside and gawk. Stopped by the vastness, the high, ornate ceiling. Forced to retch or belly laugh or both at once by the lurid, floor-to-ceiling, four-wall mural depicting mountains swathed in clouds, trees, meadows, lakes with fish jumping, bugling elk and rampant bear—someone's idea of paradise. Soft blue, plush theatre seats filled with elderly men and women in loose, white outfits, like character angels in a high school play. And they are tempted to think what a rough life it must be that drives people to such things. But Orrin's approaching siren reminds them what short lives theirs might be and they head down an aisle for the tall double doors on the other side of the room.

Orrin charges through the drapery, raises the pistol to fire at them as they run—

The Hymn is turned down; the pain, diminished, a dark, tremendous burden lifted, sifted from me as I enter and I am washed, anointed—

raises the pistol to fire at Agnew and his guards. He hollers "Wheat!" before he shoots

—feel the word "Wheat!" rising from my throat and swallow it, transfigure it before it comes out: "Wait"

They have to wait at the doors, anyway, so while one guard labors with the handles and levers trying to open the door, the other guard turns and takes a shot at Orrin—the first shot ever fired inside the Salt Lake City Temple.

"Stop it! You can't hit me. It is written. Because of my hair, my great-granduncle, prophecy of Joseph Smith, and a Destroying Angel. But even if you didn't know that, you should still know that you can't hit me."

Orrin runs down the aisle toward them as he babbles, and the guard shoots again. The sound of it is deafening, but the people in the plush theater seats haven't moved, haven't flinched. They show no sign of having any idea what's going on around them, so deep in Mormon contemplation of the Celestial Kingdom are they. They appear to be wax models of people only slightly closer to the real thing than the bull elk in the mural. Or less than that—Orrin doesn't see them there.

"See. You've demonstrated it again. How many times do you have to miss before you stop trying?"

But the door is open and they're gone. Orrin follows. He is eager for the kill now that he is so close. The Hymn, like a favorite song, is still there only not so loud; like morals written on your heart by the hand of God, forgotten, but in control; like the director of a movie, off camera, unseen and unheard by the audience, but dictating motion and emotions to the characters, then editing their lives. This time when he catches them, he'll shoot the pistol, not his mouth. Their trail takes him through the sealing room, where couples are married, sealed to each other for time and eternity, as Orrin's father has been sealed now to three different women. It is an open room with a high, celestial, padded bed or bench at which the couple kneels. But it is empty. For some reason there are no ceremonies scheduled for today, though it is the most important investment, this Temple Marriage, that a Mormon can make toward securing a glorified place, with wives and family, in the hereafter.

I know where I am as soon as I enter, and I summon all my strength—not to change the scene as I did before—but to preserve it. I kneel. Here's the alter, here's the Bishop. We have already finished most of the ceremony. I know I can't hold out for long. Laura is here, beside me, holding me. I look at her, as the Bishop asks if she covenants and promises to fulfill all the laws, rites and ordinances pertaining to holy matrimony in the New and Everlasting Covenant in the presence of God, the Angels, and those persons present? She says I do. I say I do, too, before he asks me. He doesn't have to ask me. He's gone now, anyway. We kiss. The ring is already on her finger. I see it. There is a sunflower in her hair. We are sealed to each other forever. Nothing can separate us now. I am winning! I've already won. I don't care what happens now.

Orrin sprints through the sealing room, stepping in it fourteen times, catches a glimpse of something to his right and charges in that direction, getting to the tall double doors of the Council Room just as they click closed. Though mostly concerned with finding a way out of the room they just got into, Agnew and his two guards cannot ignore the monstrous portraits, or more correctly—illustrations of illustrious Mormons on the walls. The floor is crowded with over-sized, over-stuffed chairs arranged for council and the wise, departed, leaders of the past are not left out. There is God—represented by a Mormonized representation of Jesus Christ, disguised as the Arch Angel Michael—Joseph and Hyrum Smith, Brigham Young, and others. Agnew and his two remaining body guards don't recognize any of the Council, but the tonal qualities of the illustrations indicate that someone holds the Council in very high esteem.

The doors open as easily for Orrin as they did for Agnew's men, and Agnew's men blast away at him while Agnew makes it out the only other door, which opens onto a long corridor. One of Agnew's guards, a burly giant and karate expert, decides to attack Orrin physically, but only after he empties his gun. His companion joins Agnew out of fear for his, Agnew's, safety. Carefully holstering his pistol, rolling his thick shoulders in the comfortable, vented, polyester double knit jacket, before lashing out savagely with his deadly appendages, the guard, having wasted too much time with preparatory participial phrases, finds himself alone, all the action having passed him by. So he follows them, hoping to take the assassin by surprise from behind.

"Listen," Orrin says to the other guard, when he catches him in the hall, "why don't you just stay here and be forgotten. You can't stop me."

The agent is surprised. One minute this guy's a torrential maniac, the next... But Agnew is safely behind the door at one end of the hall, and his partner is coming from the other end to help, so he stalls Orrin with, "Okay, let's talk about it." But there is nothing to talk about. Orrin shoots him, turns, and uses the last bullet in his pistol to stop the other agent before he is close enough to use his oriental craft. He throws the gun away and walks to the door behind which Agnew waits.

I pause before I open the door, turn for a last look down the corridor. It is empty. The hall is clean; I see no bodies there, no blood. In my book, I have shot no one. I couldn't possibly.

Twelve oxen of solid gold, worth their weight, twelve of them, fanned out, support the font. The font itself is gold; the water in it, baptismal, clear and pure. The pier out to the font, the stairway to the pier, the railings—all of these are solid gold. These are not Masonic oxen. These oxen represent the Twelve Lost Tribes. Orrin looks around. One other door out of here. There is nothing to be seen but golden oxen, their golden burden, golden runway, stairs.

I don't care if I never see Agnew again. I know what I have got to do, what I've forgotten—Laura must be baptized.

But he's got his order turned around. He's supposedly already had her sealed to him, and she's not baptized? He tells himself it can't be helped and doesn't matter if it can't be helped. He'll baptize her anyway. It must be done, and this font, this one, this is the font used for vicarious baptism of the dead.

But Laura isn't dead. I know she isn't.

Still, Orrin climbs the steps up to the platform.

I know this is a trick. Laura isn't dead. I don't have to baptize her this way. I thought I'd have to, once, in The Maze, but no more. A trick...

He walks out toward the font,

and I see that I am right—it is a trick.

The poor bastard is hiding in the water, completely submerged, a gutted ball point pen casing for a snorkel. Agnew rises up out of the water like a whale, to defend himself, now that he is cornered, spits the pen casing aside. He climbs out of the font to be on equal footing on the platform. Orrin takes the garrote from around his neck. Agnew snorts his derision. Orrin stuffs the garrote in his pocket and produces the straight razor from up his sleeve, flips it open. "Wheat!" he yells and leaps at Agnew's throat while he's still listening to it.

Before I hit him, in the air, I think Laura can be baptized—not vicariously either—truly baptized. This font will do. Lord knows this font...

Slashes him down across the collarbone and chest.

Laura's on the platform, ready. But somebody is wrenching my right arm almost off—without my thinking it or him. I'll let it go. I can baptize her with one arm, well enough.

If Agnew is startled by Orrin's yell, he is more surprised by the distance from which he leaps, and astonished when Orrin manages to slice him from collarbone to ribs. He grasps Orrin's wrist with both hands and chomps down on his thumb. Orrin doesn't fight to free his arm but swings up on to Agnew's back, as up onto a wet horse. And once there applies a wicked crossface, which turns Agnew's head and teeth away from his hand. Scissors Agnew with his legs.

Laura's good at that, too. Ready in her baptismal robes, she's been washed, anointed, indoctrinated, and she's ready to be baptized Mormon…Latter-day Saint. By virtue of the Authority I vest in myself… But this is silly. I hold the Melchizedek priesthood. I'm an elder, a priest. I must be. I am. I think Laura had better hold her breath. I shove her backwards, lower her smoothly into the font without a ripple. In the name of Jesus Christ—who is a priest forever after the order of Melchizedek, ancient priest-king of Jerusalem.

Agnew tries to pry loose the forearm that is smearing his nose across his face, leaving only one hand to contend with the razor. One hand cannot hold the razor back and it quickly whips closer and closer, translating his soaked suit into confetti, and bestowing upon him a multitude of painful but nonfatal, bleeding wounds. He brings the other hand back, pushes the razor away, and Orrin intensifies the crossface, clamps down with his legs and throws his body back, breaking Agnew's balance. They both fall into the font.

Laura Christianson, that's your name now. I don't remember what it was before, but I don't have to. In the name of the Father, the Son, and the Holy Ghost, by the Melchizedek Priesthood vested in me, I baptize you a member of the Church of Jesus Christ of Latter-day Saints, and I say unto you, Sister Christianson, wife and lover, I say, be humble, pray, keep your sweet spirit, stay clean, chaste, obey the Word of Wisdom and memorize the Doctrine and Covenants.

They gurgle to the bottom. Ribbons of blood spurt straight out of Agnew, turn serpentine and weak then disappear as the clear water washes him of his sins, and blushes pink. They splash water on the oxen. Thinking he is on the platform, talking to someone who isn't there, Orrin inhales red water, partakes of Agnew's diluted blood, allows him to escape.

I lose my footing and go in after her. We tumble in the water, wrestle, splash water on the oxen, kiss. Her baptismal robes cling to her. I think she wears nothing under them, and she doesn't, as can be seen. My clothes are gone, I think, and notice that a negative thought is as good as not thinking something, leaving it out. If I'd only known this stuff before... Her baptismal robes dissolve. The water is growing warmer as if Laura and I are two electric heating elements, the font, a golden water heater.

Agnew escapes over the lip of the font, drops onto the back of an ox, then slithers off it to the floor. He huffs and coughs, rubs his mutilated chest and looks around for refuge. His legs are uninjured and carry him through the door before Orrin expels the water from his lungs and recovers enough to chase him. The razor is lost somewhere on the bottom of the font, the garrote, still with him in his pocket. Orrin holds one handle in each hand, hits the closing door at the other end of the corridor with his shoulder, rolls into the room: The Celestial Room, full of people wearing tied, loose, white outfits, emerald green aprons, and flat round white hats, like tortillas. Some wear glasses. All are spiritually well-endowed, because their of works and their obedience to the Mormon Doctrine. And they think they are in heaven. They meditate on the exalted state they will live in forever, after they die, on the highest plane of existence, in the best Celestial Kingdom. They will be up there with God, and they will, if they please, travel freely among, to and from, the other celestial levels that make up Mormon heaven, even dip down into Mormon hell for a night of slumming, if they wish, and come back home, forever.

Agnew tries to hide in their midst, but he is not of them.

I don't mind being moved into the Celestial Room in the middle of our honeymoon. I mean, just think, Laura and I will be together in the most glorious kingdom possible forever. God is my witness—I've lived the Doctrine, in so many words. So has Laura, as long as she's known it. Laura's here, beside me in her long white Temple Gown with billowing sleeves. Her bosom, boobs, oh, God. Ready, ready for eternal bliss with me. She is listening to me, looking at me like she does, softly, attentively. "Wait here, Laura," I say. "There's something I can't help doing, but I'll be back." In fact, I know now that I must do it if she and I are ever to be left alone, in peace, just as we are. I know I'll do it. I'd be a fool if I thought I could avoid it. That part is written, this whole thing has been outlined in advance. If I get any bliss out of this, I'll have to make my own.

Orrin hits the door with his shoulder and rolls off it into the room, spotting Agnew immediately among the meditating Mormons, though the Greek's lifted a hat from an ancient Saint and placed it on his own wet head.

On second thought, maybe I had better make my bliss before I...

loop the wire over his head from behind, catching Agnew's fingers as he grabs for it. Orrin pulls mercilessly, bending Agnew's head back, turning the tips of Agnew's captured fingers white. Orrin puts his back into it. The Hymn pours encouragement into his inner ear. Beads of sweat burst out at Orrin's temples. Agnew's mouth is open, rasping throaty *gcaws* over his erect, extended tongue. His face pales; and the backs of his fingers sink with the wire, into his throat. His eyes blossom, the blood vessels in them swell, and the incessant *gcaws* grow more primitive.

But Orrin doesn't expect him to give his life up easily. He shuts his eyes and pulls. Imagines he is doing objective isometric exercises, pulls, yells, breathes deeply, yells, pulls harder, eyes shut, squinting, seeing kaleidoscopic colors and afterimages of Agnew's swollen eyes. He shuts out Agnew's death *gcaws* by tuning in entirely to The Hymn. He listens to it reel off stanzas, and he pulls. When there is no more resistance to his pulling, and he thinks he must have pulled the wire through Agnew's neck, Orrin opens his eyes again. There is no one at his feet. The loop in the garrote is empty, but the room is crowded with uncountable Spiro Agnews, just like the one he chased and caught. Orrin's arms are tired. But there they are, waiting. The Hymn tells Orrin to kill all of them, but Orrin's arms are tired. He looks up for relief, for an answer, something, and Orrin sees Spiro Agnews in the air, everywhere, floating up, drifting down, hovering, perching bat-like on the ceiling.

ABOUT THE AUTHOR

Born and raised in Salt Lake City, Steven Janiszewski knew he was writer at an early age, and he wrote fiction until he was thirty-three.

The birth of his second child and a so-called casual comment inspired him to go to law school. He has been litigating in Denver for twenty-seven years and writes something perfectly legal every day. He has three adult and three teenage children.